T0196488

Lou's Triumph

WINNIE ACE

WESTBOW
PRESS*
A DIVISION OF THOMAS NELSON
& ZONDERVAN

WestBow Press books may be ordered through booksellers or by contacting:

WestBow Press
A Division of Thomas Nelson & Zondervan
1663 Liberty Drive
Bloomington, IN 47403
www.westbowpress.com
1 (866) 928-1240

Because of the dynamic nature of the Internet, any web addresses or
links contained in this book may have changed since publication and
may no longer be valid. The views expressed in this work are solely those
of the author and do not necessarily reflect the views of the publisher,
and the publisher hereby disclaims any responsibility for them.

Any people depicted in stock imagery provided by Thinkstock are models,
and such images are being used for illustrative purposes only.
Certain stock imagery © Thinkstock.

ISBN: 978-1-5127-6320-1 (sc)
ISBN: 978-1-5127-6319-5 (e)

Library of Congress Control Number: 2016918508

Print information available on the last page.

WestBow Press rev. date: 11/15/2016

Dedicated to my church family
at Chapel on the Hill, Emlenton, PA.
(Matthew 5:14)

One

WHEN HE DEPARTED FROM THE family home in Alton, Pennsylvania, Derek Metcalf had allowed himself more than an hour to arrive at his destination this morning. He was headed for Clairton University, where he would park his vehicle and walk to the Orientation building.

Clairton was just twenty-five miles to the east of his hometown of Alton, so he was quite familiar with that town. He could easily have avoided Main Street. But it is not Derek's nature to rush through life. That is, surely, evidence of his earlier years in Alton. His family's home was located at the very outskirts of the town. Derek had daily walked a long mile-and-half from his home-to-town and even further to school, which is at the farthest end. Those long, daily walks had given him time to think, analyze and plan.

Derek will be twenty-one-years old in November. He is muscular and extremely fit. At 5'8" in height, his 180 lbs. are distributed in a frame similar to that of a well-conditioned boxer. His hair is such a dark brown as to be almost black. He keeps it cut short and combed back. Even so, it's common to see wavy locks fall down on his forehead. His eyes are a sky-blue color. There is no subterfuge in his personality. He's honest, straightforward and quiet but quick to smile. A young man with strong character, Derek seems destined for serious responsibility. His high school teachers were convinced they would one day be voting for him in an election.

Today, he is starting his second year in college. At times, he still finds it staggering to realize that he, Derek Metcalf, is attending Clairton University. True, this is his second year here. But he wants to remember everything about the day. It is that which accounts for his drive through the business district on his way to the college.

Clairton, Pennsylvania lists a population of 43,230. It's a small, bucolic, college town nestled in wooded terrain. In earlier years, patches of the surrounding area had been cleared for farmland. Farming is minimal now. But the citizens, who live on those acres, often keep a few cattle or horses. They enjoy their vegetable gardens and orchards. Otherwise, they share the land with deer and other wild life, which provide for hunting enthusiasts. There is no notable manufacturing in Clairton. The average income in the county is scarcely above the poverty level. But the area is neat. Buildings are modestly maintained. Most every home in the town offers a yard of substantial size. With so much greenery around, folks don't think poor. There are no large museums, symphonies, art galleries, zoos, national sport's teams or planetariums here. One must travel nearly ninety miles to Pittsburgh for those. But with modern transportation, travel isn't difficult. In exchange for that slight inconvenience, the citizens of this area enjoy country living.

Derek entered the town of Clairton from the west. When the traffic light changed, he pulled onto the main thoroughfare and drove through the business district. Traffic moves slowly down Main Street. This five-block area offers restaurants and sandwich chains, jewelry stores, a barber shop and a few specialty shops. There are two, upper-class, clothing establishments serving the conservative citizenry and one, small shop which offers trendy, teen attire and quirky outfits that are popular with the college crowd. Beyond the business district, the Moose Lodge and a senior-citizen high rise are positioned at the far, northern end of the street. The college rests at the Southern end with Al's Motorcycle Shop and several car dealerships along the highway beyond it. Gio's Pizza and a few, smaller businesses scrunch their way into the borders of the town at that far end.

The remaining, necessary businesses are located on subsidiary streets. A small mall, with a growing number of chain stores, has sprung up just outside the town limits on the west.

Folks here describe Clairton as a bustling town.

About fifty years earlier, Clairton University had mushroomed from a small college to the present status of University, with a student enrollment, this year, of nearly five thousand. There are many more students here than there are citizens in Derek's hometown of Alton.

Derek is excited to be starting his second year at Clairton University. *I'm ready to move forward,* he thought. His plan, while on campus, is to attend classes and use any free time at the library for preparation. Then, he will hurry home to Alton and his job at Skinny's Market. He has held that job since eleventh grade. He needs the money and is glad for the work. Skinny employs him Tuesday through Friday from five p.m.

until ten p.m. Derek sweeps the floor, fills the shelves and puts the place in order after the store closes at nine o'clock. On Saturdays, he works from nine-till-five p.m. That leaves him no time for college recreation. In his first year, he got to know only the other students who attended his classes. Even then, he didn't know them well. That fact saddened him. He had hoped college would be fun, as well as a course of necessary study.

By the end of his first year, class participation had brought him recognition by his teachers and classmates. But there were no actual friends. He went to class, and, then, went home.

Today, Derek put that disappointment behind him. He maneuvered the six-year-old Pontiac, jointly titled to his mother, Lou Saunders, and Derek Metcalf into a spot in the student's parking area. He still found pleasure in noticing the sticker he had been given to assure it was legal for him to park here. He never lost his sense of wonder about attending college.

He is certainly not alone this morning. The area is swarming with young people, many of whom walk with a friend or friends. A number of them look uncertain. Maybe this is their first year.

I'm ready for this, he thought. He welcomed the new challenge.

Though naturally reserved, Derek doesn't lack confidence. Bright sunlight greeted him, as he exited his car. He filled his lungs with the fresh, clean, country air and ... ...

He glimpsed the wild approach of the car and jumped aside for safety! The new, black Lexus scree-ee-ched into the space beside him! The incident drew the attention of everyone within sight. Almost before the Lexus stopped, the car door swung open, and a young man sprang out.

"He llegado!" he declared loudly to the world. He had the attention of everyone, including Derek. Then, the fellow closed the distance with Derek, held out his hand and introduced himself in very good English, "Salvatore Ridenti, from Sao Paulo, Brazil!"

"Hi," Derek responded a bit cautiously. "I'm Derek Metcalf....from Alton, Pennsylvania."

"Pleased to meet you, Derek. 'He llegado' means 'I've arrived!' he explained. "And, for me, arriving was no easy feat. I began the process many months ago. I now have a Student Visa and finally a license to drive in Pennsylvania. Purchasing the car was even more difficult. But most of that was the doings of mi padre.

"I had three, plane transfers on this trip. Even with GPS, I got lost on my drive from Pittsburgh. But that I didn't mind. I got to see more of the state of Pennsylvania in the United States of America!"

Derek had said nothing. Now, as Salvatore took a breath, he repeated the earliest information given to him. "You're from Sao Paulo, Brazil?"

"Actually, our family home is near Cacapava. But no one has ever heard of that city up here. So, I just say, Sao Paulo. Are you a student? I'm headed for the Orientation Office," he volunteered.

"As a matter-of-fact, I'm headed that way myself."

The two fell into step.

Derek took a quick look sideways at his Spanish companion.....*or, I guess he said he was from Brazil,* thought

Derek. Salvatore had a full head of dark-brown hair that blew across his forehead, covered much of his ears and swirled just above his shoulders. His eyebrows were thick, wide and equally dark over surprisingly blue eyes. The deep-tan, skin color was a shade darker than a summer tan. Several inches taller than Derek's 5'8", Salvatore looked very fit with a strong, wiry build that brought to mind a famous, polo player. Derek couldn't remember the name. A sharp nose and prominent, cheek bones gave his face a Roman intensity. But Salvatore Ridenti's eyes were friendly, and he radiated good humor.

The two, young men covered the student-parking area quickly and took the cement stairs up to the sidewalk. From that vantage point, one could see five, different buildings. They were only a small portion of the University. There was a student dormitory across the way. The next building was the library. The smaller, stone building to the left was a relic from much earlier years when this university was still just a college. The sign in front said *Herman Slagel Music Hall.* Further on, one could see the corner of another brick, campus building. In between, there were sidewalks surrounded by grassy areas. For Derek, it had all been rather intimidating last year.

Salvatore showed no concern. As they walked quickly toward the Orientation building, he exclaimed, "Esplendido! Mucho verde! Bonito!"

Derek didn't understand, of course.

"Oh, pardonen....I'm just admiring the campus. It's magnificent. Green trees, green grass.... I spent the past year in the city of Sao Paulo. There are buildings everywhere. In Clairton, there is much green everywhere. Beautiful!"

The Spanish accent was evident. "I guess Spanish is your native language," Derek observed.

"Actually, many Brazilians speak Portuguese. Mi madre was from Chili, and we spoke Spanish in our home. The two languages are similar, so I'm fluent in both.

"And in English," Derek observed with a bit of wonder. "You speak very good English."

"En realided, English was not optional for me. Mi padre.. (Salvatore stopped his sentence here to switch to English.) My father assured I'd have the finest, English instructors from my earliest years. Coming to America for my college education was not optional, either. But I'm delighted that was so," said Salvatore.

The two had arrived at the Orientation hall and hastened over to the steps. The place was jammed with students at the start of this, school year. A student counselor, with an identifying cap, stood near the stairs. She smiled at the two, young men and, when asked for direction, she advised them both to go to floor three. Once there, they were to be separated in the process of orientation.

Derek held out his hand. "It was nice to meet you, Salvatore," he said.

"My friends call me, 'Sal'," was the response, as Salvatore returned the farewell handshake, and the two moved off in opposite directions.

With so many students on campus, Derek thought it improbable he would see Salvatore again in the near future. Therefore, when he pulled into the parking area the next morning, he was surprised to find him waiting .....*for me?* Derek wondered. *Is he waiting for me?*

And indeed, Sal was waiting for Derek. Salvatore had much experience in life and was not backward in strange situations. In fact, he was quite confident and perceptive. This was his first year in this college in this strange country, and he intended to choose his friends carefully. The week before he left Brazil, he had even offered a prayer to that effect in the Catholic Cathedral, which his family attended in Cacapava. He wanted to enjoy this adventure, but Salvatore Ridenti is a serious scholar with serious goals at the end of his studies. Those goals have been stamped into him and nurtured, from earliest childhood, by his father.

And Salvatore has a strong sense of being led on his way by destiny. Upon their meeting yesterday, he had liked Derek immediately and sensed in him a compatible spirit. He had settled into his room in the all-male dormitory yesterday. The college offers a number of co-sex dormitories. Salvatore had chosen all-male, and in just one day, had met numerous, male students. He was bombarded by many, new names. But the one name that was with him still, at bedtime, was that of Derek. Strangely, he had even remembered Derek's last name....Metcalf.

This morning, Derek exited his vehicle and, remembering that Salvatore had said, "My friends call me 'Sal'," he greeted him thus. Derek thought it better not to ask Sal why he was waiting. The two just fell into step, as they moved out of the parking lot and onto the campus.

"Did you get settled into the dorm?" Derek asked.

"They gave me a room on the second floor of that building," Salvatore said with a laugh, as he pointed to the building across the way. "'The 'greats' had chosen the highest floors. It's more private up there. As I was late in arriving, I got placed on the lowest, dorm floor.

"But I don't mind. My roommate is a quiet, little guy from the western part of the state. I don't expect he'll be a problem. I have to stay in the dorm for this semester. After that, I should be able to choose my, future quarters."

"You're permitted to keep your car on campus?" Derek asked. He had understood that first-year, dorm students were not permitted to have their cars on campus. But Sal's car was new, expensive and prominent in the parking area.

"I got an exception on that," said Sal. "This is my second year of college. My first year, I studied at the Pontificia Universidade Catholic de Sao Paulo."

At Derek's puzzled expression, Sal laughed and said, "Most people just call it the Catholic University. I had intended to come to the USA for my first year of college. But there was a situation back home that required me to spend that year closer to home.....My mother is ill..." That was as much as he explained.

The two were now at a fork in the pathway. Sal needed to turn right to the Science Building, and Derek was to take the opposite path to the English Department.

"Have a good day," Derek offered.

"You, too, mi amigo." Sal offered a brief wave, as they parted.

The next morning, Sal was again waiting in the lot when Derek arrived. With no verbal agreement, the two held to that rendezvous in the days ahead.

It was obvious that Sal was, purposely, leaving his dorm early to wait nearby for Derek. And Derek was glad, for he found that he enjoyed the companionship.

Salvatore was very open about his life, and Derek quickly

gained some information about his, new, friend's background. He learned that Salvatore is the son of a wealthy, business man and land owner from an area north of Cacapava, Brazil. They are coffee growers. His father and grandfather, like his great grandfather before them, have political influence. Sal offered that information minus any pride.

"It's a responsibility," he said. "I've had a weight of expectation on my shoulders from the day I was born the oldest son of Fernando Salvatore Ridenti, III.

"My grandfather's name on my mother's side is 'Pablo'. Madre insisted I must carry his name, too. (Now Sal carefully chose the English word.) My father can deny her nothing, so they named me Fernando Salvatore Pablo Ridenti....Sal, for short. I was spared the numerals," he added with a chuckle.

"I'm majoring in the Science of Agronomy. That's the study of soil management, irrigation, warding off bacterial diseases....problems or advances that affect our coffee production..... I'm expected to excel and carry on the family business."

"How did you find Clairton University in Clairton, Pennsylvania?" Derek asked.

"Your country and South America have an exchange program for gifted, science students. Canada, also, has developed a Science without Borders program. That nation is offering a scholarship for exchange students from Brazil. I was urged, by my university professors, to apply for that scholarship. But as a youth, my great-grandfather came to Brazil from New York City."

That accounts for his blue eyes, thought Derek.

"My grandfather and father both attended New York University, and I understood that I must get my college training in the U.S. My father can afford the cost of my education here. And, in truth, your country was my desire, too," Sal continued.

"Being the favored son has some advantages," he said with a laugh. "I'm usually granted my wishes. I was permitted to choose the University I would attend...within reasonable limits. I saw Pennsylvania on the map of the United States. The state is famous for its woods. A search on-line of universities in this state, with Science impetus, brought me to Clairton University, which had just completed a major, new Science building. Everything about the area appealed to me... the surrounding farmland and the boundless, tree-covered hills. The river below the town looked as green as the forest it parted. And I liked the fact that Clairton is a small town of only 40,000 people.

"But what are your ambitions, Derek?" he asked now.

Derek was glad that Sal had omitted the questions on family background. He went immediately to his ambitions.

"I'm planning to teach school," he said. "English is my major. But I also hope to be involved in politics. I enjoy both. In my last year of high school, I was elected to the Alton Advisory Council. I had to compete for the position and found I really enjoyed that challenge. The position gave opportunity to help the other students with scholastic and social needs. It was enough to interest me in a career in civic service.

"My first year here was filled with required, refreshment courses on high school subjects. The classes were interesting enough. But I'm anxious to put the first-year studies behind me and delve into more challenging material. And I'm still hoping to integrate into campus politics."

The two, young men took no classes together. Sal, a Brazilian citizen, is a deep tan, skin coloring; Derek is Caucasian. Salvatore is wealthy; Derek is not. Sal is a dorm student; Derek commutes. It would seem they would have little in common. But the two quickly became good friends.

Each evening, following his classes at Clairton U., Derek worked his shift at Skinny's Market. He should have been exhausted. But, in fact, he was exhilarated. Beginning his second year of college was a big occasion. Tonight, instead of falling into bed, it was perfectly natural that he would first write a letter to Bill Tonkins.

Bill, a year older than Derek, had graduated from the same high school a year earlier. During their Alton High years, these two had been as close as brothers. They were involved in a harmless gang of five or six guys, who called themselves the ZONCs, which stood for Zealously Obnoxious but not Criminal. Like all good friends, they hung out together and supported one another. Derek and Bill have a special friendship. The love they share has seemed to Bill to match that of David and Jonathan in scripture.

Following his high school graduation, Bill had worked in his father's plant, NELCO CHEMICAL, as an apprentice. Mr. Tonkins naturally wanted Bill at his side in the business he had co-founded but now owned exclusively. His son was a chemistry whiz, so that seemed to be the right career. But to his dad's disappointment, Bill felt called into the ministry. Prior to entering college, he agreed to a summer apprenticeship with NELCO to satisfy his dad regarding his choice. But Bill's mind was set. He wanted to be a pastor. And honoring his agreement with his son, Mr. Tonkins wished Bill well that August, as he departed for Southern Bible College in Florida.

Fate had a different road for Bill. His father died of a heart attack that November, and Bill returned home to assume control of his father's business enterprise. The previous summer, Bill's father had merged NELCO Chemical with Eastern Mobil Chemical. Now, Bill found himself in leadership during a transitional period. He was young and had no college education. This new role offered a great challenge.

Bill had married Derek's classmate, Debbie Rudolf, the summer after she and Derek graduated. The couple reside in Redford Falls, Virginia, where the united, chemical plant is located. Company headquarters was in the previous, Amherst Tower building. The company fills the entire two, top floors of the complex. EASTERN NELCO in huge, bright letters has replaced AMHERST at the skyline.

On the highest floor, a wall of top-to-bottom windows gives an unhindered view of the city. Much of that area, nearly half of the space on the top floor, has been furnished for meeting the most important, business clients. One section has deep-brown, leather seating with compatible tables and lamps. Another portion of the room has a small table of cherry wood, with four richly padded chairs. And before the long row of windows looking out over the busy, central thoroughfare, there is a lengthy table. Hanging overhead is a huge, silver globe with tiny lights piercing through a multitude of silver disks. There are eighteen, cherry-wood chairs with elegant seats. An understated, centerpiece of driftwood and artificial flowers graces the table. The carpet on this entire floor is lush rose. The company executives meet with their most important clients here to discuss business. Bill knew his dad had done business with oil executives, senators and other high, government officials in this room.

The other portion of the top floor has a space set aside for the company's executive's offices, and includes a connecting area for their secretaries. There are two, such offices here. NELCO Chemical was considerably larger than Eastern Mobil when the two merged. It would have been logical for Mr. Tonkins to choose to have his office on the highest floor. Today, that space is held by the executive head of Eastern Mobil.

Mr. Tonkins had chosen his space on the floor beneath. The windows there don't reach floor-to-ceiling. Bill had visited the headquarters at the start of the merger. He thought it curious that his dad had taken this lesser space.

"What do I want with ceiling-to-floor windows to distract me while I'm working?" his dad had said in answer to Bill's unasked question. That choice was typical of Mr. Tonkins.

Though modest in comparison, this was no second-rate office. There are plenty of windows and a nice view, especially if one takes the time to observe. There are large, stuffed chairs and a sofa with a beautiful, coffee table and matching end tables. One wall contains shelves of books with impressive, matching bindings.

Bill had added a large, music console with shelves for his classical and spiritual, music collection. Music relaxes him. He finds that soft music in the background is helpful when working alone.

Another wall holds pictures. There are numerous, family photos, including one, large photo of Bill's parents. There is a picture of young Bill in his baseball uniform and even a photo of Derek and Bill shooting baskets at the garage hoop. A most recent addition had been a photo of Bill behind the podium at high school graduation. He had been the class valedictorian when he graduated from Alton High.

And there were pictures, of Mr. Tonkins, taken with various leaders in business and politics. Centered among the pictures of people, there is a large, aerial view of Alton, Pennsylvania. It shows the little town nestled in the green hills of Pennsylvania. The last, family photo sets on his father's large, executive desk. Today, as Bill sits at that desk, he realizes how much he appreciates his father's values.

Bill and Derek have kept in touch through letters. After he graduated from high school, Derek got his first computer. He needed it for college classwork but seldom uses it for personal communication. He bought himself a Trak phone his first year in college. It just made sense to have the phone when traveling the highways. But he rarely uses that, either.....even less than rarely. He has nearly a thousand minutes stored up now, and will add more when he buys the next, renewal card. Derek doesn't like communicating via email, and he isn't comfortable talking on the phone. But he writes to Bill rather regularly now. He finds that he can think more clearly with pen and ink in hand. In fact, he shares his deepest thoughts, just as he probably would have done if Bill and he had taken one of their, many walks together.

Bill welcomed Derek's letters.

This morning, Bill is facing a serious problem at NELCO Eastern. He had been hard at work when his secretary, Sherry, interrupted. Like Bill, Sherry is new here. His father's, long-time secretary retired when Mr. Tonkins died. Bill knew his dad had, years prior, made sufficient arrangements for her retirement years.

Bill had hired Sherry himself. He did it the old-fashioned way. Rather than have an agency, or even the company staff, send over likely candidates for the job, he posted a simple ad in the Redford Falls Tribune. It read:

For hire: A person with secretarial skills sufficient for a modern business.

He gave his home, phone number as the touch point.

The next morning, he answered the phone himself. There were seven applicants, including several men, in the first hour. But he liked Sherry right away.

"Hi," she said carefully. "I'm Sherry Hampton, and I'm interested in applying for the job you have advertised in the Tribune."

She sounded very young, and her voice was almost shaky. It was on his tongue to ask her age, but he quickly decided she wouldn't have called if she wasn't of appropriate age. Something about her youthful uncertainty appealed to him. He knew what it was to be unsure of oneself in the business world. Bill invited her in for a job interview. For that purpose, he arranged to meet her in a small, third-floor, office room in this building rather than confront her with his actual office and title.

That morning, Sherry was wholly unpretentious. She was 5'3" with a slender build. Her soft, brown hair upturned slightly and bounced just above the shoulders. Her eyes were green, her gaze straightforward. For this interview, she wore a khaki skirt with a white blouse and flat shoes. Sherry was not a beauty. Even so, she was young and attractive enough to catch some eyes as she entered the building. But her mind was nowhere in that direction. She had departed from Pennsylvania to make a life for herself. She and a female friend, who had graduated from the same, technical school, had chosen to begin their new lives here in Redford Falls. Her roommate's uncle owns a fancy restaurant downtown. The two, young women figured, that if work was hard to find, they could always become waitresses. They had arrived last week, and now Sherry was seeking a job.

Bill greeted her and invited her to have a seat. She sat very straight but showed reasonable poise.

"What skills do you have, Sherry?" he asked.

"I attended a small, technical school in Scranton, Pennsylvania," Sherry replied.

("She had a foot in the door just by being from Pennsylvania," Bill wrote that evening in his letter to Derek.)

"They taught us all the necessary, basic skills for secretarial work," Sherry assured him. "I'm willing, and I believe I'm capable of learning anything I don't know."

That's about as much expertise as I have to offer here, thought Bill.

Sherry got the job. Of course, she was quite shocked to learn she'd be the secretary to a top executive of the company. But Bill quickly saw that she had, indeed, been taught enough of the necessary skills. And when she didn't know something, she asked those who did. He found her humble, capable and likeable. She was working out real well.

He had suggested she call him "Bill", but thus far she hadn't been comfortable to do so. "You have a letter from

Derek Metcalf." Sherry said through the intercom. By now, she knew that her boss considered a letter from Derek Metcalf important enough to interrupt his day. She had noted how he set aside most business duties to anxiously receive that mail.

When she entered, Bill reached out to take the stack of papers she was handing him. Derek's letter was on top.

"Thank you, Sherry," he said.

"You have that business conference in the Redford Hotel Convention Center at 10:30 this morning," she reminded him.

"Thank you. I remembered that. But I don't recall if I told my wife I'd be out of the office. She planned to come downtown this morning. Will you see if you can reach her for me?"

Shortly, his secretary informed him by intercom, "Mr. Tonkins, your wife isn't answering," she said.

"She must be gone already..." he murmured.

"Do you want me to call her cell phone....or text her?"

"No," he said. He didn't want Debbie reaching for her phone when she was driving. He much loved his wife and hated it when he failed in these little considerations. *I'm just too busy*, he thought.

Even so, Bill reached for the epistle from Derek. Swinging his chair away from the desk to face the section of window that looked out on the skyscraper across the street, Bill opened the letter.

Dear Bill,

Well, I'm back in school. I'm still amazed that this is happening to me. And excited! I can't recall ever being more excited. I love the challenge.

This is all so different from high school. The professors treat us like men rather than boys. They are matter-of-fact about the material they expect us to learn. One quickly understands they don't mean to pamper us along.

Professor Rowe said it this way: "I'm here to teach; you're here to learn. If you don't bother to learn, our acquaintance will be brief."

Derek used several pages of paper to share his impressions with Bill. And Bill relished every bit of it. He rejoiced that Derek was in college.

But how he wished he had been able to complete his own college education. He had accomplished only one semester before his father's death. His work at EASTERN NELCO was very difficult. He wondered if he could possibly succeed in this job without that schooling. Bill smiled when he read Derek's, humorous story of getting lost when he tried to find the right building for his English Lit class. Then, Bill sighed. He was dealing with a problem that was much more serious, and he knew of no one who could give him the advice he needed.

Bill folded his friend's letter and placed it in his desk drawer.

He worked later than usual that evening. Sherry had departed several hours earlier. It wasn't terribly late, but it was dark outside the windows, and the floor above him was quiet. He was still troubled, as he wondered where to find the solution to this problem. And he was lonesome. *No, that isn't the right word,* he thought. *Not with Debbie so near and such a blessing.* But he missed his old life. In his memory, those days weren't this hard.

Bill walked to the windows to look out on the city street below. The place was never quiet. At this hour, the traffic was still bumper to bumper. But that isn't what disturbed him now.

Bill saw his reflection in the dark, window glass. He had always been a little chunky. In high school, he had been fit, but he was built much differently from his best friend, Derek. Derek had an exceptional physique. He had never worked out to achieve that, either. He was just very active. The long walks to-and-from school…often Derek ran most of the way… not to mention the hours the two of them had spent together shooting baskets, surely assured Derek got lots of exercise… and Bill got "some".

Of all the family pictures on the wall of this room, he had to admit it was the picture of Derek and himself shooting baskets that stirred the most nostalgia. He relished his memories of high school. He loved his friend. And everything had seemed easier back then.

Tonight, as he considered his reflection in the window glass, he realized he had probably added another ten pounds this past year. Bill dressed meticulously and could afford the finest, well-fitting clothes, but…..*I'm fat* he decided! *Maybe not actually 'fat' yet,* he thought. *But I'm on my way.* Debbie and he had agreed a number of times to add a scheduled workout to their days. They agreed they'd jog together daily.

But it just wasn't possible. Neither of them had the time. Debbie was in college studying to be a nurse. She was teaching a Sunday school class for twelve to fifteen-year-olds at Redford Falls Presbyterian Church.

And I have this job....

Bill turned back to his desk.

Derek and he shared their personal concerns through the years. Derek could not solve this problem. But it always helped to share with him. Bill reached for pen and ink and began his own letter to his friend.

Dear Derek,

Today, we have a serious problem in the office of EASTERN NELCO. The company has won the bid on a new and lucrative, government contract. But during the process of vetting the leadership for this job, one of our finest, most capable men has been found to have cheated on his original, job application. The deception had been covered for nearly ten years! That is alarming! The other company leaders have asked me to handle this matter. As the newest and youngest among them, I couldn't refuse. (Not that I would have anyway.)

Our employees are reluctant to give me the information I need. I'm new here and young. I suppose they consider me the rich kid who was born with a silver spoon in my mouth. And I have no college diploma.

When Dad was involved, Mr. Stevens headed the office of Personnel and still holds that position. He has been the exception. He's been most co-operative. It was he who uncovered this problem and brought it to the attention of the company executives, (which includes me....I still can't get used to that title.)

I've tried to get information from the man's co-workers. But nearly all of our staff employees are older than I and have been with the company a number of years. If they know anything about this, they have no interest in squealing on their fellow employee. Besides, the man with whom I'm concerned, (his name is Mike) is well-liked. It's clear the other employees resent the idea that I'm asking questions about him.

I'm not happy about this situation, either. I almost feel that my reputation is on the line.

I've got to leave this for now. Keep in touch, my friend. Your letters are treasured.

Sincerely,
(Bill)

He placed the letter in an envelope, added Derek's address and laid it aside on his desk. He had not solved the concern he had. Obviously, he wasn't going to solve it tonight. With a sigh, he gathered together the papers on which he had been working and placed them in the manila envelope. He opened the cabinet on the side wall, placed the papers inside and turned the lock.

Even his excess body weight was only a minor problem

tonight. *I'm in over my head,* he thought. *I have no idea how to solve this problem.*

Then, as he did every morning when he arrived at the job and every evening before he left it, Bill bowed his head and asked for the Lord's help.

When the weight of the day lifted, he locked up and headed for home. Debbie would be waiting for him.

Two

As always, Lou was sitting in the dining room alone, while Abel listened to the evening newscast. It is Lou's practice to end each day with a cup of tea, her Bible and prayer for each of her children. She knows she has much reason to be thankful.

Today, in her mid –thirties, Lou is still a beautiful woman. Her hair, a glossy brunette in color, is thick and luxurious. She keeps the upturned ends cut at shoulder-length. Her eyes, behind long, dark lashes, are a most unusual, gray color. Lou is quite reserved, but she has a smile that sparkles when she chooses to do so. And her exceptional figure is still that of a young woman.

From earliest childhood, Lou was told that she is beautiful. She would say that her beauty had not brought her blessing. She had been born to an irresponsible mother, who abandoned her. She had no knowledge of her father. An unmarried aunt had raised her.

Lou often thought that, had she been introduced to faith in God earlier, it could have spared her much hardship. In earlier years, she had no concept of how to handle boys or men. All three of her children were born out-of-wedlock and to three, different men. She had been raising her family alone.

They were living, as a welfare family, in a rented, inferior house on the outskirts of Alton.

Things began to change when Lou came to the Lord just before Derek's last year in high school. Today, the family's lives are much changed. Lou is married to retired Colonel Abel Saunders, who had been a friend of Derek's father. Abel had sought out the family. Lou and he fell in love and married. Able had built them this new home just outside of Alton. Cloaked in his respectability, she and her children are adjusting to far better circumstances. At least, most are adjusting.

Tonight, Lou is considering her thirteen-year-old daughter with concern. Rachael had entered her teen years this past summer. Her oldest daughter is uncommonly pretty, with thick, dark tresses that fall below her shoulders in soft waves. She has a creamy, caramel-colored skin tone and deep-brown, alluring eyes.

Lou found it disconcerting to realize that her thirteen-year-old daughter has "alluring" eyes. Her eyes reflect a spirited personality that is a concerning reminder of Rachael's father. He had been a carefree, rebellious drifter of Mexican heritage. Like her mother, Rachael's body had matured early. She looked older than her young age. Lou remembered the problems her own, early maturity had personally caused her.

Eleven-year-old Joy is just the opposite in looks and personality. She is of very light skin coloring with wispy, blond hair and blue eyes. Joy is tiny in features, and quiet… even shy in personality. She is sweet, obedient and a child still.

Joy attends Alton Elementary School. This will be

Rachael's first year at Alton High. Though only in eighth grade, the eighth graders are taught in two rooms on the lowest floor of the high school. Rachael and Melissa, her dearest friend, are beyond excited about that.

Classes at Alton High start a week later than Clairton University, so the girls are still home this week. But Rachael has been preparing for the big day. She has clothes scattered all over her bed. Most of the outfits are new, but she had been trying different combinations.

"What are you doing?" asked Joy as she entered her older sister's bedroom. Rachael was sitting before her vanity and busily applying makeup. For Rachael, becoming a teenager was a milestone that separated childhood from....what? She wasn't quite sure what she was at thirteen, but she definitely wasn't a child anymore!

"What do you want?" Rachael responded grumpily.

"I just wanted to talk....," Joy answered uncertainly. "Can I stay?"

"Oh.....yeah....come in..." was Rachael's impatient reply. She was busily applying mascara to her lashes.

"What's that?" asked Joy as she leaned closer to observe.

"It's mascara," Rachael replied.

Joy said nothing for a minute, but she studied Rachael as she brushed the dark mascara on her lashes. Rachael was now enjoying Joy's interest. She felt ever so much more grown-up than her little sister, who couldn't even identify mascara.

Finally, Joy asked with some concern, "Where'd you get that, Rachael?"

"Melissa gave it to me. Her Aunt Gloria sells Avon cosmetics. She has tons of it. She gives Melissa all kinds of stuff. Melissa gave me this mascara."

Rachael looked at herself in the mirror. Then, she turned in her chair and asked, "Doesn't it look great?"

Joy stared at her older sister but didn't answer. She was thinking, I bet Mom won't think so. But she said nothing.

"When I grow up, I'm gon'na have tons of cosmetics," Rachael declared, "and rings! I'm gon'na have a ring for every finger and my thumbs, too....just like a movie star! And I'll have a huge wardrobe full of ball gowns and stacks of high heels in every color! Oh! I wish I was grown-up! Don't you wish you were grown-up, Joy?" she asked with scarcely a pause between her words.

".....not really....," Joy said uncertainly.

"You'll think differently when you're older," Rachael sagely predicted. "It's still a long time till you become a teenager." Rachael had become a teenager this past June. Being a teenager now added to her self-diagnosed maturity. She studied herself in the mirror. Then, she finally put the mascara down.

"Do you want to do something?" asked Joy timidly.

"...oh.....sure..... What should we do?" Rachael finally responded. Rachael was still not so grown up that she didn't play some with Joy. As their home is outside of town, it limits them socially.

"We could play badminton," Joy suggested.

"OK," Rachael agreed. And easily forgetting the open doors and drawers, the scattered belongings and clothing, she preceded Joy down the stairs and outdoors.

The afternoon was especially hot even for August. When Lou called them in for the evening meal, the girls dropped their rackets and ran for the house. Both were sweating and red in the face from their game. As they crashed through the door and stopped just inside, the three grown-ups stared at them speechless. Then, shock gave way to glee. The heat of the game had left Rachael's eyes in circles of black with murky lines running down her cheeks.

Abel's eyes were twinkling. Derek dropped his head to control his urge to laugh. Rachael's plight finally registered with Joy, who looked at her sister with concern.

Lou stifled her impulse to laugh and quietly said, "You girls wash up, please. Dinner is ready."

The girls were longer than usual in the bathroom.

"You should have told me!" Rachael complained.

"I didn't notice it, Rachael," Joy said defensively. She felt as guilty for Rachael's plight as she might have felt had she been the one with the streaked mascara. When they came to the dinner table, both girls were subdued.

The grownups said nary a word about the incident. But with the start of school just days away, Lou decided she wouldn't need to worry about her oldest daughter wearing mascara to school…at least not yet.

When Bill Tonkins awakened this morning, he had some thoughts toward solving the work problem that so concerned him. He was anxious to get to his office and set the process in motion. Though he arrived earlier than usual, he found Sherry was already busy at her desk. He was never quite sure what time Sherry figured her work day should begin or end. He actually didn't recall discussing that with her. *That's how inexperienced I was in hiring a secretary,* he thought.

But Sherry had her own ideas about this job, and she was always there before him. *I sure picked a good one,* he thought.

He took a few minutes to get settled. Then, he reached for the intercom button and summoned her.

"Sherry," he said, "Would you please reach Marge for me?"

"Yes, sir," she responded.

Shortly, his phone rang and Sherry said, "Marge is on the line, Bill."

"Thanks," he said.

He liked that she called him "Bill" rather than "Mr. Tonkins". *This is the start of a good day,* he reasoned.

"Good morning, boss," said Marge cheerfully. The company's Assistant Personnel Manager had, from the start, been as casual with Bill, as she was with his partners. Marge was a very capable, thirty-nine-year-old, career woman. She had never married, other than to be married to her job. She had been the Personnel Manager in Eastern Mobil Corp. When the company merged with NELCO, Marge came along as Assistant Personnel Manager. Mr. Tonkins, who was co-operative concerning many changes which occurred in the merger, had insisted on keeping Mr. Stevens, his own man, as head of the Personnel Department. But Marge easily fit into the merged company and was trusted with authority beyond her position. She handled her role so efficiently that it was thought she could probably run the business.

Bill came right to the point. "Marge, I need a copy of the files on any of our employees who were hired between..." Bill looked down at his notes and located the date Mike Sabitini had been hired. He provided the dates by including the preceding and following month surrounding Mike's hiring so as not to reveal the purpose for this search.

When EASTERN NELCO CHEMICAL was awarded the government contract, the executives had asked their Senior Personnel Manager, Mr. Stevens, to have his office vet all the leaders who would be involved. After that, there should be a thorough re-examination of anyone hired for this particular job and then later, all who held positons of authority on this job. But this contract was so important that it was decided a covert recheck of the leaders by the very head of the Personnel Department, Mr. Stevens himself, was in order.

Mr. Stevens had discovered a serious discrepancy when he did a background check on Mike Sabitini. The other partners assigned Bill to follow-up on this matter. Bill needed to determine who had approved Mike's original application for hiring? Then, how did Mike escape the vetting done prior to his present role in leadership? This was a most serious concern as the work on the new contract was scheduled to begin in less than three months.

Bill's request for those files was curious to Marge, of course.

"All of them?" she asked cautiously.

"Yes, please," said Bill.

As Marge hesitated, he could sense her increased concern. After all, she was the Assistant Personnel Manager and was accustomed to being included in the workings of the inner circle.

But Bill offered no further information.

Marge reluctantly responded with, "Yes, of course. I'll get right on that."

Ordinarily, Bill would have asked how things were going in her department, but this time he just said, "Thanks, Marge," and ended the conversation. This was no minor infraction that he was investigating. Who was responsible for failing to expose this discrepancy in Mike's application, and why? Was it carelessness or deliberate? And are there other such deceptions among the company's personnel? A very large, government contract was involved, and he needed to quickly expose anyone among them who would put the company at risk by improperly vetting employees.

It wasn't long before Marge delivered the files he requested. She needed a small cart for that. After she left, it took only a few minutes for Bill to locate Mike's file and to ascertain that his original, employment application was missing. He had suspected that might be the case.

Bill bowed his head and prayed for wisdom.

Only then did he call Mike Sabitini into his office. He had some ideas now on the source of the problem. Later, he wrote this to Derek.

> Dear Derek,
>
> I'm too busy to write to you. But I find that expressing my concerns on paper often helps to unravel the problem. That's especially true when my letter is to you. I find such comfort in our relationship, my friend.
>
> And I'm in need of comfort at the moment. I'm sure aware of my lack of college training in this job.

We were gifted with excellent instructors in Science, Chemistry and related subjects at Alton High. Mr. Hallman, my Physics teacher, was my favorite. If you recall, I had him as an instructor in his first year at Alton High. How glad I was that he had been hired. I learned so much from him. With his teaching and those of the other science instructors at Alton, I have no problem with the scientific expertise needed in my job. Then, too, the Lord has gifted me in this area. Where I feel the great lack is in human resources. I wish I could have had some college courses in that. Dealing with the integrity of the employees is a big part of my job.

With the present-day scruples in the country, even college courses might not have prepared me for the fallen morals I find in some. It's usually the younger employees ....our generation... that I find wanting. They are well trained in the fields of science. But too many of them lack good work disciplines and morals.

I was told that, when my dad was still here, someone had leaked a confidential paper to an environmental group that was endeavoring to sabotage a company project. They were attempting to prevent it from ever getting off the ground. I guess my dad easily saw through their ploy. He identified and exposed the deceitful employees. And our company completed the work a few days ahead of schedule. My dad was held in high esteem here.

But he had years of experience and was familiar with the employees. (I'm making excuses for myself.) My age is a drawback. The employee, with whom I spoke today, is older than I, as are most with whom I deal. Even so, it isn't optional that they accept my authority.

We are presently involved with a government contract that requires skill and integrity from our firm. This morning, I interviewed a man who had been chosen to oversee an important part of that work. Mike is said to be quite capable and was recommended by more than one in authority here. This man is thirty-three-years old, married and the father of two children, ages three and five. Mike had been with Eastern Mobil for eight years and has added almost two more with the merger. He's a stellar- looking guy, dresses well, and is neat and polite.

We shook hands when he entered. After he settled across from me, I said to him, "You know, Mike, that the job we are starting next month is a sensitive, government job?"

"Yessir," he said. "I do know that."

"Well," I said, "without exception, we have had to vet all the leadership connected with this job."

I could see some wariness in his eyes.

"Our Senior Personnel Manager was asked to recheck the background of all the chosen leaders," I said.

Now, I sensed that he was definitely wary. I can't tell you how disappointed I was to see that. Our Personnel Department is usually thorough in matters like this. I hoped against hope that there might have been some mistake. But now I could see that there probably wasn't. So, I said, "We checked with the University of Maine regarding your professed, college diploma, Mike. They tell me you didn't graduate from there. I've been told that you dropped out in your third year."

"Well….that's a mistake…..the college is mistaken….they've lost my records or got them mixed up with someone else…," he stammered.

"Are you sure about that, Mike?" I carefully asked.

"Yessir," he mumbled, while shifting in his chair.

Do you know, Derek, if he had come straight when confronted, I'd have had some leverage? I didn't want to fire him. He has a family, and his work has been satisfactory, even better than satisfactory, during the years he's been with us. That, plus some real, seasoned ability is why he was chosen for this important job.

Besides, I stepped into this leadership role by reason of my father's death and without the college background that most of our employees have. If Mike had just been honest with me, I'd have considered looking for another, less sensitive position in the company that would give him some time to redeem himself. But he continued to lie.

I had to let him go. That's the hard part of this job.

Of course, the big story here is how he got through the security check in our Personnel Department when he first got hired. That's why I became involved. We have a Human Resources Department. But the partners asked me to investigate it. I need to find out how he escaped our earlier, background check. He said he couldn't remember who had interviewed him for this job. So I find it necessary to go back through the files and learn how, or why, someone missed this easily-discovered deception.

Say a prayer for me, my friend.

Some other news: I'm signed up at the local Community College here in Redford Falls for a night-class course in The Psychology of Human Resources....what else?.... which starts in a few weeks.

Debbie is doing very well in her nurse's training course. She is excited about this. We're blissfully happy in married life. That sounds trite, but it's so true. I sincerely hope you are as blessed in finding the right mate, my friend.

Back to work. Please stay in touch. I await your letters impatiently.

Your friend,
(Bill)

Bill folded the letter and found the stash of envelopes that he kept especially for his letters to Derek. His secretary took care of his other correspondence. He sealed the letter and entered the address. Then he laid it in his mail bin, and with a sigh, turned back to present duties.

Derek entered the kitchen carrying an armload of books. This was his second week of classes.

"Do you want me to bring you home later?" he asked his

mother. She didn't drive, so Lou depended on Derek or her husband, Abel, for transportation to-and-from her Remnant Shop uptown. There, she sold sewing supplies and offered instruction on sewing and related crafts.

"That won't be necessary, Derek," said Abel, who had just entered the kitchen from outdoors. "I'll be here today."

Abel filled his coffee cup and sat down at the table to watch his, new family start their day. Having been a bachelor in a military setting for so long, he relished the morning activity and interaction of Lou and children.

Abel, in his late forties, is several inches taller than Derek. A retired, military officer, he exudes an unconscious authority. His hair is now mostly gray, and the prominent lines on his face seem wholly natural. Those lines deepen with his ready smile. Colonel Abel has seen bad times. But he has trained his character to hold to the positive.

His stepchildren quickly learned to love this man their mother had married just over a year ago.

Derek has great respect for Abel. When Lou and he married, Abel had taken Derek aside and suggested he'd like to help him with his college expenses. The Colonel could well afford to do so and would have welcomed the opportunity.

"I appreciate your offer, Abel. But this is something I'd like to do on my own," Derek had replied.

Abel understood.

The young man and his elder share a mutual respect.

Joy came in just then and stopped for Derek's hug. A tiny, delicate child, her unremarkable, blond hair, is too thin and unmanageable to retain body. She commonly wears a headband to keep the wisps of hair off her face. Joy is nearing her eleventh birthday, but hugging her older brother is a ritual she has not outgrown, and Derek welcomes it.

"Is Rachael ready for the big event?" he asked. The family had heard much from Rachael in recent days about her promotion to the high school.

"I wonder if they're ready for Rachael at the high school." Abel offered with a laugh.

"Yeah," Derek agreed. "They're in for a rough time. I've got to go," he said.

"Tell her I said 'goodbye'." And with that he left the house.

"Rachael, it's time to catch the bus," Lou called. But her voice tapered off as a sullen Rachael was just entering the room. She was not happy to have to ride the bus today, and she was very inclined to let the others know that.

"Why can't I ride with Derek?" she asked.

"Derek has his own schedule to keep," Lou responded.

"Well, Uncle Abe could take me," she complained.

When the family first got to know Abel, he had suggested the girls call him Uncle Abe. They were delighted to do so. They still call him that, and he is still at peace with it.

"Rachael, you will be riding the bus this morning and every morning," said Lou. They had had this argument a number of times this past week.

Lou's recent marriage to retired Colonel Abel Saunders found the family in a new house that was a quarter of a mile further down the road from their previous residence. Rachael admittedly loved this new home. But it was outside the town limits, and she was required to ride the bus to school. Previous to the move to this house, she and Joy were permitted to walk to the elementary school, which was only a short distance away. In years past, Derek had walked all the way to the high school. In their new home, Joy took a bus to the elementary school. But Rachael was going to eighth grade this year, and grade eight was in the Alton High School building. Therefore, Rachael had to ride the bus that took the out-of-towners to the high school. Rachael considered this advancement to the high school a "big deal", but she much disliked the thought of exiting a bus there.

"It makes me look like a rural hick!" she complained. "Melissa will get to walk to school. So will most of the others!"

"There will be nearly as many riding the bus from the country and the small towns around here," said her mother, reasoning with her.

"And they're all 'country bumpkins'!" Rachael stormed.

Lou turned away from her oldest daughter and busied herself at the kitchen sink. Rachael's thirteenth birthday this past summer had inspired a maelstrom of teenage controversies.

"She is a handful!" Lou complained to Abel often. Rachael was developing early. At thirteen, her figure was already formed, with the enticing appeal of a maturing, teenage body. Her dark hair, thick and shining, bounced well below her shoulders. Long, thick eyelashes fluttered over flashing, brown eyes. With her soft, caramel coloring, this daughter was an early attraction. It was a real concern to her mother, as Rachael accompanied that beauty with a fiery disposition. Lou's oldest daughter was very inclined to make her wishes known.

Realizing her mother was finished with the argument

this morning, Rachael stormed toward the door. She brushed past Abel, who called after her,

"You have a good day."

"Thanks," she murmured. Then, without a word for Lou…or Joy, who was studying her big sister intently, Rachael exited the house. Joy kissed her mother and Uncle Abe and followed her out the door. Lou went to the window to watch her girls walk down the short lane. Joy's ride arrived first; she boarded meekly, and the bus pulled away. The second bus pulled in just then, and Rachael took her first, bus ride on her first day at Alton High School.

"Well…no 'good morning' from Rachael," remarked Abel, as he walked to the counter and filled his coffee cup.

"She's her usual, cheerful, cooperative self," said Lou glumly.

Abel put his arm around Lou's shoulder and kissed her neck from behind.

"You are more tasteful than this delicious coffee," he murmured, as he nuzzled her. He found the temptations he enjoyed, because of his lovely wife, were well controlled by their busy household. Lou hadn't bothered to turn or even to answer him. Her mind was still occupied with getting her children off this first day of the school year.

Rachael felt an unfamiliar shyness as she stepped onto the bus for the first time and saw the many faces all turned toward her. The other students were seated further back. The first, two rows from the front were unoccupied; she quickly slid into the aisle seat, second row and faced forward. It was little more than a five minute ride from her place to the school.

She was first off the bus, and, with relief, saw that Melissa was waiting for her in the school yard.

Rachael and Melissa have been good friends throughout most of their grade-school years. Rachael is uncommonly pretty and always attracts attention. Melissa is cute. Melissa is several inches shorter than Rachael, but then, so are the other girls their age. Melissa's hair is dark and naturally curly. She wanted long hair like Rachael has, but her tresses had always been too curly for that. She kept it cut short until this past summer, when she learned that one can straighten the curls. Now, she spends much time doing just that. Today, her hair brushes her shoulders, and it is straight!

Melissa's green eyes sparkle with personality. She smiles easily and walks with a bounce. Burgeoning maturity is beginning to shape her body into womanhood. Like her best friend, she, too, easily attracts male attention.

Melissa comes from a secure home with great parents. Her mother works at the bank and her dad is well known and respected, which gives her a standing in town. Melissa is the All-American teenager, who knows very little of the dark side of life. Her friendship has always been stabilizing for Rachael. It influences their classmates and has prevented many of the barbs that might otherwise have come Rachael's way.

As Rachael exited the bus and hurried over to her friend, her poise returned. The two girls turned to watch the others leave the bus.

"Gee, Rachael," said Melissa. "It must be exciting to be on the same bus with upper-class students."

"Yeah,....sort-of...," Rachael responded. In truth, she had

felt more intimidated than excited. But she'd not let Melissa know that.

"There's Roger Adams," whispered Melissa as she nudged Rachael to look down the street.

Rachael didn't reply. But she, too, noticed Roger, who had practiced with the football team all summer.

The men in town had, for years, insisted there was a need for Alton High to have a sanctioned, football team. They finally convinced the authorities that their students were missing out on a sport that was much enjoyed in the other schools. The year after Derek graduated, the school board finally agreed and football was added to the extracurricular roster. That summer, some land was purchased. It was on the outskirts of town but within walking distance of the school. The men pitched in to prepare the field. Fund raisers and donations had been sufficient to provide wooden bleachers. They would need to play all day games their first year. But, this fall, Alton High was prepared to put their first, registered team on the field. The enthusiasm of the students was at high pitch.

Roger, a tenth grader, had won a uniform. Roger is the son of Doctor Miles Adams, whose medical complex is in Burnswick. Roger's dad had won a position on the football team at Pitt during his first, two years as a student there. He had not really excelled; in fact, Miles had spent most of his time on the bench and was dropped from the roster in his third year. But the men of Alton held him in high esteem. His son, Roger, was known to be an excellent athlete and much was expected for his future. His fellow students just knew Roger was destined to be a star.

Melissa and Rachael followed him with their eyes, as he started up the steps of the school.

"Hi, Cal," Roger said and hesitated beside the janitor, who was standing at the top of the stairs.

"Morning, Roger," said Cal.

Calvin Carson has been janitor at Alton High as long as anyone could remember. His work here is more than a job; it is central to his life. He makes an effort to know the students by name and succeeds reasonably well. But with each advancing year, it is getting more difficult. He does know the outstanding students, such as those involved in sports. Today, he was faced with a new bunch of eighth graders. If they are from the town, he probably knows them ...or at least their parents.

Roger Adams is known by most everyone in Alton.

"Are you ready to hit the books again?" he asked the young man.

"I guess so," Roger replied.

Keith Stuart and Doug Rupp, both in eleventh grade, stepped to Roger's side. Keith greeted Roger with a slight punch to the shoulder. Both boys greeted Cal. These three friends are football players.

"How's practice going?" Cal asked. He knew the football team had been practicing most of the summer. The other, two guys were starters on the team, and Roger was a hopeful. As he was only in tenth grade, there was a good chance he'd spend most of the season on the bench. Even so, his talent was recognized, and he chose his friends among the team players.

The small group was still clustered there as Rachael and

Melissa made their way up the steps. Uncannily, all three boys turned to watch the two girls pass them and enter the building. Cal noticed that, of course, but said nothing.

The entrance of the girls had silenced the talk about football. As the door closed on Melissa and Rachael, the guys seemed to collect themselves. They said an offhand "See you" to Cal and started into the building.

Mr. Harriger, the tenth grade Math instructor, had arrived earlier to get his material in order. Now, he was stepping outside to visit with Cal, for a minute, before the start of the school day.

"Morning, Mr. Harriger," each of the boy's said as they assumed single file past him. When he first came to Alton, the kids had shortened Mr. Harriger's name to Mr. H. They meant no disrespect by it. Even so, they didn't use that nickname this morning, as they exchanged a greeting with him.

David Harriger was in his seventh year of teaching at Alton High. An ex-Marine, he had added nearly twenty pounds since his military days, but his deportment still reflected the authority, training and values of that era. He was 5'11" tall and had thick, dark hair, a square jaw and a confident, straight-forward manner. The handsomest of the male teachers at Alton, David is still unmarried. The school girls tend to think of him as a heartthrob. The boys respect him.

The janitor here knows him as a friend. Mr. H, as the kids call him, had arrived in time to notice the effect Rachael and Melissa had on the young athletes.

With a smile to Cal, he said, "High school is when the boys notice the girls and vice versa. Those three guys spoke, but I don't think they even saw me. They had their eyes on the girls, who preceded them. They were pretty, young girls. I seldom get to know the eighth graders."

"The shorter one is Melissa Jordan. Her dad works at the courthouse in Clairton. Mr. Jordan is an elder in our Baptist church. (That was Cal's church, so he knew Melissa some.) Melissa's mother works at the bank."

"Oh, sure. I know who she is."

"The other one is Rachael Metcalf. She's Lou Metcalf's.... excuse me. She's Lou Saunder's daughter."

"Oh. She's Derek's sister?"

"Yes."

"She's very attractive. Of course, her mother is a beauty," he remarked thoughtfully. "...though Rachael doesn't appear to look like Lou. Still, she's pretty striking for as young as she is," said Mr. H. "Apparently, the boys have already noticed her."

"Do you ever see Derek," he asked in a change of subject. The high school teachers had little association with the eighth graders. "I guess this is his second year at Clairton U, isn't it?" he continued.

"Derek stopped in this summer. That was before his college classes began this semester," said Cal. "He's doing well. He's still working at Skinny's, so you'll, no doubt, have a chance to talk with him."

"He's a young man with a future," said Mr. H.

The warning bell rang just then. Without further comment, Mr. H. made his way through the conglomeration in the hallway. There were already three or four students waiting at his door for entrance. Most of the students spoke, as he hurried past to start day-one of this year at Alton High School.

On the second day of school, Lou was grateful to see Rachael had resigned herself to riding the bus. In the future, that controversy was quieted. But Rachael, in her teen years, seemed to be on a roller-coaster of emotions.

Lou knew her family had suffered socially because all three of her children were born out-of-wedlock. She had shared, with them, nothing about their fathers, and she kept their birth certificates hidden. Then, one day, she had carelessly placed Derek's certificate in a cabinet temporarily. Her twelve-year-old son discovered the document and learned his father's name.

At age eighteen, Derek sought out his grandparents. That brought Abel, a close friend of Derek's father, into their lives. Derek now had comforting information about his now-deceased Dad.

But neither of her girls knew even their father's name. Lou could offer them no family ties other than herself and their siblings. She realized that Rachael was reaching an age when that could become an issue with her.

After her marriage to Retired Colonel Abel Saunders, Lou much hoped for a normal, family existence finally. She hoped this would bring stability for all her children. Abel had built, for them, this lovely, stone house just outside the borders of the town of Alton. Uncle Abe was loved by her children, and the family was now enjoying an above-average standard of living.

Alton citizens had begun to refer to them as the Saunders' family. But her three children still bore their mother's, maiden name of Metcalf. Abel suggested adoption. The girls were excited about that. That is, until Derek was considered.

"I'm grown," he said reasonably. "I'll be a Metcalf for the

rest of my life. And I hope to bring honor to my mother's, family name." There was no belligerence in his statement. It was just matter-of-fact.

When the girls realized Derek was to remain a Metcalf, they chose the same.

"I'll keep the same name as Derek," they each said.

Abel was not about to allow this to cause hurt feelings. The subject was dropped.

Following his retirement, Abel's new work with the military was not incidental. It was detailed and challenging. It was his military job that solved a problem they had with Rachael at this time.

Derek and Joy had shown no strain in settling into this new life.

But Rachael was different. She was in her room again for another night. At age thirteen, moodiness isn't unusual for any teen. *But it's becoming too common for this child*, thought Lou, as she considered Rachael's state.

Since learning about his father, Derek was in touch with his grandparents. He had visited them in Howenstein, Ohio several times in the past year. In fact, he had recently returned from a visit. Always, he had stories to tell of the Derekson's, family history. Abel had been like a son to the Dereksons, so he relished the stories Derek would share.

Tonight, as Abel and Derek talked, Rachael listened quietly for a short time. Then, without a word, she turned and went to her room.

In spite of such wonderful, recent changes in their lives, Rachael was moody and separating to her room too often.

Lou was troubled. This evening, she chose to visit Rachael in her bedroom. Lou had entered the room unnoticed, and she quickly glanced around. Her oldest daughter enjoyed her own, luxurious bedroom graced with lovely furniture. Her closet was full of the nicest apparel. She was surrounded with comforts she never had before.

Rachael was seated at her desk, though obviously not studying but staring morosely without focus. Lou had not entered the room silently. The problem was, Rachael was in a mood. Lost in her own desolate thoughts, she had not heard her mother's footsteps.

"Rachael, why don't you stay down with the family this evening?"

No answer.

"Is something wrong, honey?" asked Lou.

"No."

"You and Melissa often have sleep-overs on Friday night." Lou's marriage to Abel had brought respect to their home. Melissa visited in this new home often. "Did you have a fight?" Lou asked.

"No."

Lou waited. Then, she said, "Derek is home tonight."

"I know."

"You love Derek, honey. Are you upset with him about something?"

"No." Then, in a torrent, Rachael said, "Everything good happens to Derek. Derek goes to college, and Uncle Abe wants to hear all about his college stuff. Derek visits his Grandma Derekson, and Uncle Abe wants to hear all about that, and about his Aunt Rose and, and, and..." she said. Her words were between anger and tears. Then, she murmured, "Melissa is excited. She's going to her grandma's house in Hershey this weekend. Everybody has relatives but me!"

"That isn't any fault of yours," said Lou softly. "It would be useless to try to place blame for this. Sometimes life is unfair." There wasn't much she could say to help Rachael.

Finally, Lou took her hand and suggested they go down with the others. This time, Rachael was willing.

Lou discussed Rachael's problem with Abel that night. The following week, Abel said at the dinner table, "I need to return to Washington for a few days. My former commander has asked me to stay overnight at his home."

Lt. General Luter and his wife were good friends of Colonel Abel. The family had met them at Abel's retirement celebration. How happy that couple was when Abel finally took a wife and had a family of his own. They did, indeed, ask him to stay overnight. When Abel suggested he might have one of the girls with him this time, Mrs. Luter was overjoyed.

"I hate to make the trip alone," Abel said to his family this evening. "Mrs. Luter has suggested I bring Rachael with me."

The school year had just started, so he added, "Do you think we could arrange for Rachael to miss school for several days to accompany me?" he said to Lou. "Of course, that's only if you want to do so, Rachael."

"Yes! I'll go!" said Rachael in excitement

"Can I go, too?" asked Joy.

"Not this time," said Lou, who guessed Abel's purpose. "But we'll find something special for you to do here."

Joy was not inclined to fuss.

Colonel Saunders made the request to the principal himself. Rachael had a very respectable, class standing during her school years, and the request was granted.

They left early the next, Monday morning. Rachael, who was rarely shy, chatted on the drive down to Washington. She was delighted when Abel stopped along the way for restaurant food.

When they arrived at the Luter home, Abel was greeted enthusiastically. Rachael was introduced and welcomed. Then, Lt. Gen. Luter suggested that Abel and he leave at once on their business matters.

Just as the men left the house, there was a ruckus from another room, and they were suddenly invaded by a miniature Schnauzer named Bruno, who had been given entrance by the maid. The Metcalf house had always enjoyed the presence of a cat. The exuberant greeting from the dog was new, and Rachael was enchanted. Shortly, their hostess suggested she would show Rachael to her guestroom. The circular stairway they climbed continued up to the third floor. But they stopped at the second floor, and Rachael entered the designated room. She saw that her suitcase had been placed on the cedar chest by the maid, who was waiting there lest further services were needed. As Mrs. Luter spoke with the maid, Rachael quickly acquainted herself with the beautiful furnishings. She walked over to the window that looked out on an upper-class, residential area with fancy houses and big yards. The street just beyond the Luter lawn was busy with traffic. This was so different from country living.

That afternoon, the two of them went to the mall. What an excitement! Rachael was delighted with the bright lights, escalators and shops....four stories high with a glass ceiling above them! They had lunch in the food court that surrounded the atrium. Mrs. Luter explained that "atrium" is what you call the central part of the mall with the overhead skylight.

Finally, Rachael chose gifts for her family. Then, they went to the movies. By now, she was so comfortable with her hostess and so delighted by this day that she forgot she was thirteen-years-old and skipped down the street afterwards!

When they returned home, they found the men were awaiting their return. The kitchen staff had prepared the evening meal. Rachael was getting very tired and sat quietly at the dinner table listening to the grown-ups talk. She played with Bruno until bedtime, which wasn't far away. It was only as she crawled into the strange bed in this fancy bedroom that she felt a little uneasy. But she was so tired, she fell asleep immediately.

They didn't have a lot of time, but, in the morning, after saying goodbye to their host and hostess, Abel took Rachael to visit a few of the memorial sites in the city. He took her picture in front of the Jefferson and the Lincoln Memorials. A nice lady offered to take a picture of Abel and Rachael together beside the reflecting pool of the Lincoln Memorial. One could clearly see The Washington Monument in the background. Rachael would prize that picture in the years ahead.

They viewed the Treasury Building, the Capital Building and a few others from the van.

Mostly, Abel handed Rachael the camera and let her take

whatever pictures she chose. Rachael took a picture of a little boy trying to save his hot dog from a real dog, which was obviously friendly, though circling around and behind him. She took a photo of a homeless man digging through the waste can in the park. She snapped a picture of two teenage girls, with their faces pressed into the glass storefront of a large, window display. She took many pictures. And, as she did so, Rachael inadvertently captured, in her mind, scenes that would one day find expression in the stories she would write. For, Rachael was destined to be a writer.

But one picture had the greatest impact for her on this trip. It happened on their final stop. Abel and Rachael visited Arlington Cemetery. They had to walk a little ways to get the best vantage point. Then, Abel grew quiet and somber. He slowly moved forward, and Rachael realized he was forgetful of her. And, in fact, he was. As Colonel Abel Saunders looked down the long rows of markers, he pictured the faces of young men....*Ah*, he thought, *so many were just boys.....laughing and clowning one day. In battle the next..... He had commanded some of them. There are young women, here, too.....*

He stood there unmoving, lost in his thoughts.

Rachael had dropped back a little. She was awed to see the rows and rows of pristine, white, grave markers. But she was equally awed by this moment in Abel's presence. She finally understood that this is an exceptional man. Rachael always looked for words to describe the moment... she searched for the word or words that would define Abel's character and settled for "noble", though she knew it was wholly insufficient. As he stood there alone, with the backdrop of all those graves, Rachael snapped the picture.

Soon, he turned and motioned for her to stand beside him. "Rachael," he said, "this is the most important moment of your visit to Washington." He let his hand circle the area of gravestones. "These are the graves of men and women who gave their lives so you can freely enjoy this trip and all the other good or challenging days of your life in this wonderful nation.

"Do you understand what I'm saying?" he asked.

"Yes," she answered sincerely.

Just outside of Washington, Abel and Rachael had sandwiches and fries. She slept most of the way home.

Melissa stayed over the following, Friday night. Rachael took Melissa to her bedroom, and Joy followed along. That was not unexpected. Joy followed her older sister like a shadow. She had heard the story before, when Rachael shared her adventure at the dinner table. But Joy was excited to hear, again, all that Rachael saw and did in Washington. Of course, along with her enthusiastic tale, Rachael had many pictures to share.

Her bedroom door had been left slightly ajar. As Lou walked past in the hallway, she heard Melissa say to Rachael, "You're sure lucky, Rachael, to have Uncle Abe for a dad."

Later that evening, when Lou shared that with Abel, he only smiled.

The following week, Rachael and Melissa were walking down the hall at the close of classes. Ordinarily, Rachael would catch the bus, while Melissa walked home. That fact much bothered Rachael. She would look out the window of the bus to see Melissa walking with different kids, even some from upper classes. Mostly they were girls. But once she saw Melissa walking with an eleventh grade guy! True, he wasn't anything special, but still......

Rachael was resigned to the bus ride, but never happy about it. *Here I sit in a stupid, school bus! ...ever so much like I'm slow-witted!* Those were Rachael's frustrated thoughts, as the bus rolled past her friend and walking partners. *I wish we still lived in the dumb house,* she would think. *At least I could have walked to the high school like Derek did.*

But today was different. It was Friday and Rachael had permission to go home with Melissa and spend the night. The two were excited about that.

"Hey, Melissa! Wait up!"

Both girls heard the voice calling to Melissa. It had come from Melissa's cousin, Keith Stuart. Keith and Melissa had played together when they were younger. Keith was in eleventh grade now and the relationship had changed a bit. But he still thought of Melissa as someone special and looked out for her.

Melissa turned and intended to wait for Keith, but two girls came up to him just then and distracted him. The one girl was Ms. Conrad's daughter, Clara, who was in ninth grade. The other girl, whom Rachael didn't know, was in eleventh grade.

"Hi, Keith," the girls said almost in unison.

Keith said, "Hi" in an offhand way, while turning again toward Melissa.

The pretty, eleventh-grader nudged Keith. "Let the little girls alone," she teased. "They're just kids."

"Hey, lay off the 'kids' stuff," said Clara

"Well, you don't act like a kid," said her friend in appeasement.

And indeed, Clara didn't act her age. Still two months shy of fifteen-years-of-age, Clara had no common interests with the girls in her class. She made her friendships and spent her time exclusively with kids seventeen or older. Her present company, Dana, who was nearing her seventeenth birthday, was her best friend.

"Melissa's my cousin," Keith explained to the two girls.

School had just dismissed, so there were bumps and disturbances, including two other guys, who came up beside Keith. Roger Adams and Doug Rupp greeted the group, who then seemingly forgot about Melissa and Rachael.

Even Keith now ignored them.

The two, younger girls were a bit deflated by the unintentional brush-off.

"Does Clara run around with that crowd?" Rachael asked as the others thoughtlessly moved away.

"Yeah," Melissa responded.

Rachael knew Clara only in passing and thought her unfriendly. She had never spent any time with the vice-principal's daughter. Living on the outskirts of town all these years had limited her association with the town kids. Besides, Clara had always seemed a bit snobbish. *Maybe that's because of her mother's position in the school,* Rachael supposed. She hadn't given it much thought before. But now she noticed that Clara seemed to be accepted into the society of older students....some of the choicest older students, it seemed, for Roger Adams was in the group.

It was apparent the guys were occupied with Clara and Dana.

"He's cute," said Rachael, as the two walked toward town.

Melissa looked at her in some surprise and asked, "Do you mean Keith?"

Keith's straight, brown hair fell across his forehead and nearly obliterated his left eye. The other eye was green but not very noticeable beneath eyebrows that were prominent and bushy. His friendly smile showcased one slight tooth overlap. But, Keith Stuart had the strong build of a weightlifter. He got his muscles working in his dad's, lumber business. He was a good student, well-liked by his classmates and a major player on the new, football team. He had no problem getting a date when he was interested, but sports eclipsed girls for Keith.

When Rachael didn't answer, Melissa said with discernment, "Oh,….you mean Roger? Yeah. He's real cute. Keith is my cousin, you know," she added.

"I didn't know that," said Rachael. "I guess he's a good friend of Roger?" The statement was really a question.

"They're both on the team," said Melissa. "Keith says Rog will be signing up for basketball, too."

"Do you ever see Roger outside of school?" Rachael persisted.

"Forget it Rachael! He's too old for you," said Melissa with a laugh.

"Well, Clara doesn't think so," Rachael reasoned.

"No one is too old for Clara," said Melissa sarcastically.

They both laughed at that. When they reached the heart of town, Melissa stopped for the family mail at the post office. How Rachael wished she had those things to do in town. She hated being a country girl….though admittedly she did live in the prettiest house in-or-around Alton now.

That was as long as these two would lament a missed

opportunity, even if it involved Roger. They headed for Melissa's home and a Friday night of endless talk and giggles.

When the group around Keith broke up, Roger chose to walk away with Keith. He had been aware of the two girls off to the side. He knew Melissa, for she lived in town. But he was not familiar with Rachael.

"Who's the girl with Melissa," he asked.

"That's Rachael Metcalf," Keith answered. "Rachael and Melissa are good friends. She's in eighth grade, too.

"She's too young…." Keith added, punching Roger in the ribs. "You'd better stick with Clara."

"Spare me," said Roger with a laugh.

Nothing more was said about the two girls. But both of the guys had taken notice.

In the days ahead, as school was dismissed, Roger would make occasion to speak to Rachael. He would be waiting for Keith on the steps, when Rachael left the building to catch the bus. Invariably, he would initiate conversation.

"Hi, Rachael," he said. "How was your day?"

At first, Rachael was surprised…shocked even. *Roger knows my name!*

"I had a good day," she said. Then, with some embarrassment, she hurried off to catch her bus.

But Roger was often in that spot as she left school for the day. Always, he spoke to her by name. She began to think the rendezvous was planned. *Oh, that couldn't be….,* she thought.

The school janitor, Calvin Carson, always watched the students exit at dismissal. He made it his business to be in the hallway, or, in nice weather, just outside the entrance door. He noticed the attention Roger was giving Rachael, as did Mr. Harriger. Neither of them thought these were accidental meetings.

"They're both nice kids," said Mr. H. "At least, that's what I'm told. Rachael is a good student. She's bright, like Derek. Her teachers like her. And, of course, she's so pretty. It's easy to see why Roger is interested. But she's too young for him," he added thoughtfully.

"It's a concern," said Cal. "Hopefully Roger will be too busy with his sport's practice soon to bother with girls."

"Does that ever happen?" asked Mr. H. with chagrin.

"I guess not," Cal agreed. *I wonder if I should speak to Mrs. Price,* he thought. *She and Lou, are good friends. Maybe she could share the concerns with Rachael's mother.* But then, he decided that wasn't necessary....at least, not yet.

It was fall, and Roger was occupied with football. Melissa and Rachael attended the first game. Roger took notice of Rachael when he perused the stands. On rare occasion, he caught sight of her in the hallway at school. The relationship went no further than a smile. But Rachael dreamed of Roger as young girls are apt to do.

Apparently, everyone...students and teachers alike... were noticing the uncommonly pretty, little eighth grader, Rachael Metcalf. One day, amidst the rush of students changing classes, Roger saw Rachael in the hallway and walked over to speak with her. Clara Conrad noticed. Clara grabbed her friend's hand and pushed through the crowd to within earshot of the duo.

"You better be careful, Rog..!" she said loudly. "You know what those Metcalf women are like!"

Roger looked around, as did Rachael, to see who was talking to him.

Now, Clara had the attention of a number of students in the area, as well as Roger and Rachael.

"Like-mother-like-daughter!'" Clara taunted sarcastically.

As the implication of that struck her, Rachael gasped and her cheeks turned red.

A few of the student onlookers laughed. But most were embarrassed for Rachael and quickly turned away.

JerriLynn Smathers was the Home Ec teacher here. Her room was at the very end of the long hallway that offered teaching rooms on either side. JerriLynn was just three years into this job and was very interested in the well- being of the students. She was a careful observer when classes changed and was familiar with most of them.

This day, she heard Clara's, taunting remark to Rachael. As Rachael hurriedly turned away to escape her tormentor, JerriLynn noticed the tears in Rachael's eyes. Reaching out an arm, she drew the young girl into the privacy of her empty classroom and closed the door. Rachael was now sobbing as JerriLynn helped her into a chair.

"Oh, Rachael," JerriLynne said soothingly. "That was so unkind and unfair. I'm so sorry."

Rachael was sobbing now. In her elementary years, living out of town as she did, Rachael had spent very little time after class with the towns' kids. And, unlike Derek's experience, the elementary teachers were kind to Rachael and Joy. "They're such sweet, little girls," they would say to their fellow teachers.

Rachael knew her home life was different from most of her classmates. The other kids talked about their dads. Sometimes, the dad would come to school for some reason. Or, the teacher would ask questions about family. At those times, Rachael felt awkward. And the looks she received from her classmates was evidence that her less-than-proper home life was known.

Melissa Jordan had become an early friend. In the youngest grades, they were only together during school hours. Several years prior to this, Lou had begun to attend the Baptist Church. Of course, she took her girls with her. It was the same church that Melissa's parents attended with their family. Melissa's mother encouraged her daughter to befriend Rachael. And now the two girls were best of friends. With Melissa's friendship, Rachael seldom thought about her family background.

But today, she was confronted in a way she'd never experienced before. This was the first time she had really felt the shame of her mother's past reputation. She was overwhelmed with embarrassment for something about which she was personally blameless.

As JerriLynn handed Rachael tissues and a damp cloth, she sought for words that would take away the hurt from those, hateful words.

"I'm so sorry, Rachael," she repeated. JerriLynn knew Rachael's name. This pretty, young girl was noticeable in her class. It was known she was Derek Metcalf's sister, and Derek was well remembered and respected by the teachers here. She waited in silence until the girl stopped sobbing. Then she said to her, "Sometimes people can be very mean. We've all been victims at times, Rachael. I make it my principle never to remain a victim. If you do, the nasty person wins. I rather think you are stronger than that... ...aren't you?..." she asked hopefully.

Rachael looked up then. JerriLynn could see the resolve rising in her countenance.

"Oh, good," said JerriLynn. "I believe you're like me, Rachael. You're a fighter."

Yes! thought Rachael. A tide of anger was replacing her shame, but not completely. She still cringed to think she would have to go back into the school scene.

JerriLynn handed her a damp cloth to wipe her face. She located a mirror in her handbag and some powder. Then, she watched quietly as the girl patted away the shine on her face.

Finally, Rachael squared her shoulders, and with a sincere "Thank you" to JerriLynn, she stood up, walked to the door and out into the hard world. Rachael left that room a bit more mature.

Several teachers, who were monitoring the change of classes, saw the exchange between Clara and Rachael, but didn't actually hear Clara's unkind remarks. They observed Rachael's changed countenance and knew something bad had occurred. They also saw JerriLynn's quick response. The incident was discussed among the teachers in the lounge the next morning. JerriLynn let them know what Clara had said.

The lounge crowd was incensed. For many of her childhood years, Clara had been comfortable in the high school setting because of her mother's position. But she was not held in high regard. From years of observing her, the teaching staff knew Clara to be arrogant. They all agreed there was no point in bringing the matter before Ms. Conrad. Clara's mother would receive it as an unwarranted criticism of her daughter.

Nothing was resolved that morning. But the teachers would be on guard now to prevent any recurrence of such unkindness. JerriLynn was lauded for her compassionate response toward Rachael. Mr. H observed that JerriLynn responded to their praise in her usual, modest way.

The incident changed Rachael. Years into adulthood, she would remember that hallway incident in her eighth-grade year. It had awakened her to her own vulnerability brought about by her mother's past reputation. That day, Rachael lost a tender innocence. And, especially, she disliked Clara.

The ninth-grader, Clara Conrad, now took special notice of Rachael Metcalf.

The two girls were a notable contrast. Clara was barely five-foot-two in height, slim and small in features. She was attractive enough. Clara had a light, delicate skin coloring, blue eyes and a pert, little, turned-up nose. Her brown hair was bleached blond, permed and purposely un-styled. The thick, long mass of tangles, intentionally wild and disorderly, accentuated her short stature. But it did make her stand out among other, female students.

That is, with the exception of Rachael Metcalf. Rachael was unquestionably the prettier of the two girls. Though only thirteen-year-of-age, Rachael was five-foot-five inches tall. Her body was surprisingly mature. She had a light, caramel skin coloring that reflected her Mexican heritage. Lou insisted her daughter's long, dark hair be cut to a disciplined length, so it fell just a bit below her shoulders in a carefree style. Rachael had always been pretty. But in her blossoming maturity, she was becoming beautiful.

Clara's father was a plant manager in Burnswick. Her mother was Vice Principal at Alton High. An only child, Clara moved with ease socially. She was quite confident and spoke with boldness.

Rachael exhibited great confidence when talking to her younger sister, or even with Melissa, but she was most unsure of herself among the school crowd. She had little, social preparedness for the period ahead. It was innate pride that kept Rachael's head high after that encounter with Clara in the hall.

Jealous pride was Clara's forte. She had ignored Rachael Metcalf through the earlier years of school. But now, with Roger showing an interest in her, Clara took notice, also. And she began the work of undermining everyone's opinion of Rachael.

"Lou Metcalf always dressed well....She must have charged a nice rate," she would say with a laugh.

"I've been told there was a steady stream of men visiting Lou's trailer back then....," she whispered.

"It's been said that old man, Norwell, (who was the town's notorious drunk) spent a lot of time out at that trailer before Rachael was born..."

Clara's campaign bore fruit. Rachael was more and more ostracized. The other students said, "Hi" when they passed her in the hallway, but no one tried to befriend her.

No one, that is, except her good friend, Melissa, who

realized what was happening. Rachael wouldn't talk about it. And rumors travel on the wind with no way to apprehend them. In spite of Melissa's efforts at friendship, Rachael was becoming more withdrawn and even falling into increased disrepute. Roger no longer made any effort toward friendliness. In fact, he was now showing a definite interest in one of his classmates.

Rachael built her walls of self-protection ever higher.

Lou's oldest daughter was much different at home now. And Lou was quick to notice. Always, she had greeted her girls after school and asked about their day. Always, both girls had shared enthusiastically. But now, Rachael only murmured, "It was fine", and went to her room. Though Rachael had always been more temperamental than Joy, she had previously been part of the family. These days, she stayed in her room excessively. She wasn't even very nice to Joy.

After opening her shop in town, and especially after her marriage to retired Colonel Abel Saunders, Lou was accorded respect in town. But these were the same townsfolk that had whispered about her and avoided social contact in earlier years. She knew her past choices were shameful. She had her three children out-of-wedlock to three different men. *They have a right to whisper about me,* she thought. *But my children have done nothing to deserve this.*

She knew Derek had suffered because of her reputation. But she believed her daughters had been spared….that is, until now. With Rachael so isolated and wounded, Lou could only suppose herself to blame.

Derek held the same suspicions. He well understood

how hurtful the gossip about his mother could be. Through the years, he had been so grateful that Rachael and Joy had not experienced similar prejudice from teachers and schoolmates.

But Rachael has matured, and she's pretty, he thought. *She and her classmates are older now. Some might be jealous of her. Others might be nasty just because they delight in gossip.*

The family said little, but they were all concerned. Until they knew the problem, they couldn't help. When Rachael offered no explanation in the days ahead, Lou was disheartened.

"If Joy is anything like Rachael in her teen years, I don't think I can bear it," she said to Abel one evening.

"Rachael's different," Abel acknowledged. "Something is bothering her."

Abel had been a military commander. In that role, it was necessary to have insight when dealing with a troubled youth. Many of his soldiers were just that. They were barely beyond childhood. He found he was gifted with that insight. And years of experience had sharpened his understanding. He knew intuitively that something beyond the ordinary was troubling Rachael.

One morning, as Abel and Derek visited at the breakfast table, Rachael came down for school. She was dressed in a very short skirt. Lou took one glance and said, "Rachael, you're all legs! That skirt is too short to be worn outside this house."

Glowering at her mother, Rachael shot back, "What do you care what people think of me?"

The sharp exchange brought Abel and Derek to attention. Words were not found, as their mouths dropped open.

Lou's face turned white. Rachael whirled around. The three grown-ups exchanged shocked glances, as they heard her run up the stairs. A minute later, dressed in blue jeans, Rachael came through the room and went out the door in a run. The bus had pulled in at the foot of the lane. She had to hurry to catch it.

Lou's head noticeably dropped, as she turned back to the sink. Derek picked up his book bag, and with a quiet, "Goodbye, Mom..." and a nod to Abel, he left the house.

Rachael's morning outburst troubled Derek all day. When he returned from college that afternoon, he received the letter from Bill, in which he discussed his problem at work. *There are troubles enough to go around*, Derek thought. And, he had no way of solving any of them.

He felt especially bad for his mother. Her past indiscretions had brought damage to him during his earlier, school years. But he knew her to be a wonderful mother.

What is happening in Rachael's life, he wondered?

Three

AT HOME, NOTHING WAS SAID about Rachael's rudeness to her mother. Derek knew his mother was hurt as well as concerned, but she didn't discuss it with him. Once again, Lou withdrew into her private world. She never denied her mistakes, and she kept her pain to herself. But this daughter's problem did not go away. Rachael remained withdrawn, uncommunicative.

Derek determined he had to seek some answers. A talk with Cal, the janitor at Alton High, might help. Calvin Carson's "den" had been a refuge for Derek during his four years of high school, and the janitor had been his confidant and counselor.

When he left college this day, Derek drove directly to Alton High School. There, he made his way down the stairs, past the boiler, the water heater and further in to Cal's private "den". The head janitor at Alton High School had fashioned an office for himself amid the equipment of the boiler room in the basement. He had a small refrigerator. His coffee pot, a radio, and a simple, desk lamp, left just enough room on the stand for his work schedule. The radio was always tuned to the weather channel in the morning and turned off when Cal went home.

This day, as Derek rounded the furnace, he realized how much he had missed the comfort of this place. His old friend was seated on the familiar, straight-back chair with the now-faded, comfort-pillow. Cal was bent over some paperwork on his desk. The weather station, sounding in the background, was loud enough to muffle Derek's entrance.

Derek spoke early so as not to alarm Cal, who was deeply involved in the paperwork. "Good afternoon, Governor." Derek resorted to a familiar title for the janitor.

The old man turned quickly, and with a big smile, rose and reached out his hand to Derek, whom he hadn't seen for some months.

"Derek! Well, my young friend, how are you? How good it is to see you."

"Same here," said Derek, and their hands clung for a moment.

"Have a seat," said Calvin. "Will you have coffee or a coke today?"

"The cold drink sounds good," said Derek. It all sounded so touchingly familiar.

Cal reached a coke to Derek, who had seated himself on his stool. He had fashioned this seat from cement blocks back in ninth grade. It hadn't been moved or altered. Cal poured himself a cup of coffee. Then, he seated himself and said, "Well, how is college going for you this year? It's been some time since I've seen you."

"Yeah. I'm sorry about that," said Derek. And he really was sorry to realize how long it had been since he had visited with this dear friend. He was, in fact, a bit concerned to realize how old Cal looked. The janitor was a little man, with a noticeable stoop in his posture today. His thin hair was gray now, his face lined in wrinkles, and he walked with an obviously painful gait.

"It's gon'na rain," said Cal, who had noticed Derek's look of concern. "I don't need the weather report anymore to tell me that. My arthritic knees are a dependable sage.

"But tell me how you are doing in college?"

"Everything is fine," said Derek. "I've had no problem with my studies."

"Well, that doesn't surprise me," said Calvin. "Are you finding the experience a good one?"

"It is an experience," said Derek with chagrin. "It sure isn't like high school. Not many of the students seem to have had an Alton High background. With a lot of them, anything goes. I'm glad not to be living on campus. With so much activity all around, I don't know how they study there.

"Well, you've entered the real world now," said Cal. "The administration here tries to engrain the students with good morals and work ethics to prepare them for the cultural shock of the outside world."

"Yes," said Derek. "I do realize what a good education I received here."

At Cal's urging, Derek then shared some of his experiences.

Cal listened with great interest. "It sounds like you're finding your place there," he said. "And I'm not surprised."

Then he asked, "How's your family doing? What a beautiful home Abel and Lou have! We're all so glad to see Lou blessed. I speak with Abel most Sundays at church...."

"Yes, Mom's doing well. I'm very glad Abel came into her life," Derek said.

"And the little sisters?" Cal asked. "I guess they're not so little anymore?"

"Well.....Joy's still a child.. But Rachael… …"

Derek hesitated for a moment. Then, he attempted to introduce the subject of his concern carefully.

"Maybe you've noticed, Rachael and Melissa Jordan are good friends," he said. "But then, I expect she's making other friends now, too?" It was a hopeful question. He hoped to hear something positive from his old friend.

Rachael's ordeal with Clara was known to Cal as well as the teachers. They all knew that Ms. Conrad's daughter was an unfair adversary for Rachael. And they could see that Rachael was hurt and withdrawn. She was not the cheerful, young girl who had come to classes at the start of the school year. Cal was quick to discern Derek's concern and came right to the point.

"Derek," he said. "I understand Rachael is struggling with something. JerriLynn Smathers has taken her under her wing. She will be a good influence. You know the administration and teachers look out for all the kids. And your mother has the girls in church. That will help," Cal said reassuringly. "Our best bet is always to take our concerns to the Lord in prayer."

Abel had told Cal that Derek confessed Christ to him before he graduated from high school. But Cal had not seen Derek in church. As he had no way of knowing the reason for that, he said nothing more on that subject.

Derek dropped his head. He realized Cal did not feel at liberty to talk about this matter. Maybe he really didn't know what was happening with Rachael. Derek changed the subject. "I was told Miss Roberts is gone," he said.

"Yes. That was quite a surprise," Cal responded.

"I expect Mr. Harriger misses her," Derek said.

"We all do," Cal was being cautious again. Indeed, he and the others knew that Mr. Harriger had been much wounded by that turn of events that found Cindy Roberts married to another man.

"Well, I'm still working at Skinny's after classes. So, I need to be going. I just wanted to stop by and say 'hello'."

As Derek rose, Cal stood quickly and the two hugged. "Do stop in again soon, Derek. I'll be anxious to know about your political role." Then Cal added, "It's nice to have Rachael here at Alton High. We'll all do our best to look after her."

"I'll be back soon," Derek promised. As he turned to leave, he was shaken by how much Cal seemed to have aged. There was scarcely anyone in Derek's life who meant more to him than this, high school janitor. He determined he would stop more faithfully in the future.

As he exited the basement, Derek understood that unless-or-until Rachael shared her problem, his only recourse was prayer. *It should have been my first recourse,* he thought.

He had solved nothing. But he was in his old school. Class dismissal for the close of the school day was just minutes away. He still had a little time and decided to visit the teachers, who had been so helpful in his life.

He gave a brief visit to Mr. Harrison, his former history teacher. Mr. Scott, who taught Biology, greeted him enthusiastically. He intended to visit Miss Smathers. He had really hoped to talk to her. But she had other company, so he had to content himself with a wave.

School was ending just as Derek walked down the hall. Mr. Harriger's door swung open, and Mr. H. stepped into the hallway as the children filed out of his room. He and Derek shook hands. Like the other teachers, he was truly glad to see this, past student.

Derek could not help but notice the absence of Cindy Roberts. Cindy had taught the subject of Business at Alton High. Her home room was next door to Mr. Harriger's home room. The two of them had always stood together, beyond congenial, as students came or went to classes or dismissal. Now, Mr. H. looked so incomplete standing outside his doorway without her there at his side.

Derek hesitated a moment but said nothing.

David recognized Derek's unspoken concern. "They'll be gone in a minute," he said, indicating the children who were quickly moving out of his room.

"'Bye, Mr. Harriger," he heard from many.

Derek waited as the children filed out of the classroom. Finally, the noisy dismissal was complete, and David turned his attention to this, former student. Derek was questioned about his college experience. They talked a few, more minutes. The absence of Cindy was so noticeable, but neither of them had broached the subject.

Finally, with a self-deprecating smile, Mr. H. voiced what they both were thinking. "Yeah. It's different without Cindy. And I'm finding it hard, Derek," he admitted. "You probably knew my feelings for Cindy were deep. But....life can give some hard knocks."

Derek nodded in agreement but didn't comment. They visited for a minute more before they shook hands and parted.

As he walked away from the school, Derek thought about the parting words of Mr. H. *"Life can give some hard knocks".* *I sure understand that,* he thought sadly. His own memories drifted back to Penny, the girl he had dated in eleventh grade....the girl he loved...and lost. Penny had married Michael Houston, another classmate.

Yeah, he thought. *I understand about "hard knocks."*

Mr. H. watched Derek Metcalf walk away. The classroom was empty now, and he went back inside to set everything in order before departing for the day.

Two of the blinds had been lowered to shield eyes from the afternoon sun. He adjusted them to conform to the others. There was something bright back there under that desk. He reached down and retrieved a red, basketball jersey that was rolled into a ball. Had the kid left his room with no shirt on? With kids, anything was possible.

This certainly wasn't the strangest thing he had ever found. Once, he picked a toothbrush off the floor. More than once he had found something of concern. He turned such things over to the principal.

With everything in order, he walked to his desk slowly and sat down. There was no reason to hurry home. *"Home" and "house" describe two very different places,* he thought. *I live in a "house"; I don't have a "home".* That thought was discouraging. He had imagined that with Cindy.

As he sat here today, he let himself remember. He thought back to those years when Derek had been a student here. *They were happy years*, he remembered...*years when I had Cindy Roberts at my side.*

They had never dated,...Cindy's choice....But he looked forward to seeing her every morning, looking into those beautiful, blue eyes and chatting with her in the hallway as classes changed. He loved Cindy and believed the feelings were mutual. *Strangely, I still believe that,* he thought. But back then he had garnered hopes of winning her hand in marriage.

Alas, now he knew what hindered that hope.

The scene was indelibly sketched on his heart. He would not likely ever forget the way it started. Even the date was firmly fixed,...it was April 3, which was the final, school day before the Easter break last spring.

JerriLynn had arrived at the teacher's lounge early to make the coffee that morning. For some reason, he always smiled when he thought about JerriLynn. Even this afternoon, with his melancholy fixed on Cindy, he smiled, as he remembered JerriLynn busy at the coffee urn. That self-imposed duty was typical of her. She was the Home Economics teacher, and from the time she began working at Alton High three years prior, she had assumed the role of hostess in the teacher's lounge. Cheerful, kind, self-forgetful, and most helpful...those were the thoughts of JerriLynn that always brought the smile to his face. *She's attractive, too,* he thought now. *It took me a little time to realize that. It helped when she abandoned the pony-tail or whatever it was she did with her hair when she first came. She now wears her dark curls cut short. She replaced her glasses with contacts and one can see that she has really pretty, blue eyes.*

Like Cindy, JerriLynn is tiny....
  ..like Cindy.....
   ...like Cindy....
  Ah, but there's no one quite like Cindy... ...

Cindy was small in features with golden hair tinged with brown. She had a porcelain doll look, with big blue eyes and a beautiful smile. No one could remember ever seeing her at school in anything other than heels and skirt or dress. Cindy was genuinely friendly, and she laughed easily. She was a favorite with teachers and students alike. She was a favorite with David simply because he was in love with her and couldn't remember a time when he wasn't. He had long held out the hope that she might admit the attraction was mutual, for he truly believed it was.

Anyway, ...on that fateful, April day, JerriLynn had exited for a brief time to attend to a personal matter. The others began arriving for the day. When JerriLynn re-entered the teacher's lounge a short time later, she registered the same look of surprise the others had evidenced when the seat beside Mr. Scott and across from himself, was still empty. Cindy Roberts always sat in that seat. The others knew that he and Cindy were almost a couple. At least, it's probable they all knew he was in love with Cindy.

This morning, the group was discussing Miss Robert's absence.

"Mr. Ashton stopped me in the hall and asked me to fill in for her second-period, study hall," said Mr. Wilbert. "I understand she had an unexpected visitor just now and Principal Ashton is excusing her today. With no advance warning, her substitute will be a little late. Cindy is always dependable, so he made an exception for her in this."

There was a general murmuring as those present considered Miss Robert's, unexpected visitor.

Just then, the door opened and Cindy Roberts entered ahead of a well-dressed man, who was a stranger to them, but obviously not to her. Cindy was all smiles as she looked up at him. The fellow was lanky and noticeably tanned. His dark hair was combed back, and showed a distinguished-looking streak of white across the top in front. Gray hair interspersed with the darker hair above his ears.

A yellow tie and yellow, striped shirt showed beneath the gray tweed jacket. The immaculate slacks were a darker shade of gray. He wore dark rimmed, larger-than-stylish glasses.

Stopping just inside the door, Cindy announced, "Friends, I'd like you to meet Professor Clifford Edelson."

Her announcement was met by stunned silence. Mr. Scott was the first to recover. He rose quickly from his seat and walking over to the man, he shook his hand said, "It's a pleasure to meet you, Professor." Though no one else had risen, the others then offered a delayed but equally gracious greeting…everyone that is, except Mr. Harriger. A tide of red, which had begun at his neck, now rose to cover his face. He remained silent.

"Clifford is Professor of Egyptian Archeology at Keenan University in Ultima, Illinois," Cindy explained.

He's sure playing the professor role to the hilt, Mr. H had thought grudgingly,….*complete with the dark-rimmed glasses and suede patches on the tweed, jacket sleeves.*

"Clifford has been in the South Karnak region of Egypt these past three years working on a project that is co-sponsored by the Museum of Egyptian Antiquity in New York City. The work is sanctioned by the Egyptian government. But I'm sure you've noticed the turmoil in Egypt…in fact, in the entire Middle East in recent months. They've endeavored to keep their project out of the spotlight."

"Well, that might have been impossible if you had been around," said Clifford, with less than humor in his remark.

"Oh! I'm so sorry, Clifford! Did I say something I shouldn't have?" Cindy asked in concern.

No one spoke into the uncomfortable silence that ensued. Those seated at the table had never seen Cindy Roberts this flustered.

JerriLynn, who had stationed herself by the coffee machine, heard that exchange and spoke to ease the awkward situation.

"Would you two like coffee?" she offered.

"Oh, yes, that wou…." But Cindy's words were interrupted.

"No! ..no..," Clifford softened the second refusal, as he reached over and took Cindy's elbow to turn her back toward the door. "We won't have time for that today," he said curtly. "It was a pleasure meeting you all," he added properly. And then, he propelled a docile, obviously confused Cindy Roberts out the door.

Mr. Scott again found his manners first and spoke to Clifford's retreating back, "It was a pleasure meeting you, Professor." There were some general murmurs from the others. But they surely weren't heard, for Professor Edelson and Miss Roberts were already disappearing down the hallway.

The normally vocal group of teacher-friends sat stunned

and silent. Just then, the bell rang with a warning for the start of classes, and they all rose in haste to exit the room. Mr. H recalled that he was first out the door.

That morning, on the break just before the second period, Cal, the school janitor, was walking down the hallway near Mr. Harriger's room. Cal had been the janitor here for more than thirty years. Everyone respected and liked Cal...Ms. Conrad, the vice principal being the possible exception. As the last kid exited, Mr. H remembered that he had called out to him, "Hey! Cal!"

When Cal walked over, David asked, "Do you have a minute?"

"Oh, sure," the janitor said agreeably. "How are you, Mr. H?"

"I've been better," was his gruff reply. "Did you happen to meet the guy Cindy brought around this morning?" he asked.

"Well....no. I didn't actually meet him," Calvin responded. "But I did see him as the two of them came through," he said. "I was sweeping up some paper in the hallway at the time. Miss Roberts curiously seemed a little upset," he said with some concern. "When she noticed me, she stopped and tugged at his arm. I expect Miss Roberts was intending to introduce us. I set the broom aside to meet him. But apparently her friend was rushed and hurried her away without stopping," Cal explained.

He suspected Cal knew it was a deliberate snub. But he would not risk slighting Miss Roberts by expressing that.

"Is he somebody important, do you suppose?" Cal asked.

"Cindy sure seems to think so," Mr. H said glumly.

Cal, as well as all the other teachers, knew of Mr. Harriger's affection for Cindy Roberts. Not knowing what to say, he said nothing.

"It wouldn't be so bad, if he was a nice guy. But he's an arrogant, stuffed-shirt!" said Mr. H angrily.

"Maybe he has some redeeming qualities," Cal offered gently.

"Not a chance!" was the reply. "And he didn't treat her well. If I ever see him push her around again, I'll give him some instructions!" he said angrily.

The janitor didn't know to what he was referring. Cal could see that he was upset and tried to offer some encouraging words.

"They did stop when Principal Ashton greeted them further down the hall," Cal offered. "I saw Cindy introduce the two men. Her friend appeared to be at ease with Mr. Ashton, and they talked for a minute. Their meeting was interrupted by the ringing of the bell announcing the start of the school day. The hallway was jammed with children and teachers seeking classrooms. Miss Roberts and her friend bid the principal a good day and exited the building.

"I notice we have a substitute in her area now, so I expect she's gone for the day?" The last was a bit of a question.

"She won't be back," David had replied curtly.

Just then, the bell rang signaling the time for the next class, and the kids began to swarm down the hallway. Mr. Harriger gathered his calm.

"Thanks, Cal," he said. "Thanks for listening." And he went into his room.

Cindy Roberts has a beau! And it isn't Mr. Harriger. The

next weeks were a blur for David. When Cindy returned from that weekend with Clifford, she was wearing a big, diamond ring. She had entered the teacher's lounge as usual. She got a cup of coffee and then seated herself across from Mr. H. But it took only a moment for her ring to be noticed. It was Mrs. Blake who commented first.

"Cindy! Is that a diamond on your finger?" she asked in surprise.

That was followed by a chorus of excitement from the others. They gathered around to view the ring....everyone, that is, except David. He just sat there stunned. As her friends admired her ring, he knew his emotions were registered on his face. When Cindy looked over at him, she showed obvious concern. Cindy and he had locked eyes, and then she quickly looked away.

I suspect she felt pity for me, he thought in remembrance. He had never, in his lifetime, been more embarrassed. It seemed all his friends were looking at him now.

The room grew silent. But he had collected himself and said quietly, "Congratulations, Cindy."

"Thank you," she responded softly.

Cindy didn't return to the teacher's lounge that day. It was probable that all the teachers knew he was in love with Cindy. *Maybe like me, they assumed she returned my affections,* he thought.

Cindy and her beau were the subject of conversation anytime the teachers met in the lounge the remainder of that day.

"I never even heard her speak of Clifford," said Mr. Scott. The others acknowledged their shock at this turn of events…that is, everyone except for Mrs. Blake. Cindy's best friend was Mrs. Blake, the librarian. When the clamor ceased, she spoke quietly.

"I knew about Clifford."

She had the attention of all.

"Clifford and Cindy were in college together. They dated through her last, three, college years," she explained. "He graduated a year before Cindy. She told me she had expected that he would ask for her hand in marriage after his graduation. But he didn't.

"A year later, when he applied for and was hired as an assistant to Professor Georges, an expert in archaeology, she was sure they would marry then. And, in fact, he called her that night to say he got the job and would drive down to see her that weekend. Cindy said she was so excited, and she dressed so carefully for that date.

"They went to an exclusive restaurant for dinner, and, after pouring her a glass of champagne, Clifford reached into his pocket and retrieved a jewelry box. She breathed a sigh of relief, as he handed it to her.

"But when she lifted the lid, she was dismayed. Clifford supposed she was overwhelmed by the beauty of the gift. But that just wasn't so. He had bought her an expensive watch with a black, Egyptian cat twined around the band. She told me she had nearly cried.

"To this day, she hates that watch. You've never seen her wear it. She said she wore it only enough to keep Clifford satisfied."

Clifford. All these years, Cindy had been waiting for Clifford, thought David.

David couldn't even remember the days of that Easter break. He figured he stayed in his apartment looking blankly at the TV screen.

The morning they returned to class, he had arrived at the teacher's lounge early. JerriLynn had already made the coffee and had left the room on an errand. Mrs. Blake was the only one present yet.

"The coffee is ready, David," she said as he entered.

He filled his cup and sat down at the table, not knowing what to say.

Mrs. Blake broke the silence, "I'm sorry David. I'm almost as shocked as you probably are. I really thought she'd make a wiser decision."

"She pitied me," he mumbled almost to himself. He was still deeply wounded as he remembered Cindy's engagement announcement and how she had dropped her head and couldn't look at him.

"Oh, no, David…that wasn't it," Mrs. Blake replied sincerely. "Cindy is in love with you. I can see she's still torn by her decision."

But he couldn't believe that.

The next weeks were a fog for David. Cindy was excited about her plans to marry in July.

She told her friends in the teacher's lounge, "We will be married in Ultima. My parents will fly up there, as Clifford wants us to be married in that city's old, historic cathedral. His parents attend that church. We plan a short honeymoon in Alaska. Clifford says he has baked in the sun for three years in Egypt. Now, he wants to enjoy the cold.

"We will live in Ultima, of course. Clifford will be

teaching in the university there in September. Clifford says he has friends in the educational hierarchy and will suggest my name as a Business teacher in the nearby high school."

Mr. H was so sickened hearing about "Clifford" that he wished he could avoid the teacher's lounge in the mornings. But his absence would have been especially noted. So he forced himself to tough it out.

Cindy surely understood how hard this was for him. She stayed in her room between classes.

The kids noticed the change. They soon heard about Miss Robert's engagement. They were especially considerate of Mr. H, which he found embarrassing. He hated the thought that he was pitied.

His friends understood. One morning, when Miss Roberts didn't make it to the lounge, the others spoke freely.

"It's hard to believe this is the same Cindy Roberts we've known all these years," said Mrs. Blake.

"I guess love will do that to a person," Mr. Scott said wryly. "How about you, JerriLynn? Are you hiding a serious beau somewhere?"

"There's only one Clifford," said JerriLynn. "And Miss Roberts got him. I guess I'll just be an old maid."

"I don't think you need to worry about that," said Mr. Scott. "And you can thank your stars you didn't get stuck with Clifford."

"Amen," said Mrs. Blake.

David recalled the day Cindy chose to seek him out for a personal word. The school year was winding down. She would soon be gone from his life. He weathered the heartache, endeavoring not to let it show.

Classes had been dismissed for the day. The last of the students were receding down the steps to the outside world. Cindy had waited. When all were gone, she stepped across to David's room. He was sitting at his desk, with his head down in his hands. That picture would stay with Cindy in the years ahead.

He sensed her presence, looked up and then rose to his feet. Neither offered a greeting as she walked toward him and stopped in front of his desk.

"David….," she said softly.

She caught her breath as she looked into his eyes. She had come to express her sadness about … ……about what? Cindy had no words…no correct words. She loved David as her dear friend. She knew he loved her. But she had waited for Clifford for so long. She had waited all these years for him to propose….

Finally, David spoke. "It's alright, Cindy," he said softly. "I wish you well."

"Thank you," she whispered. She turned and walked away.

The students all congratulated Miss Roberts and fussed over her ring. At one of the final, student rallies for the year, Principal Ashton called Cindy up on stage. Mr. H thought her more beautiful than ever. She was wearing the soft, blue dress that caught the blue of her eyes.

Cindy… … … … oh, Cindy, don't do this… said his heart. But he remained silent, of course.

She was given a hearty round of applause in appreciation for her service.

The teachers gave her a farewell party in the lounge. He didn't attend.

Even the worst of times pass eventually. Finally, it was June. At the end of each, school year, he would spend a two-week vacation at the Outer Banks. Following that, he assumed the role of visiting Editor of his father's small newspaper in Weston, TN, while his parents took a much-needed vacation. That was the routine he had followed since locating in Alton, Pennsylvania. The Weston News reached towns circling an area of fifty miles in any direction. It was a challenging job. But he was capable and found the work interesting, though not on a level with teaching. He knew he had found his niche in life as a math teacher at the high school in Alton, Pennsylvania.

He couldn't actually think of anything he had experienced in life that had hurt him more than that experience of losing Cindy. But he had endured. When summer was over, he was back in Alton, PA.

He had returned to Alton on the 25th of August. Alton High would resume classes for the new, school year on August 26. He probably should have allowed two or three days to prepare his living quarters. But the ending of the last, school year had been most difficult and returning to Alton was not easy.

The apartment he was renting was upstairs, with an outside entrance, in the widow Faller's house. He had three rooms and a really nice bath. In fact, all the rooms were large, decorative and comfortable. The kitchen was modern; the bedroom offered a king-size bed and other amenities. In the living room, three, large connecting windows look out on the main highway and the high school across the way. The widow Faller, a woman in her seventies, was very nice, too. Though

his board was not included, she often brought him food…
lasagna and other casseroles. He finally realized his landlady
must keep these single-serving bowls to prepare for him when
she was cooking her own meal. And there were sweets for any
taste. Mrs. Faller often expressed how glad she was to have
such a nice boarder.

When school was out in June, he had paid his rent for
the summer, asking her to reserve the apartment for him for
the next, school year. He could well afford to do that, and he
didn't suppose he could find a better arrangement.

But he had returned in August with a heavy heart. His
mood had nothing to do with his living quarters. Correction,
it had everything to do with his living quarters. He was tired
of living alone in a rented apartment. He could well afford to
buy a home of his own. But he had the old-fashioned idea that
a home needed a woman…no…not just a woman. He could
always find a woman. He wanted a wife.

Since coming of age, he had no problem attracting
women. He hadn't bothered to date in high school. But in
college, he went out with a number of different girls, many of
whom let him know that she was available. But none inspired
him to form a lasting relationship. He had his own ideas about
marriage. First, it was to be founded on love, the kind of love
that consumed one. He kind'a believed there was a perfect
mate for each person, and that he would know when he found
his mate. He figured they'd both know. For the love would
be mutual.

Following college, during his years in the military, he
parked that goal and concentrated on the duty at hand. After
his discharge from service, he began his permanent career
as Math teacher in this, little town. Alton suited his ideals so

well. When he met Miss Cindy Roberts, teacher of Business at Alton High, he thought the puzzle was coming together just right.

But, alas, that hope had died the previous spring. Cindy had other plans. His heart had been crushed...as was his pride. He had never been slighted by a woman before. And Cindy's rejection and preference for another was played out before all his fellow, teacher friends and students. It was humiliating. Almost sufficiently humiliating to make him forget his broken heart. Almost....

That had been the reason for his discouragement as he unpacked his belongings at his apartment.

He responded to the knock on his kitchen door. Mrs. Faller stood there with a plate of cookies.

"Thank you, Ma'am," he said as he took the tray. "How was your summer, Mrs. Faller?"

"Welcome back. And I had a good summer, thank you," she said with cheer. "Do you find your apartment suitable still? Have you any needs that aren't met?" she asked.

"Everything is great," he said, knowing she had no possibility of solving his problem with loneliness. As Mrs. Faller departed, he turned back to his rooms and walked over to the windows that faced Alton High School.

He had approached the new, school year deeply humbled. That first day as he hurried to his classroom, he realized he was a few minutes late, and the kids had taken quick advantage. They were clustered in the hallway just outside his door and making far too much noise. But he was happy for the confusion at the doorway. It took his mind off the one who wasn't there this year. Cindy Roberts had always been first to her room. Then, she would stand in the doorway to greet the kids…and me. How he looked forward to her smile, which seemed to say so much, though words were not spoken.

But this was a new era, a new life without Cindy.

It's the old habits that are the most painful, he recalled. He faced an immediate problem as he entered the lounge that first morning. Who would sit in the chair across from him? That had been Cindy's chair for these many years. He had taken pleasure that his friends realized that he and Cindy were a pair. At least, in his eyes they were a pair. And Cindy had always chosen that seat just as if she thought so, too. Now, as he took his coffee cup to the table, the empty chair was another, painful reminder.

He figured it was awkward for the others who entered the lounge, too. But the regulars wandered in and each took a regular place at the table. What makes us all gravitate to the same seats, he wandered. Even after the summer away, we all do so. He looked around. Sure enough, Mrs. Blake sat on his right. Art Peterson sat on the opposite side, one chair further along. He always separates himself by one chair, he noted. This morning, that one chair was filled by the new, ninth-grade, History teacher. Mr. Wilbert sat across from Mr. Scott, as usual….and so on.

The seat across from David had always been Cindy's chair. They were a duo, and everyone recognized that. Everyone, except Cindy, it seems….. Now, that vacant seat cast a pall on the morning's gathering. He knew his own demeanor was revealing. He'd always been a man of good humor and cheer. Mr. Scott once said, "Dave and Cindy together are as cheerful as the morning sun…"

Aw, well, ...life goes on...

But just as he pulled out his chair to sit, JerriLynn, who had finished her efforts at the coffee machine, walked across the room, nonchalantly pulled out "Cindy's" chair and seated herself. Her movements were so unaffected, she made it look natural. The others breathed a collective sigh of relief.

"I don't know if I'm ready for this," said JerriLynn. "...another year down in the dungeon." That's what she laughingly called her Home Ec room, which was under the stage and adjoined the gym.

"How many kids have signed up for Home Ec this year?" Mr. Scott asked.

"Principal Ashton told me I'd have twenty-three in one class and fifteen in the other," she responded.

There was much commiseration about the twenty-three, which was a considerable number for one Home Ec class. After that, the conversation flowed easily into other subjects. JerriLynn was up and down several times fussing with cups and napkins over by the coffee machine. The counter, under the coffee urn, tended to get messed with spilled liquids and sugar. JerriLynn wet a cloth and wiped it.

More than once, she refilled someone's, coffee cup. Mr. Scott had once teased JerriLynn about being a Home Ec teacher who made no cookies. After that, she often brought home baked cookies for the lounge crowd in the morning. Occasionally one of the other, female teachers did so, too. Last year, Mrs. Blake made some tasty brownies, and Art Peterson's aide, Dotty Sloan, brought chocolate chip cookies one day. But JerriLynn was the most dependable. She just seemed comfortable in the role of hostess.

On this morning, he had observed her casually at first. Then, he noticed her more carefully. She still had the short hair style which replaced the ponytail. It made her look older. And this summer, she had gained a deep tan which was most attractive. When Mr. Scott teased her about spending the summer on the hammock, JerriLynn laughed and replied, "I spent the summer chasing my sister's three, young hoodlums around the yard, while Emily and Blaine toured Bermuda for their tenth wedding anniversary.

He had smiled at JerriLynn's animation as she recounted some incidents she had while babysitting those children. He enjoyed the sparkle in her ever-so-blue eyes. The problem about the chair opposite seemed to have been forgotten by everyone, even by him.

"Have you all seen the new arrangement in the gym?" she asked the group.

"Yeah," said Mr. Wilbert. "What are they doing there? It appears they're making the area smaller."

"They've partitioned a little off both ends," Mr. Scott contributed. "They plan to enclose that space for costume changes during the plays. The opposite end will allow room for instruments or other side stuff, when needed on stage."

"That will sure help," said JerriLynn. They had always requisitioned the Home Ec room when they had an event on stage that necessitated extra space. When there was a school play, the kids changed their costumes in her Home Ec room between acts, and then hurried up on stage. Instruments cluttered up the room during certain, special events. Always, she had to rearrange her schedule and plan her material during that time. She had to keep her students seated at the tables. It was usually the one space left unhindered.

The conversation was flowing easily now. Even he had a few comments to offer. Then, the bell rang for the teachers to leave the lounge and be attendant in their rooms for the start of the school day. JerriLynn was slow to rise. As he left the room, he glanced back and saw Mr. Scott squeeze JerriLynn's shoulder and whisper something to her. He suspected JerriLynn had acted intentionally. But it helped.

He knew he was different now. The students realized it. His teacher friends looked at him sadly. He sure didn't want their sympathy.

Cindy didn't deceive me, he thought. *She made it clear all along that she didn't want a romantic relationship with me. But we had a relationship.....The spark was there for her, too....I wasn't wrong about that.*

Forget it, David! He shook himself. *Let it go! It's over. She's married to him now!*

And I am six years older and....hopefully....wiser.

He had spent six years of his life supposing a different ending than this. He wasn't familiar with a lot of the Bible, but he recalled the story of Jacob in the book of Genesis. Jacob had worked seven years to gain the hand of Rachael in marriage only to be cheated into marrying her sister, Leah. The story says he worked seven more years to marry Rachael. But his love for Rachael was so great, the long wait seemed like a day. David Harriger understood a love that powerful. But there was no happy ending for him.

Mrs. Conners had been hired in Cindy's place to teach the Business courses. Mrs. Conners was in her middle fifties. A native of Alton, she had lived all of her married life in

California. Her late husband had worked in Silicon Valley. She had three children. All were married, and she had several grandchildren. But all were located in California. Thus, she seemed a bit like a displaced person.

However, she had family in Alton, too. Her elderly father was still living here, and she had several siblings, both older than she. She seemed nice enough... ...*just rather dull after Cindy,* he thought. Mrs. Conners never came to the teacher's lounge in the morning, and rarely any other time. She stayed in her room and was usually seated at her desk with some paperwork.

When classes changed now, as often as not, he stayed in his room, too. Previously, this had been a bright spot in the hall. The area had radiated good humor as Cindy and he stood together greeting the kids between classes. Now, the area had a heaviness about it, which seemed to absorb the cheerful chatter of the kids as they walked down this hallway.

Fortunately, the days were busy, and gradually he knew some ease as they passed.

Nights were the hardest. His apartment felt so empty. Early into the morning, he would stand at the windows and look across to the school from his apartment. He was anxious for morning. He liked the personnel at Alton High and enjoyed the work. Always, he would think, I'll feel better when I get back into the grind.

And indeed, his classes had been going well.

You don't die from a broken heart, David thought wryly.

The brief visit today, from Derek Metcalf, had been a sharp reminder of happier days and burgeoning hope. It was a fresh reminder of Cindy Roberts. And it had re-opened the wound. But then, it didn't take much of a scratch to get it oozing again....

He rose from his desk and walked to the door. Across the way, Cal and his aide, Jason, were working on a door that kept jamming.

"Well! Mr. Harriger! You're keeping late hours. You'll miss your dinner," said Cal.

"I can afford to miss a few meals," said David, with a pat to his stomach.

"Goodnight, sir," said Jason.

"Goodnight, fellas," said David. And he left the building.

Four

IN RECENT MONTHS, DEREK HAD decided to follow his mother's example and read a few chapters in the Bible before retiring for the night. His plan was to start at the first chapter and read through the book. He had progressed to the book of Samuel, but there was much in scripture that was a mystery to him. Even so, there was plenty that he did understand, and it was helping him to deeply appreciate the gift of salvation he had received from the Lord Jesus Christ.

That understanding was helpful to his prayer life, too. Rachael's problems at school weighed heavily on Derek. His friend, Bill Tonkins' problem was a concern. He had no answers for either of these. But he prayed for them.

He was overjoyed to receive this letter from Bill in the following days.

> Hi, my friend,
>
> This is just a short note to tell you how my personnel problem was resolved.
> The error...or intentional cover-up.... occurred in Eastern Mobil's Personnel Department. If not for Mr. Steven's careful

oversight, that employee's deception would have continued unnoticed.

I think I already told you, Mike's original application was missing. Those responsible for securing the files insist they have no idea how that could have happened.

At the time Mike was hired, Eastern Mobil had only three employees in the Personnel Department with the authority to give final approval on the hiring of an applicant. Two of them were lesser, staff members and the third was Marge, our Assistant Personnel Manager. The two, lesser members were no longer with the company when a second vetting took place to raise Mike to his present authority. Yet, Mike's deception was not discovered at that time, either.

The closer I came to unraveling this matter, the more concerned I became. I checked all the applications that were conducted that same week Mike was hired. I learned that Marge had been the one to interview every one of them.

The same was true for the week before and after Mike was hired. Marge was obviously doing most....or all...of the final interviews at that time.

I had no choice but to question her. This woman holds high prestige here. She was seated in all the executive meetings, including those that led to the merger. Mr. Stevens, our chief, Personnel Manager is due to retire in two years. Marge was to be his replacement.

When she answered my summons, Marge was not the confident, cheerful woman who usually greeted me. I'm sure I wasn't displaying my usual demeanor, either.

When she was seated, I said to her, "Marge, do you want to tell me why you did it?"

I hated the moment. We both knew the truth. I wouldn't waste her time by pretending otherwise.

Her face had turned white, and there were tears in her eyes. Even so, she didn't answer me.

"Will we find other workers you've hired that have been falsely investigated, too?" I asked.

Finally, she responded in a small voice. "No," she said. She reached for a tissue on my desk to stop the tears that were about to flow.

Marge finally confessed that Mike and she were involved in an affair that had been going on for the last ten years, even before Mike came to work here. She had met him through a friend. They continued the relationship on-line and otherwise. She falsified his application to get him the job with Eastern Mobile.

When the second vetting took place, she deceptively concealed the truth again.

She said to me, "Mike is so capable...." It was a plea.

"I agree," I said. "But you know we can't keep him....or you, either, Marge."

She nodded. She did understand that. Then, as she turned to leave, she looked at me kindly and said, "I wish you well, Bill."

"And I you," I responded sincerely.

This has turned our Personnel Department into a bit of a nightmare. There will need to be a multitude of reviews done in the days ahead.

One problem solved....and, no doubt, many more ahead. But something positive has come from this. It has helped to establish my authority. I sense a new respect from the co-leaders and our employees.

God is faithful, my friend.

Sincerely,
(Bill)

Derek was delighted that Bill had solved a serious problem. He wasn't surprised, though. He had the utmost admiration for this good friend. Bill was smart, moral and dependent on God.

Derek hoped his own faith would prove to be as solid.

And he hoped he might conquer the challenges he would face in life. Presently, Rachael was the biggest concern he had. He still had no idea how to help her.

At school, Melissa and Rachael had different schedules and different lunch breaks. During her lunch hour, Melissa easily melded into a social group with the other classmates. But following the bad experience with Clara, Rachael's confidence was gone. Even so, she walked with her head high and determined not to let her insecurity show. In the lunchroom, she avoided the crowd and took her tray to an almost isolated area. The other girls noticed that, but no one called out to ask her to join them. The boys also took note but none approached her.

JerriLynn made it a point to observe Rachael after the incident with Clara. She went to the cafeteria to see if Rachael was blending in and quickly surmised the young girl's isolation. She made it a point to be in the hallway as Rachael left the lunchroom and stopped her to chat in a friendly way.

In the days ahead, Rachael began to visit with JerriLynn during her noon break…not every day, of course, but rather often. This period was JerriLynn's lunch break, too. And she had found the time useful for preparing her afternoon classes. But she set aside her own needs and always made Rachael feel welcome.

Occasionally, Melissa and Rachael would stop by Miss Smathers' room before leaving the school. She found the two girls typical of thirteen-year-olds. They were both attractive, both newly interested in boys, and both enamored with Roger

Adams. It made JerriLynn smile as she remembered her early "crushes".

But Roger Adams had quickly lost interest in Rachael Metcalf. The football season was giving way to basketball. It seemed there was always practice of one kind or another. He no longer stopped to talk, and he no longer waited outside the door when the school day was over. Roger's interest had turned to his own classmate, Judy Langdon. He could be seen hurrying to catch up to Judy after class. In her room under the stage, JerriLynn saw the kids in the hallway and noticed things like that.

One noon-day, Rachael was visiting with JerriLynn when Roger and Judy walked past her door. They both spoke to Miss Smathers....but they ignored Rachael, (she was still only an eighth grader, after all.)

Rachael muttered, "What does he see in her?"

The unkind remark took JerriLynn by surprise. She looked at Rachael and asked, "In Judy, do you mean? Are you asking me what Roger sees in Judy Langdon?"

"Well,....she's fat," muttered Rachael, whose jealousy was obvious.

JerriLynn was surprised by this animosity in Rachael. She looked beyond her to where Judy and Roger were moving down the hallway. Roger had stealthily taken Judy's hand.

"Well.., Judy is a little overweight, I guess...maybe twenty pounds," she reasoned..... "She was in my Home Ec class last year. Judy's a real nice girl," she said.

Rachael only glowered.

JerriLynn reached around to the stand behind her and retrieved a photo.

"These are my grandparents, Rachael," she said as she

offered the picture to Rachael. "That's Grandpa Smathers and Granny Mae, as we call my Grandma."

In the picture, the elderly couple was smiling at one another. They both looked very old to Rachael, with their gray hair, wrinkled skin, vein-lined hands and bent backs. Granny Mae was heavy and shapeless.

Rachael had never known her grandparents and her lack of interest was apparent.

"That's nice," Rachael murmured without comprehension, as she handed the picture back to JerriLynn.

"The photo was taken this past summer at their fifty-eighth, wedding anniversary," said JerriLynn. "They are still very much in love. The outward appearance isn't the reason for their love…not after all these years. When Grandpa sees Granny Mae, he sees the woman he has known for more than fifty years. He loves the person she is.

"It appears that Roger is interested in Judy. I expect he sees what a nice person Judy is. It's the person inside who really matters Rachael."

Did Rachael grasp the lesson, she wondered as she watched the pretty, young girl walk down the hall to her next class?

Clara's smear campaign tapered off rather quickly. But most of the students now, who gave her any thought, considered Rachael "stuck-up". After all, she was uncommonly pretty, so what other reason could account for her lack of friendliness?

But it was shame and fear that held Rachael aloof.

In the days ahead, as Derek had relied on the janitor's counsel, Rachael was inclined to lean on Miss Smathers.

JerriLynn lamented that she was unable to penetrate the hard shell of resentment she saw in Rachael.

The Saunders household was a busy place. With Lou running her sewing shop, there was always someone coming or going. It was some time before Abel finally had an occasion to talk with Rachael alone. Derek was away that evening. Lou was teaching a class on crocheting at her shop. Joy had learned to crochet simple patterns and was much interested in learning more. This night, she chose to attend her mother's class. Rachael was in her room when her mother called out to her, "Goodbye, Rachael. We'll be back soon." As usual, there was no response.

Abel dropped Joy and her mother at the shop. He often stopped in the restaurant to visit on similar nights. But this time, he returned to the house, poured himself a cup of coffee and sat down at the table with the sports section of the newspaper.

About ten minutes later, Rachael came downstairs and wandered into the room. He busied himself with the newspaper and said nothing. She cut herself a brownie and poured a glass of milk. Then, she chose to sit down at the table. Abel was encouraged. Perhaps, she was ready to talk about it....whatever "it" was. He laid the paper down and smiled at her.

"You've got enough cookies there for three girls your size. I thought girls always worried about their weight," he teased.

"What does it matter if I get fat?" she muttered, while not bothering to raise her head.

What do I say, he wondered?

Finally, he just asked, "Do you want to tell me about it, Rachael? What's troubling you?"

Finally, she looked up at him. "No one will ever like me anyway," she said. "I'm Lou Metcalf's daughter. They all make fun of me for that." She was almost crying now.

"Whoa-a," said Abel. "Who has ever made fun of you?"

"All the kids do," she murmured.

"Because of your mother?" he asked.

"Because Mom had all of us without a husband," Rachael's voice broke, as she said it.

"Oh." Abel now understood in part. "Will you tell me what happened, Rachael?" he asked quietly. But he wasn't feeling quiet inside. "Did someone say something unkind about your mother?"

"Clara did....Clara Conrad...Ms Conrad's daughter." The words were rushing forth now. "She said it real loud in the hallway. All the kids heard it. She made fun of me because of my mother's reputation," said Rachael.

Anger... a deep, riotous anger was his first reaction. Abel calmed himself. Years of training had given him that strength. He believed Rachael. Abel knew how unkind others can be.

Finally, he asked,   "Rachael, did you ever hear your mother say anything unkind about anyone?"

After a moment, Rachael responded. "No," she admitted.

"It was one of the first things I noticed about Lou," said Abel. "She doesn't talk a lot of nonsense. And I've never heard her say anything unkind about others. That's pretty remarkable," he said.

"We don't know your mother's earlier years." Lou had still shared very little with him. "I don't know why she had her children out-of-wedlock. But I do know she loves you all very much. And I know something of her character just by association these last years.

"I find her an admirable woman. She raised this lovely family all alone and in this little town where gossip is commonplace. There are some who are as mean as Clara was to you. But I've never heard Lou complain or retaliate.

"I do hear her thank the Lord for you children. She's so grateful for her family. And she has every reason to be proud of all of you.

"You can choose who you want to be like, Rachael. You can be like Clara and fight your way through life with vicious and unkind words. Or you can be like your mother and be a kind and gracious person who chooses not to strike back."

Rachael said nothing. Uncle Abe was someone she trusted and had learned to love. His words had reached their mark.

Abel waited quietly. Neither said anything for a few minutes.

Then, "I'm sorry," she murmured. "I'm sorry I've been so awful, Uncle Abe."

"It's alright, Rachael," he said.

Derek had agreed to stop by the shop that evening for Lou and Joy. When they returned home a little later, Abel and Rachael were watching a game show on TV.

"You beat me again!" Abel was saying. "I need to sharpen my wits, if I want to compete with you."

When Rachael went to bed a short time later, she bid Abel goodnight.

Then, "Goodnight, Mom," she said.

Lou was practically speechless. "Goodnight, Rachael," she offered.

Abel had brought about changes in Rachael's thinking, and it was soon obvious at school. After the incident with Clara, Rachael had hurried through the hallway in a most unfriendly manner. Now, Rachael began to walk with confidence again and even smiled at others. The other students responded in kind. The teachers and the janitor were delighted to see the spirited, young girl emerge from her darkness.

Rachael had been too embarrassed to share with Melissa the unkind words hurled at her by Clara. Of course, Melissa heard about it from others. And she had seen the sorry change in Rachael and was grieved. Now, finally, she had her old friend back.

In no time at all, Rachael returned to her cheerfully feisty self. Derek was relieved to see Rachael's normal disposition restored. One evening, his two sisters were at the kitchen table looking at a ladies' magazine. He heard Rachael say to Joy, "When I'm sixteen, I'm going to wear four-inch heels like these with my jeans!"

"Will you be able to walk in them?" Joy asked with real concern.

"I'll be able to dance in them!" declared Rachael.

Roger and Judy became an established couple at Alton High. Rachael scarcely noticed. At thirteen, love doesn't usually last very long.

Derek had a purpose for being at the college this Saturday. He had taken half a day off his work at Skinny's Market to attend a meeting of Professor Graff's, political committee. As he left the meeting, he met Sal and two friends. The four were chatting when they heard a female voice call out, "There's Derek!"

Derek and his friends turned to see who was calling. The exclamation came from Rachael. Abel had brought the family to town for some shopping. Lou was sitting in the passenger side, front seat. Directly behind her, Rachael had her window down. Joy had crowded over to Rachael's side, so both were looking out that window.

"You know the girls always insist on driving past 'Derek's school'," Abel explained as Derek stepped over to the car.

"Are you having a good day?" Lou asked him at the same time.

The young men with Derek had quickly turned their attention to the people in the car. With her window down, the male interest zoomed to Rachael in the backseat of that car. She was aware of their interest, too. Ignoring Joy, who was leaning against her, she smiled at Derek's friends. The simple scenario didn't escape Derek's notice, and it upset him.

"Yeah, Mom'" he responded to her question about his day. "But I can't visit right now," he replied gruffly.

Is Mom blind to the interest the guys have in Rachael, he wondered?

Abel was not, and discerning Derek's discomfort, he said, "We'll leave you to your duties, Derek." Windows were rolled up again as the car pulled away.

Derek turned back to his friends.

"How old is your sister?" Phil asked the question they all considered.

No surprise in his interest, thought Derek. *Rachael is only thirteen, but she attracts male attention.*

All three guys were looking at Derek, awaiting the answer.

But he didn't answer. The camaraderie, that had permeated the group, before his family stopped to speak to Derek, was gone.

Derek mumbled, "I've got to go."

The three, young men exchanged puzzled glances. As he turned and walked away, two of them began to walk in the opposite direction. But Sal hastened to reach Derek's side.

He said nothing as he caught up to his friend. They walked a space hurriedly and in silence. Finally, Sal asked, "You don't like to talk about your sister... ....?" He made it a question.

Derek again said nothing. His friend had it figured. The girl is pretty. That was apparent immediately. She young... but she's a knock-out; Sal had seen that.

Finally, Derek muttered, "She's just a kid."

With no further exchange with Sal, he turned toward the steps that would take him to his car. *She's only thirteen, but Rachael looks older, and she has our mother's beauty,* Derek mused. Remembering his mother's history, that concerned him.

He could hardly keep Rachael from maturing. How was he to protect her?

He met Sal and the others again, of course, but no mention was made of Derek's family....namely, his sister,.... with these friends. And his actions that afternoon had closed the door on future questions from them.

That is, until one day Sal convinced Derek to join him for a coke at the student lounge. During his first year at college, Derek had spent little time at this favorite hangout for students. He knew that was rather foolish. *College should be more interesting than I've made it,* he thought at times.

But this semester, Derek was spending more time with Sal. They were commonly seen together. This late September day, the weather was warm. Sal was wearing bright, red shorts, a navy "CLAIRTON U" t-shirt, blue socks and Nikes. Derek was dressed more conservatively. For classes, he often wore a short sleeved, button-down-the-front shirt and jeans. Today he wore a light blue t-shirt with his jeans. They visited the student lounge together frequently now. Derek enjoyed the noisy chatter of the place...the interaction of girls and boys....*No,* he corrected himself, *these are young women and men.* The interaction wasn't really any different than some of the experiences he'd had with the ZONCs (the name for his gang of friends in high school) and the girls with whom they mysteriously connected at times. *The world's not such a big place,* he decided.

He much enjoyed Sal's company. His friend was very outgoing and knew most of the students milling around the cafeteria. Sal had a roughness about him. He was more virile than handsome. With his Spanish looks, that brilliant smile and easy friendliness, Sal was always surrounded by others... girls notably. It was obvious the guys liked him, too.

This day, both Sal and Derek exchanged greetings with a number of students. Derek was becoming known to them but still seemed a bit unapproachable. Even so, their greetings were friendly. They both stopped to speak to one group and another as Sal led the way to a more private area in the back.

Obviously, he had something on his mind. They spoke casually at first. In these weeks, Sal had shared personal stories about his family. Derek surmised that the relationships were close and loving. This day, Sal said, "You know a lot about me, Derek. I talk too much and too often about myself."

"I've enjoyed getting to know you, Salvatore. I've much enjoyed it," Derek said sincerely.

"But I know very little about you, amigo," said Sal cautiously. He knew Derek was the strong, quiet type. Even so, it seemed there must be a reason why he shared so little about his home and family background.

"You said you live in Alton. Last Sunday, with nothing of importance to do here, I drove down and toured your home town. I could have been on the other side of town in the time it takes to sneeze," he said with a laugh.

Then he graciously added, "Everything is well maintained, and it looks like a very nice town."

Oh, thought Derek, *I should have invited him down to meet my family before this.* During his school years, he never invited his friends to his home. *But our home life is different now,* he thought. *I've shared nothing very private with Sal,* he realized. He felt a bit ashamed of his hesitancy to share his life with this friend.

"I'm sorry, Sal," he said carefully. "Of course you need to know something about me."

"Well, it's not a 'need', exactly," said Sal. "I discerned your character that first day and determined I'd like us to be friends. I know you're intelligent and a man of good morals. But I am curious. Is there a reason why you don't like to share your life?"

"Yes," Derek answered quickly. "But no....no.."

Sal was confused. They were quiet for a moment. Then, Derek said,

"My mother had three children. I was the oldest. Rachael

is thirteen, and Joy is eleven. I love them very much. I love my mother, too...."

Sal was quiet and waited.

"My mother had the three of us out-of-wedlock," said Derek. He still felt the shame of that.

"Do you all have the same father?" asked Sal carefully.

"No....three different men.....," said Derek. He did not look up.

"That had to be hard," Sal said quietly. He could see that Derek's shame and pain were still palpable.

"She's a good woman...." But Derek stumbled on that and quickly said, "She's a good mother....and last year she married finally."

"Did she marry one of the fathers?" asked Sal.

"No. My dad died a month before I was born. The other, two men disappeared soon after my sisters were born. Mom has married a fine man...retired Colonel Abel Saunders. He was my dad's best friend. After eighteen years, Abel finally got in touch with us. Mom and he fell in love and married just this past summer."

"Sounds like your story has a happy ending," said Sal.

"It's working out real well. I'm so glad my sisters will have a stable, family situation. Abel has built her a new house just outside town. The family seems to be in the good graces of the town now."

"But not when you were little," Sal perceived.

"It was hard the early years. Then, I made some really good friends. And the teachers and Administrators at Alton High ....and the janitor," he quickly added, "maybe especially the janitor...were just excellent. They're the reason I'm at Clairton University. That and several scholarships, and my job at Skinny's Market in Alton," he added with a smile.

Sal was quiet. *What a different upbringing from my own,* he thought.

Now, Sal understood the scene at the car with Derek's pretty, younger sister. *He's protective of her,* he thought.

Then, he said, "Well, now I know why you have such a strong character. You've overcome a lot. I find you very admirable, my friend. (This time he used the English word for 'friend'.)

Derek never considered himself admirable. "I'm grateful to God for the good changes in my life," he said.

Derek had never invited his friends into his childhood home. Now, following the marriage of Abel and Lou, both the home and the home life of the Metcalf family were radically changed. The new, stone house, Lou's graciousness and the authority engrained in Abel's character assured that guests to their home would be welcome and comfortable.

Derek made arrangements with Lou, and that Friday, before they parted, Derek invited Salvatore Ridenti to have Saturday-evening dinner with his family.

It was Sal's nature to meld with others easily. And that was so on this visit. By the time they sat down at the dinner table, everyone was at ease. Naturally, Sal's background invited curiosity. The family wanted to know about his home in Brazil. He shared stories of his parents and siblings, and it was obvious the relationships were close.

Then, Abel asked him about his father's occupation. To this, Sal responded rather carefully, "My family owns a coffee plantation in Southern Brazil."

A plantation? Even Derek hadn't known that. Sal was driving a new Lexus, so he assumed the family was affluent.

But as Sal answered the questions that followed, Derek surmised that his friend was from a very wealthy family.

Rachael and Joy had a multitude of questions about life on a plantation. To each, Sal answered courteously. He told of the hundreds of thousands of coffee plants that are grown from seedlings into trees.

That explains Sal's choice of Agronomy for his major, thought Derek.

"All of those coffee trees must be trimmed to a reachable height for picking the beans," Sal offered. He described the red earth beneath the mature, coffee plants, when the berries have turned from green to red. And he spoke of the little villages interspersed throughout the land, "where the workers and their families live."

The girls were excited and evidenced no end to their questions. Sal was being gracious, but the grown-ups were sensitive. They weren't happy to be grilling their guest this way. Lou's defenses had always been high, and she never questioned others on private matters.

Abel moved the subject to a more general theme. "I spent a brief time in Brazil during my military years. Much of that time, I was in-or-near Sao Paulo."

Sal was obviously delighted to meet someone who had some understanding of his country. Abel and Sal were soon conversing like old friends.

The conversation turned to life in the little town of Alton. The girls had adventurous stories about their goat and picnic baskets along the creek near their, old home. Abel had humorous tales of some of the townsfolk who regularly had breakfast at the restaurant. Even Lou, rather shyly, spoke of her class, at her Remnant Shop, for first-time knitters.

"Some of the older ladies, in town, come just for the fellowship," said Lou. "But three in the class are of high school age. And, of course, Joy is also learning to knit and is doing very well in the art."

As they shared their simple lives in this small town, Derek could see that Salvatore was sincerely interested. *Strangely, he seems almost envious,* thought Derek. *But that can't be.*

They all had an enjoyable time. The evening had a down-moment, though,…at least in Derek's mind. Rachael sat on Derek's right side at the dinner table. Sal and Joy were seated across from them. At one point, Derek noticed that Sal, who had looked across at Rachael, had quickly lowered his head and was trying to mask an amused smile. Derek turned to glance at Rachael in time to see that her eyes were lowered in a seductive way, and she had a teasing, little smile on her face. His thirteen-year-old sister was flirting with Sal!

Derek's mouth dropped to his chin.

Abel had been observing the scene with some amusement. When he saw Derek's reaction, he struggled not to laugh aloud. And Sal's eyes were sparkling with merriment to see his friend so flustered by the antics of his little sister.

Lou had gone to the kitchen for something. When she returned, she noticed Derek's face was red, and Abel appeared to be vastly amused. Abel recovered in time to open a new line of conversation.

The family enjoyed dessert and another hour with Salvatore, before he left.

Later that night, Derek considered that scene. He still could hardly believe that Rachael was flirting with Sal!

Derek feared that she favored her mother. It wasn't actually in outward features, for Rachael possessed the caramel-colored skin and dark hair of her Mexican father. Her dark eyes were sultry and flashing, and at age thirteen, her figure was already shapely. Rachael is very pretty, he admitted.

Derek possessed knowledge of his mother's history that wasn't known by his sisters. His mother's beauty and early experiences had left her vulnerable to the most disreputable men. He well recalled his sister's fathers. They never married Lou but abandoned her to raise the children alone. Derek was very protective of his sisters. As he replayed that dinner-table scene, he realized Rachael was maturing. *She's shedding the cocoon of childhood so quickly... too quickly,* thought Derek.

When he saw Sal next, neither of them mentioned that incident. Derek was simply too embarrassed by his "little sister's" antics to do so.

Salvatore became a regular, Saturday evening guest at the Saunders home in the months ahead. There were no more background quizzes. As for Rachael's flirtations, it may be that Abel said something to Lou about her actions that first evening. On future occasions, Rachael behaved with reasonable modesty when Sal was around....at least, somewhat modestly. Derek wished she'd dress a bit more discreetly. But then, he had to admit, Rachael simply wore a pair of jeans and a tight shirt. She chose a similar outfit most evenings. *Why does it look so alluring when Sal is here,* Derek mused?

Five

DEREK HAD SLOWED HIS PACE outside the Science Building. He was expecting to meet his friend here following their 2:30 classes. A surge of chattering students exited the building before he spied Salvatore, who was, as usual, surrounded by laughing, enthusiastic, fellow students. Sal jogged to his side.

"Have you been waiting long?" he asked.

"I just got here," said Derek. The two increased their pace along with the other students.

"You must know everyone on campus now," said Derek. He was a little envious.

"Well, not quite. But they're a friendly bunch," said Sal. "You live off-campus. That's why they still don't know you very well," he said.

As they walked together down the sidewalk, Sal was bumped and greeted by numerous students.

"I've always been surrounded by people," he explained. "At home, we were a very competitive family. I was challenged in sports and everything else by my siblings..... three sisters and a brother. There were always friends around.

"During my first, six years of school, I lived with my family on padre's southern estate and attended the Catholic school in Cacapava.

"It is good to be in America to perfect my English," he said. "The nuns and priests who taught us were strict. I was schooled in Catholic doctrine. As I'm the oldest son, much is expected of me. For the grades from seven through twelve, my father enrolled me at Regency Middle School in Morumbi, Sao Paulo. I lived in an all-male dormitory there. Regency Middle School has a reputation of combining the best of Brazilian and American education with an excellent, academic program. It's similar to a U.S. college-preparatory school.

"The lessons were challenging; the discipline was strict. I got a good, scholastic education," Sal continued. "I also got a lesson in human foibles. Just put a teenage dormitory of hearty, young males together in one place separated from the female sex, and they learn fast. There was an all-girls' school across town. We guys knew a multitude of ways to escape the perimeters of Regency, find the means of transportation across town to socialize with the opposite sex and get back to school before we were missed!

"I spent my first year of college at the Catholic University in Sao Paulo," Sal continued. "It still amazes me that I can walk from the far, eastern side of Clairton to the far, western side of town in one day. In fact, I can do that in one afternoon!" he said laughing. "In Sao Paulo, there's little possibility of seeing even a small portion of that city in a day."

They had reached their place of parting. Derek headed for the parking lot, and Salvatore turned toward his dormitory.

"See you tomorrow, amigo," said Sal.

Derek could now interpret some of the Spanish that seasoned Sal's English speech. *My good friend*.... He had known Sal only a short time, but *yes, Salvatore Ridenti and I are becoming good friends,* thought Derek.

115

Derek had made no actual friends his first year of college. He knew some of the kids in his classes, but spent no time with them after class. Commuting, plus working at Skinny's Market four evenings and Saturday each week, gave him no time to further friendships. Sal became helpful in that matter. Their daily walk in the mornings gave opportunity to pass on information about their respective lives. Lately, as Derek left his last class on Tuesday afternoons at 2:30, Sal had been waiting nearby to walk with him to his car.

The pattern continued with Salvatore waiting at the end of the sidewalk, and as usual, he was not alone when Derek exited the building.

His new friend was a natural leader. Clairton College now had many, foreign exchange students. But Sal was prominent. He spoke excellent English with a charming accent and was obviously comfortable in these strange surroundings. In this short time, Salvatore had become known on campus and seemed to be well-liked.

One afternoon, Sal met up with Derek at 1:45 p.m. "Don't you have Physics class next period?" Derek asked.

"Professor Arnold's class was canceled today. I thought maybe you'd have time to check out my dorm room," Sal suggested, "as you don't start to work until 5."

After momentary consideration, Derek agreed. *I've never been in any of the dorm buildings,* he thought. *I need to get more involved here.*

As they opened the outside door, Derek was taken aback by the noise. There were voices and other rackets coming at them, as they climbed the two flights of stairs to the second floor.

They moved to the side when they met up with four, noisy guys hurrying down.

"Hey, Sal!" said more than one. They had all come to a stop.

"This is Derek Metcalf, amigos."

Reasonable greetings were exchanged.

"There's a poker game tonight at 10. Can you make it? You owe us. You come, too, Derek," invited one.

"Sorry," Derek said in decline.

"Not tonight," said Sal with a laugh. "I don't want to take any more of your money."

"I bet he's got nothing but centavos in his pocket, anyway," joked another guy.

The incident was brief. Sal's room was second floor on the left. His door was one of the few, closed doors. And it was even locked. Salvatore removed a key to gain entrance.

He motioned for Derek to go in ahead of him. As he closed the door behind them, the noise level was less pervasive but still noticeable.

"Hey, Jake," said Sal. "I want you to meet my friend, Derek Metcalf."

Jacob, who had been sitting at his desk, had turned toward them as the door opened. Now, he gave an almost shy greeting.

"Hi," said Derek in return.

"How are things going today, Jake?" Sal asked kindly.

"Everything's ok," Jacob replied.

Salvatore walked over to his bookcase to collect something, and Derek looked around the room. There were twin beds, one on each side of the room. Each had a dresser, a desk and a walk-in closet. There was only one TV. There was a small, music center off to the side. The place was neat, though sparsely furnished. As Sal was driving a new Lexus, the simple furnishings surprised Derek.

Sal handed him several photos and identified his family. The one, large photo showed Sal's parents and the five siblings. It was easily apparent they were beyond a middle-class family. Sal's father looked as though he was born into a suit and vest. He had light, brown hair, Caucasian, skin coloring. (....and blue eyes, Derek noticed.) His mother, like Sal, was darker and appeared younger than Derek would have expected. She was smiling for the camera and showed no sign of illness in this photo. Sal's sisters were all pretty. At least, if they weren't actually pretty, they all had such style that one would think so. All but one had dark hair like Sal. The middle girl had light, brown hair and a quieter smile than the others. She apparently took after her father and looked less Spanish. Sal's younger brother appeared to be about twelve-years-old. He was kneeling beside a very large, Sheep dog.

"That's Bruiser." Sal was pointing to the dog. "He was my dog, and I suspect I miss him more than any of the others," he said with a laugh. "I turned him over to Garcia, mi hermano.... my brother....ah, I miss him, too," he added softly.

The family was stylishly dressed. And all were obviously accustomed to the camera. Sal and his siblings exuded an easy confidence. It was a handsome family. In the background, at the entrance to the large veranda, Derek could see a prominent, decorative sign: *Abundante Lugar*

Sal chose to interpret for Derek. "In English, you would say, 'Abundant Place'."

There were large, colorful stones underfoot. Vines and plant greenery offered shade for the setting of comfortable, outdoor furniture. A small portion of the white, brick building that was obviously their home, could be seen off to the side.

"You have a nice family, Sal," said Derek sincerely. *What would my life have been if I'd had such a background?* he thought. But he didn't let his mind linger there.

"I'll be going to the cafeteria, Jake," said Salvatore. "Can I bring you something?"

"No, thanks, I had lunch earlier," Jacob said.

"I won't be long, then," Salvatore said, and he indicated Derek and he were going to leave.

Sal pushed the lock on the door and they re-entered the hall. Once again, Derek was struck by the noise. The place appeared to be a beehive of active, vocal, young men. The two of them hurried down the stairs and out the door, where it suddenly seemed very much quieter.

"How do you study with all that noise?" Derek asked.

"It's pretty bad," agreed Sal.

"Couldn't you make other, living arrangements?" asked Derek. It seemed apparent money was not an issue with his friend.

"Sure. I could..." said Sal. "I've been invited to join the Catholic College Fraternity next semester. They rent that really big, old house on the corner of Fourth Avenue and Plummer. You pass it going home. They're nice guys, and all of them are serious about their education...and their faith, too."

"You plan to do that, then?" asked Derek.

Sal gave a short laugh. "Actually, no....no, I don't," he said.

Derek stopped walking and looked at him.

"I'll probably stay right where I am," Sal continued.

"Why would you do that?" asked Derek. He was confused. "It has to be difficult studying in that dorm room."

"Yeah, it is," Sal agreed. "But I manage. And I'll probably stay for Jacob's sake."

They had stopped walking. Derek waited for some kind of explanation.

"You see what a quiet guy he is?" asked Sal. "The jerks in the dorm raze him a lot. They call him 'Jakie' and suppose he's .....maybe different..."

Derek was beginning to understand. He just listened quietly.

"Jake is shy and out-of-place. He's the only child of his widowed mother, who lives in Pittsburgh. His first year of college was spent in a community school near his home. But his father was killed in an industrial accident last year. His mother got a settlement for his death and arranged for Jake to be in college here.

"Actually, he's a technological whiz. He can fix a computer problem in a snap, program anything technical in minutes. He loves that sort of thing. She should have let him attend a Vo-tech school down there. But she took her settlement funds and declared she wanted her son to have a 'real' education. So, here he is in Clairton University, over his head in his studies and too shy to make friends. If I move out, I fear the gorilla-jerks will destroy him."

Derek was stunned. Salvatore would willingly sacrifice reasonable comfort to help Jake, whom he only met earlier this school year....a kid who seemingly had little to give in return.

They walked toward Derek's car in silence. Finally, Derek asked, "How do you study with all that noise?

"I have a set of ear mufflers, like they wear when operating loud machinery. And there's a ten o'clock curfew. Things get a little quieter after that. I'm doing alright," he said. Derek surmised that Sal had said all he wanted to say about his choice of living quarters.

"See you tomorrow, Derek," said Sal. He turned away and was walking toward the cafeteria, as Derek pulled out of the parking area.

Not long after, Sal again asked Derek to walk with him to his room.

"You have some time, don't you, Derek? Come up to my room while I drop these books off. Then, we'll grab a soft drink at the Student Lounge."

As they reached the second floor, Sal said with a hint of alarm, "The door to our room is open!"

Derek didn't understand his concern, but Sal had moved forward quickly. Derek hurried along with him. When they got to the room, it was empty, and Sal looked distressed.

"Where would he go and leave the door ajar?" Sal pondered to himself.

Derek realized he was talking about his roommate, Jacob. Just then, they heard raucous laughter down the hall.

"That's Grunge's voice!" said Sal, and he exited the room in a rush. With no understanding of Sal's concern, Derek hastened to follow him. He had stopped in front of the closed door to the equipment room.

As another eruption of male laughter came from inside, Sal slammed into the door which burst open! Inside, there were four guys holding Jacob. The guy, whom Derek later learned was "Grunge", was pulling a girl's skirt over Jake's head. Grunge looked like a TV wrestler. The sleeves of his shirt were torn-off at his large shoulders to allow space for huge biceps that were almost totally adorned with tattoos. One slender, snake tattoo climbed the side of his neck and rested its tail behind his ear.

"Let me go!" Jacob pleaded.

"Jakie makes a right 'purty' girl," said Grunge, who belatedly noticed the other guys had grown positively quiet. He turned to assess the reason just in time to get Sal's fist in his face. Blood spurted from his nose. Curses streamed from his mouth, as he started forward, intent on returning the blows.

But his friend, Leo, and the other guys rose to the occasion, as did Derek. Two of them twisted Grunge's arms behind him. Derek and Leo grabbed Sal's arms. Just then, someone said in a loud whisper, "The hall monitor is coming."

Jacob, in the skirt, was pushed into the closet. He was so embarrassed that he offered no resistance.

"What's going on in here?" asked Les Irwin as he entered. Les was in his late forties. Four of these guys were taller and bigger than he. A small, wooden staff, hanging from his belt, was his only weapon. But he wore a blue, work suit with the school insignia on the front, which indicated he carried the authority of the school on this job. The possibility of suspension kept these guys under control....usually.

"How'd your nose get bloody, Grunge?" Les asked. As Grunge was already well known by the hall monitor, he didn't bother with formality but used the nickname the others called him.

"I bumped it on the door just now," was the reply.

Les looked from one to another of the young men. No one offered any other explanation.

"Well, break it up in here. Get back to your rooms," he ordered the group.

"Yes, sir," was the general reply. Grunge and his friends departed quickly. Les could be heard still talking with them as they moved down the hall. Derek and Sal waited as Jacob quickly removed the skirt. Then, they left the room immediately.

"Thanks, Sal," Jacob said when they were in their own room again.

"How'd they get in?" Sal asked.

"I guess I forgot to lock the door," he replied.

"You've got to be more careful," said Sal more gently now. He was quickly gaining control of himself.

"I will be, Sal. And thanks again."

Sal reached an arm around Jake's shoulder in affirmation. Then, he motioned for Derek that they should leave.

"We're going to the lounge, Jake. I'll be back soon."

"Jake never will come with me," said Sal as they left the room.

When they were out of the building, Sal explained, in part, the incident in the equipment room. "Jake is small, quiet and a bit shy," he said "That's enough for a bully like Grunge to torment him."

"You've got blood on your shirt." Derek had just noticed it.

When Sal looked down, he saw the large streak of red on his sleeve and down the front of his shirt.

"I need to change," he muttered. "I guess we'll have to go to the lounge another day."

"Sure," Derek agreed.

"Sorry for that…" and Sal nodded in the direction of the dorm building.

"It wasn't your fault," said Derek.

"See you in the morning," Sal said and turned back to the steps.

Derek headed for his car. But he was troubled about this incident with Grunge.

The next day, he questioned Sal. "There are seldom less than three of them. They'll try to get back at you," he warned.

Sal's eyes narrowed as he glanced at Derek in response. That look told Derek a bit about his friend.

"I was in a Catholic, boy's school in Morumba," Sal said curtly. "They weren't all choir boys."

"Do you carry a weapon?" Derek asked in concern.

Again Sal didn't answer. From the tight jeans and tee-shirt he wore today, Derek knew he could not be carrying a gun.

When Sal offered no more, Derek dropped the subject but his concern remained.

When he enrolled at Clairton U., Derek had included in his application, his tenure as Student Advisory Counselor at Alton High. At the start of this second year at Clairton U., he was contacted by Professor Eldridge, the head of Student Affairs. She had carefully selected ten students, from the 2nd year class, to monitor out-of-class difficulties of their classmates. Derek was commuting, which might limit his knowledge of campus problems. But after observing him in his first year of college and reviewing his character with the instructors, who taught Derek that first year, Professor Eldridge decided to include him.

Derek was glad for the opportunity to use the lessons he had learned at Alton to help his classmates here.

He attended several meetings and had learned a bit about what was involved. He had even been enlisted to help a girl in his Communications class. She had transferred to Clairton U. this year and had not yet made close friendships. She expressed, to the counsel, her fear of walking to the library alone at night. Derek spent Monday afternoon after classes (time that he could have spent at the library) locating two other girls in the same, dorm building, who regularly studied at the library in the evenings. He brought the three together and was pleased to learn, in his follow-up, that the solution was working well and friendships had evolved. The three girls were regularly seen together at other times, too.

Another student had lost his wallet during a stop at a restaurant in downtown Clairton. It contained a few dollars, his driver's license, credit cards and medical information. Professor Eldridge asked Derek to aid him in his search. They tried the restaurant first with no success. Then, he took the student to police headquarters to file his loss. Derek and he went to the courthouse and spoke with the College Affairs contact there. She promised to do some checking.

Later that same day, a passerby discovered the wallet almost hidden in a sidewalk planter near the restaurant. The student's few dollars were missing, but the thief obviously wasn't interested in serious crime. The credit cards and other vital papers were still intact. Derek stayed with the student as he filed the necessary paperwork to close the case at the police station. Privately, he lamented that he had missed classes that day, study time at the library and even had a late start on his job at Skinny's Market.

But this problem with Jacob and Grunge went beyond any concern he had about the time involved in helping. *What should I do about this incident with Jacob,* Derek wondered? *The hall monitor did nothing more than scatter the guys. Is that the way to handle this? Should I take this matter to Professor Eldridge. If I do, will I get Les in trouble…maybe cause him to lose his job? Les' intervention had restored the calm quickly. Maybe that was sufficient.*

Derek didn't report the incident.

Grunge's nose was not broken. The soreness eventually went away, but his anger didn't. He now hated Salvatore Ridenti…. "that black Brazilian", he called him.

Following that incident, Derek observed how his friend shadowed and protected Jacob. He feared Grunge would see that as an even greater reason for revenge. But he had no idea how to help in this situation.

Salvatore showed no special concern.

Six

DEREK HAD BECOME ACCUSTOMED TO having Sal meet him after his last, afternoon class. Today, as he exited the building, he noticed Sal was chatting with two girls. They stopped talking, as they watched Derek walk down the sloping sidewalk to join them.

"Derek, meet Diane and Mandy," Sal said. "They've both been pestering me to introduce you to them."

"Stop it!" laughed Diane, as she gave Sal a punch in the arm.

Derek meant to offer a greeting, but he found himself nonplussed by the girl standing beside Sal. She was tall... surely five-foot-six, and glowed with healthy vitality. She had long, blond hair that was being ruffled by the wind this day. Her complexion was beautiful, her eyes were a sky-blue color and her smile literally sparkled. Diane was wearing brief, white shorts and a sleeveless top that ended about an inch above the waistline. A lovely tan covered the exposed skin, which Derek endeavored not to notice. Diane had recently won a position on the football, cheerleading squad. He was rather speechless that Sal obviously knew the girl.

"Hi, Derek," the other girl, Mandy, said quietly. Only then did Derek notice her. In truth, standing beside Diane, most girls would have been unnoticed. Mandy was of average height and carried a little, excess weight. Today, she was dressed in dark, pedal pushers and an oversize, gray jersey with a picture of a white cat on front. "FURR-EVER YOURS" was printed there. No particular style was obvious in the short cut of her common brown, albeit thick and fit-looking hair that she wrapped behind her ears. She had friendly, hazel-colored eyes. Altogether, she was just rather common looking. But being young and healthy makes most girls attractive enough. And Mandy was that.

"It's nice to meet you, Mandy," Derek responded politely.

"You know what a con this guy is," Diane continued, indicating Salvatore. "But I, too, am glad to meet you, Derek," she said. "I think you take Modern Politics with my friend, Alison Brinker."

"Yes, we're in the same class," Derek said. "She's kind of a favorite of Professor Graff."

"I'm not surprised," said Diane. "She's smart…and pretty, too."

Derek thought so, also, but didn't comment on that.

"We're headed for the cafeteria. Do you guys want to come along?" asked Diane. Derek quickly perceived that Diane was definitely interested in Salvatore. Thus far, Mandy had offered nothing more than a greeting.

"Sorry," said Derek. And he really was sorry. He knew he should make more friends. "I have a paper due tomorrow in World History. I need to use this period to accomplish that." He usually spent this free period in the library, where he could study between classes.

Salvatore shook his head, No, to Diane's questioning look.

"Another time, then," said Diane, with a twinkle in her eye for Sal, and the girls walked away.

Sal seems to know those girls rather well, thought Derek as they moved on.

"Mandy is the one who introduced me to Diane," Sal explained. "Mandy is a Spanish major. She hopes to teach the subject in high school in the future. One day, when she was in the library, I was in the aisle nearby. She apparently knew who I was....or maybe I just look Spanish," said Sal with a laugh. "Anyway, when I stopped near her, she spoke to me in Spanish.

"Naturally, that sounded great to my ears. Her Spanish is excellent. We walked to the desk together. Diane was waiting there for her, and Mandy introduced us," he explained.

Considering how pretty Diane is, it's not surprising that Sal would take an interest in her, thought Derek.

But neither of them commented further on the two girls they had just left. Salvatore had received news from home. He shared with Derek a bit about the happenings in his family. Derek understood that his mother's illness was a concern to Sal. The two parted ways at the library.

Later, on his drive back to Alton, Derek's thoughts were on Alison Brinker, the girl Diane had mentioned. Yes, he did know Alison...kind'a. They were both in Professor Graff's Modern Politics class this year. But he knew her from his first year at Clairton U, too. She had been in his English class last year. And they met on campus several times. He rather suspected that a few of those times were at Alison's instigation. Maybe not the first time, though. She had been behind him as he left the campus building after their English class, and, of course, he held the door for her. They started down the walkway together, and Allison introduced herself.

"Hi, Derek. I'm Alison Brinker," she said.

"Yes. It's nice to formally meet you, Alison. I know a bit about you from your class participation."

"I feel the same way...that I almost know you," she said. "I'm impressed with your knowledge of nineteenth century writers. You obviously read a lot."

"Thank you, and yes, I do read a lot," he responded. Derek wasn't shy about class participation. He had always been a reader and found he had a multitude of thoughts he much wanted to share. When Derek would have turned right at the next walkway intersection, she turned also.

"You, too?" he asked, meaning, Are you going to the Library, too?

"Yes," she responded. "When I have a free period, I usually get my studying done. The days aren't long enough, are they?"

"I commute, and I have an evening job," said Derek. "So I use the library for study before I leave."

"That's pretty much my routine, too," she said with a slight laugh. "I work at Wendy's four nights a week. What's at the end of your commute?" she asked.

"I live in Alton," Derek replied.

"Oh, I know where that is. I'm local, too. I live about four miles beyond the river ....in that direction," she said pointing south east, "near a little village called Clifton, population 210."

They chatted easily on their walk that day.

In the next days, they left the building together, and it just seemed natural to walk to the library together. On those walks, he learned that Alison's family lived on a farm just outside Clifton. She was the youngest child of her parent's, eight children and the only one who ever went to college. Her father had developed a disability, and social-net programs gave her some aide with college tuition. She supplemented with the job in the fast food restaurant.

Alison shared easily; Derek, as usual, listened. He was truly interested. But he offered little about his family.

Not long after, he was at the library and involved in a paper he was writing, when Allison sat down at the neighboring computer.

"Hi," she said with a pretty smile. Alison was attractive. She wore her brown hair short and uncurled but in a stylish cut. Her blue eyes were shielded with long lashes. She was slender almost to the point of "too-thin", but she looked great in slacks and a tight jersey.

Furthermore, she was nice. Derek had learned that quickly. This day, they worked quietly side-by-side for another twenty minutes. Then, Derek closed his notebook and looked up only to discover Alison was sitting quietly and watching him.

"You really concentrate when you're studying, don't you?" she observed with a smile. She rose when he did, and they left the building together. He was headed to his car for his return to Alton. Alison was apparently going to her car, too. They walked together toward the parking lot. He knew he still had nearly an hour to spare. He could ask her to spend that time with him at the lounge or somewhere. With that gut feeling one has about these boy/girl relationships, he knew Allison would be willing to date him. And he considered it that day. He was so lonesome so often.

Alison was in charge of the details for the voter registration event. Whereas, she had previously seemed to avoid him, she surprised Derek one day by stepping alongside, as he exited the classroom. Alison showed perfect poise as she said to him, "Hi, Derek. How have you been?"

"I'm fine, thanks," he said masking his surprise. Before they went any further with the social correctness, Alison interjected, "I expect you're well informed now about the voter, registration drive. We've talked of little else in class all week," she said with a laugh.

"Yes," he said. "But it's important and worth the time spent."

"You're no doubt acquainted with the Festival activities, too,...including the voter registration booth we operate in the park that weekend?" she said, in what was really a question.

"I've been in the area at that time," Derek replied. "But I can't say that I've ever given much attention to Professor Graff's doings."

"The purpose is to register voters for the November election," she explained. "The town encourages our participation. They allow us a prominent platform. There's a small group of musicians on stage, lots of banners and excitement. Anyway, I wonder if you would like to be involved. I think you have a lot of good ideas to share."

Alison's composure never wavered. She was so straightforward in her gaze, that momentarily, he wondered if he had imagined the attraction last year. He quickly brought his mind back to her question. *Registration really does matter,* he thought. *Maybe I can finally find some legitimate, political involvement.*

"It sounds interesting," he replied.

"Is there any chance you can make the planning meeting this Friday night?" Alison asked. "We meet at the Stalwart Center at seven o'clock."

It was on his lips to say, No chance. But he hesitated. *Maybe I can work something out with Skinny,* he thought.

"I don't know," he said cautiously. "I'll see if I can make it."

As they went their individual ways, Derek considered his surprise that Alison had asked him to participate. And right then, he decided this was something he really wanted to do.

That evening, he explained his need to Skinny, who never hesitated in his response. "You attend that meeting, Derek," he said. "You can come in a little earlier on Saturday to accomplish the clean-up if you like. Or, I can hire some other help. There's a young kid at the high school who's been asking for some work.

"We'll find a way," said Skinny. "You let me know what evenings you want off."

There wasn't much Skinny wouldn't do to help Derek Metcalf on his way. Anyone could see this young man would have an impressive future ahead of him. He had been an excellent employee for nearly four years now. In truth, Derek seemed more like a son than an employee.

Derek was a bit excited to be involved in something of political substance, finally. And in fact, he thought voter registration was quite important. Along with that, he lay in bed considering Alison's words. He realized Professor Graff had put her in charge of recruiting the right participants. As a student in the professor's class, he always had something to contribute. Today, he suspected Professor Graff had steered Alison to ask him. But it was still an encouraging surprise.

"I think you have a lot of good ideas to share," Alison had said. His musing on that moment was depriving him of sleep.

Salvatore was his good friend, now, and he would, of course, tell him of this adventure into politics.

But this was an experience he needed to share with his friend, Bill Tonkins. He got out of the bed, reached for his tablet and paper and wrote:

Dear Bill,

This is my second year in college, and I'm only now ....finally ....branching out into politics (albeit in a minor way). I'm excited. I've been asked to participate in an endeavor headed by Professor Graff, my Modern Politics teacher (and a man I greatly admire).

I am to be included in the group who will handle voter-registration during the Fall Festival event. The college organizes the Registration Rally, which is held at the city park on the first weekend of October. For that occasion, the activities in the park comprise a number of booths, including a display by the prize winning, college artist, who exhibits his (this year, the winner was a male) art. The winning sorority shares their prize winning crafts, and there are always food booths and a few, carnival rides for the kids. You are aware of the patriotic fervor of the town of Clairton. It's a big rally that is well attended by the citizenry.

But I'm sure you remember that.

Professor Graff's group will have a booth in the park on Friday and Saturday evenings. I've agreed to help, and I'm excited to finally be doing something worthwhile politically.

Alison Brinker, a friend,....sort-of..., from last year's English class, is the professor's, chosen leader in this. That's kind of interesting, as Alison and I "almost" connected last year. Did I tell you about that? I don't think I'm being vain when I tell you that it was my fault we didn't connect. I just couldn't get past the affection I still hold for Penny... ...

How ridiculous is that?

My "friendship" with Alison lasted only about a month. Then, when I offered no encouragement, she found other places to be than where I was.

This year, we are both in Professor Graff's Modern Politics class. Thus far, she had rather avoided me. You can imagine my surprise when she asked me to take part in this rally, and I plan to do so.

(Did I tell you, Alison is attractive and quite nice?)

I'm plenty busy and thankful for that.

(*Maybe, in time, I'll forget Penny,* he thought. But he didn't include that thought in his letter.)

Derek didn't need to explain his loneliness to Bill, who knew his best friend still loved Penny Crawford. Penny had married another classmate shortly after they graduated and was now Penny Houston.

When Bill read about Alison Brinker in his friend's letter, unlike Derek, he gave it little credence. He knew Derek's, loyal heart so well.

Ah, my friend, thought Bill, *I wish you could find someone else. But... ... .*

Derek had concluded his letter with,

That's enough about me. I'll keep you informed.
> My best to you, my friend.
>> Please give my love to Debbie.
>>> (Derek)

The registration booth was to be occupied on Friday and Saturday evenings beginning at 7p.m. Derek had attended the preparatory meeting at Stalwart Center the previous Friday. Tonight, as agreed, he arrived at the park at five o'clock. The town was bustling with excitement. There were banners high above the streets. The park, in which this rally was being held, was situated in an area of land that was located at the junction of the main roads that flowed into Main Street. A good-sized chunk of ground had been carved out of a city block to establish this grass-covered sanctuary. Half-a-dozen, oak trees and a few, original maples were growing here. The oak leaves were turning to fall colors slowly, but the maples were ablaze in orange and yellow. The remainder of the shrubbery and flowers, in that area, were plotted and planned by the Clairton Garden Club. Those ladies had included a line of dogwoods, facing the courthouse across the way. This day, in early October, all the trees were partially changed in color and the ground in the park was strewn with fallen green, yellow, red and burnt-orange leaves. A line of Mums, that had escaped the early frost, added their brilliant color to the scene. Wooden benches were scattered about.

Ordinarily, this area was very restful and picturesque. Tonight was a balmy, October evening. The sun had gone down an hour earlier, but the park was so well lighted, it seemed as bright as day. This Friday evening, the area was already jammed with people.

Vendors lined the sidewalks on Main Street, and there were novelty and food booths inside the park and along the walkways outside. The registration booth was located in a prominent, easily-accessible place.

The chosen, half dozen, energetic, college students, whose purpose was to register interested voters, lined the railing on three sides of the 12' by 12' wooden, elevated platform. Classmate, Kurtis Bahaman, stood beside Derek. A big man, Kurtis was taller and just generally more muscular than Derek in form. His hair was trimmed to about an inch in length. He had a close-cropped, black beard and mustache. A chill wind had set in after the sun went down. Most everyone in the park was wearing a sweatshirt or even a jacket. Kurtis appeared to be comfortable in a short-sleeved, Clairton U,

T-shirt with his jeans. Obviously well-known and liked, he was continually greeted by other students. Derek knew Kurtis to be a good student. At least, he was noticeable in Professor Graff's, Modern Politics class, which surely accounted for his inclusion in this booth this weekend.

A small band, which consisted of a guitarist, a bassist, a keyboard pianist and the drummer, was producing a loud and discordant sound as instruments were being tuned. Derek wasn't fond of the beat of their music. But The Cosmos, as they called themselves, was a college band, and they were popular on campus. He now knew that most, college music is loud and energizing. That's the best he could say about it. But it did keep folks awake. And tonight, he didn't want them sleeping. He hoped there would be much activity around this booth. He personally found the purpose for this activity was vitally important. Those, who were not yet registered to vote, might be made to realize the importance, take a moment to register and thus be able to vote in the November election. Professor Graff's students anticipated a busy weekend.

"The weather is sure co-operating," said Kurtis.

Before Derek could answer, Professor Graff came onto the scene and the students all gave their attention to him. A native and much respected citizen of Clairton, this professor was known and appreciated by most of the established citizens in town as well as the college students. He was small in stature… barely five-foot-seven inches tall. His personality easily eclipsed his height. He had an exceptional gift of humor, was congenial, outspoken and uncommonly clever. His signature on tonight's doings assured a good turnout.

Alison Brinker had walked across the park with him.

She appeared totally at-ease at his side. They chatted easily with the different folks they met along the way. When they reached the booth, greetings were exchanged. Then, Alison hurried over to the stand and proceeded to pass out papers and orders.

Tonight, Professor Graff stopped to speak to his student aides. During class period, he had recognized Derek's, quiet strength, and his ability to influence people with softly-spoken, persuasive words. Each volunteer had been asked to provide a large poster to enlighten the crowd of their responsibility to vote. Those signs had been pinned all around the outside of the booth. Derek was a little surprised, and embarrassed even, to see his sign directly in prominence in front.

One of the signs read:
IT'S YOUR CIVIC RESPONSIBILITY TO VOTE!

Another read:
LET YOUR VOICE BE HEARD !
REGISTER TO VOTE!

For his sign, Derek chose to quote an 18th century, political philosopher:

ALL THAT IS NECESSARY FOR EVIL TO TRIUMPH
IS FOR GOOD MEN TO DO NOTHING
Edmund Burk

Register and vote!

"That's an excellent sign, Derek," the professor said, as he looked over the others without comment. Then, they quickly became busy with a stream of visitors to the booth.

Kurtis remained at Derek's side all that evening. It was his choice. But Derek didn't mind. Though they were in Modern Politics class together, Derek hadn't really known him before tonight. He seemed like a nice enough fellow and was doing a good job at the booth.

Kurtis was apparently well known on campus, as a number of college students visited with him during the evening. He always introduced Derek, who was less talkative but made an effort to be friendly.

By nine o'clock, the stream of visitors to the booth had lessened, and the two, young men stood watching the others finish with their paperwork. Alison was talking with Professor Graff again. He was laughing at something she had said.

"She's cool, don't you think?" asked Kurtis, nodding toward Alison.

"Alison is attractive and intelligent," Derek responded, while thinking, *Those words make me sound like a stuffed shirt.* But what else could he say? Alison was quite attractive tonight. A jacket was draped over her arm. She was wearing tight jeans and an almost equally-tight, red jersey with a rather low neckline. She had the figure to model those clothes. Her hair style was simple. A pair of brief, black boots completed the outfit. The total understatement of her attire only served to draw attention to the very attractive, young woman.

"She's smart, too," said Kurtis.

"Yes, she is," Derek agreed. He was wishing they would drop the subject soon.

"It appears Professor Graff thinks so, too," said Kurtis slyly.

Before Derek found it necessary to respond to that,

Alison turned and walked toward them. She stepped onto the platform and over to where Derek and Kurtis stood. She had a form she was completing and wanted to know how many potential voters they had registered this evening and any other pertinent information they could share. When she was done writing, Kurtis spoke up. "Can I give you a ride home tonight, Alison?" he asked.

She looked at Kurtis and remained quiet for just a moment. *Is she as shocked by that as I am,* Derek wondered? But Alison turned to Derek and focused deliberately on him...waiting. Derek caught his breath. He realized she was giving him first choice!

Then....

He did it again!

He let the moment pass!

"Sure," Alison said, turning to smile at Kurtis. "I rode over with a friend, and I'll be glad for the ride." And with that, she turned and walked briskly away.

Well, that will be the final straw, thought Derek. *I like her. Why did I do that?*

But he really didn't feel badly about it....not really.

Just then, Salvatore came into view. He suggested the two of them get a sandwich before calling it a night and Derek agreed. Derek had never told Salvatore about the troubled connection with Alison. He had never mentioned her at all. Now, of course, there would be no need to do so.

He had never mentioned Penny to Sal, either.

Sal had said to him more than once, "You need some female companionship, my friend."

And Derek always responded, "There'll be time for that later."

On Saturday evening, Derek noticed that Alison apparently showed Kurtus, who was on the opposite end of the platform, no special attention. The booth was busier than before, and the aides had little time to talk among themselves. Some of the visitors took the opportunity to register. Some were just curious; others wanted to visit. As in the previous evening, the group was kept busy. The weekend event was coming to an end, and Derek helped gather up the material and the debris in-and-around the area. It was then that he caught the rare sight of Alison standing alone just outside the booth. She was watching the crowds slowly vacate the park.

He walked over to where she stood and spoke to her from behind.

"Alison."

She turned instantly and her eyes became wary. He was sorry to see that.

"I just wanted to thank you for including me," he said. "It was a lot of fun."

"I'm glad you came. Of course, you realize that Professor Graff requested you personally," she explained.

Is she being defensive, Derek wondered. "But I was happy he did so," she added graciously, "as I knew you'd do a good job. And you did,"

"Thank you."

The two of them looked at each other without speaking. They had never quite connected, but neither of them could deny the unique awareness of the other. Derek was suddenly uncomfortable, wondering how to bring this moment to an end. The problem was solved when several of the others interjected themselves into the situation. Alison turned her attention to them, and Derek turned and walked away.

I'm very good at walking away, he thought. *I seem to have done that a lot with Alison.*

It was after 9 PM. The cleanup was complete and the project was at an end. Derek had told Sal he needed to get home tonight. As he walked some blocks to where he had parked his car, he considered again the way he had treated Alison.

I really like her, he thought. *Why am I like this?*

That night, as he lay in bed, Derek reflected on his failure with women. *Since Penny, there has been no one. And since Penny, if I am honest, I don't want any other.* With that depressing thought, he finally went to sleep.

In the days ahead, it wasn't Alison who haunted his dreams. It was Penny. People say young love doesn't last. And they're mostly right. But occasionally, it does last, and when it does, it's tenacious. Penny had been his first girlfriend…his first…and only love.

He lay in bed and thought of Penny as he had known her in high school. Derek got mostly "A's" in his high school subjects.

Penny was more of a "B" student, he remembered. *"B" students are above average but not noticeably so. The teachers all liked Penny, as did her classmates. But no one fussed over her. Penny's best friend, Debbie Rudolf, was prettier and smarter than she. Debbie was the one who got the attention.*

But I noticed Penny, thought Derek. *And I fell in love with her. That love had begun to form about tenth grade. It came to fruition in the spring of our eleventh grade year..*

He could still picture her clearly.

Penny has brown hair, small features. Her eyes are bright and direct.

That always surprised him, as he knew she was shy in those days.

She still is, he thought. *She's married and has two children, and she's still shy.*

She had been raised without a father. Her dad abandoned the family when she was much younger. No doubt, that made her insecure. He could relate to that certainly. He knew the insecurity of a child raised without a father. Penny and he had that in common.

She needed me, thought Derek. *Even back then, back in high school, Penny needed my male strength. Penny isn't the modern, career-type of girl.*

Derek had no problem with women who wanted a career. Bill's wife, Debbie, was studying to be a nurse. Alison was career-minded, politically ambitious and very capable.

Penny's mind was never on achieving great things in the world, he recalled. *Penny had just wanted to please me. She could have done other things. She was smart enough… smarter than many of the other girls, but she didn't think that way. She's just a homemaker-type of woman.*

Their eleventh-grade-year was the spring he campaigned for the role of Student Advisor on the Alton High Advisory Council. Penny had worn a supportive, campaign sign for him on her white shirt. That was enough encouragement so that he finally asked to walk her home from the market one day. Penny had agreed! Derek remembered how awed he was that Penny actually wanted to be with him. They spent the rest of the school year and the following summer together. They were in love.

Yes, I know that Penny loved me, too.

But before that year was over, she had begun dating their fellow classmate, Michael Houston.

That was my fault, thought Derek…again.

But was it?

He had become so fond of Penny, and she was so willing for his caresses and increasingly-fervent love-making, that he feared he would go too far. They weren't ready for that. She wasn't, nor was he. When he prayerfully considered how to handle this, it seemed best to keep the relationship more casual until they were older. He had tried to explain that to Penny. It wasn't because he didn't love her. It was because he loved her too much!

Having been raised without a father, apparently male rejection was engrained in her heart. When Derek stopped dating her, Michael had stepped right in. And Penny accepted the attention given her by Michael. By the time the three of them graduated from high school, Penny was already expecting Michael's child.

And Derek was heartbroken.

She has two little boys now, but I love her still, he thought sadly. *I guess I always will.*

No, he didn't tell Salvatore about his "close encounter" with Alison Brinker. He hadn't told Salvatore about Penny, either. That was something he couldn't talk about.

But his friend, Bill Tonkins knew all about Penny. He would write to Bill. He needed to let him know there was no "connection" with Alison. And there never would be.

Bill would understand.

Whatever spare time he could arrange on the weekend, Derek spent it with Salvatore now. Tonight, he finished up at Skinny's at 9:30 PM and drove up to the college. Sal was waiting for him in the student lot. Derek parked his vehicle and climbed into Sal's Lexus. They went to Gio's Pizza. That eatery was a short distance to the south of the college. Gio's is always busy with college students, and tonight was no exception. The two, young men entered and looked for seating. The place was dark, jammed and noisy. Sal bumped Derek to get his attention and motioned toward Diane and Mandy, who were in a booth further back. He led the way. Diane had seen Sal enter, and now she readily slid in to make room for him to sit. Mandy followed her lead, and Derek sat beside her.

This was the third evening the four of them had met away from the college recently and supposedly by accident. As previously, the two girls were together. As they slid into the booth, it again occurred to Derek that this meeting might have been by Sal's design. He shook off the irritation that was trying to surface. *There is no harm done,* he thought.

By now, when these two guys showed up at the student lounge or the pizza place, there was soon a flow of visitors to their table. Sal was always sought after. But Derek was respected now and knew a number of students. The scene was no different this evening at Gio's, and they visited for a time.

It was still only 11:00 PM. Tomorrow was Saturday. Derek had work at Skinny's Market, but there were no classes. "You won't go to work until ten tomorrow, Derek," said Sal. "We can spend a little more time tonight…if that's ok with you?" he added in what had become a question. Or was it a plea? Derek understood that Sal wanted some time with Diane...again.

"Would you walk Mandy back to her dorm?" Sal asked. "I'll drop Diane off soon."

Derek really didn't like being put on the spot this way. He decided he would definitely talk to Sal about this....later. But for now, he courteously replied, "Well.....is that alright with you, Mandy?"

"Sure," she replied.

The four of them left the restaurant and split up. Diane crawled into Sal's Lexus.

Gio's Pizza was off a busy highway and almost out-of-town. Derek and Mandy parted from the other two and began the rather long walk back to her dormitory. The day had been summer-like. But this was October and the night was cool enough for a jacket. The days were shorter now. The evening was quite dark.

They walked past a Dairy Queen, a car repair shop. There was a tattoo place on the far side of that building. The car dealership, like the motorcycle shop beside it, was closed for the night. Then, they were on campus and walking by the first, large dormitory. Mandy's dorm was almost on the other side of the campus. After he got Mandy home, Derek would still need to walk to his vehicle which was parked a considerable distance away in the student's parking lot. He was a bit bothered by Sal's maneuverings tonight.

Fortunately, conversation was easy with Mandy.
She was actually quite bright and had an understanding of politics and sports and most everything it seemed.

They talked companionably for a time. Then, they

walked a space in silence. Finally, Mandy cautiously offered this thought.

"Diane really cares for Sal," she said.

"I'm beginning to realize that," Derek replied.

But Sal's reasons for dating Diane had become a concern to Derek. From their conversations now, he realized Sal felt no real attachment to her. He was beginning to suspect that the occasions when Sal wanted to be alone with Diane were possibly not for the best reasons.

Those thoughts had weighed on him lately. But he told himself he had no proof of what he was thinking.

Ah, he thought. *I'm not naïve, either.*

Tonight, he said nothing more in response to Mandy's statement. They continued a little further in silence. Then, Mandy asked in a quiet voice, "Do you have a girlfriend somewhere, Derek?"

Her words surprised him. He and Mandy had never discussed anything that personal before. He was puzzled, wondering what she was thinking.

"Why do you ask that, Mandy?" he questioned.

"You….just….never… You know, we don't hold hands or anything…"

Now, he stopped walking. Derek had never, for a minute, considered holding hands…'or anything'… with Mandy!

Finally, he said firmly but as kindly as he could, "We're just friends, Mandy."

"….oh…." she whispered and dropped her head.

There was an awkward pause. Derek walked a bit faster after that. He did most of the talking the rest of the way. And that wasn't a lot. But he suspected Mandy was embarrassed.

I know I am, he thought. He saw her to the outer door of her dormitory, said a quiet "Goodnight, Mandy," and left at once.

He didn't wait for Sal's return but hurried to his car and drove home. His thoughts were in turmoil. He sure didn't want to hurt Mandy. But if she supposed they could ever be more than friends, she was very wrong.

Now, he had to reconsider his friendship with Sal. They had become good friends. He didn't want to end that.

Sal is a nice guy, a decent man, he reasoned ...*but... can that be right considering his relationship with Diane? Sal seems to know the Lord.... in a Catholic sort of way.*

Relationships sure get entangled, thought Derek.

He had agreed to handle the market for Skinny, who had a special occasion on Saturday evening. Derek actually didn't see Sal again until Monday afternoon. Sal was waiting for him when he exited his last class that day. As they fell into step, Derek shared what Mandy had said about "holding hands".

"You can see that I won't be able to occupy Mandy anymore. She's a real nice girl, but I'm just not interested."

"You're right," said Sal, who sounded embarrassed. "I need to break off with Diane. She's getting too serious. If Diane and I stop seeing each other, you'll not need to say anything to Mandy, will you?"

"I guess not," said Derek. "But I don't want to cause trouble between Diane and you.

"It's not like that, Derek," Sal mumbled and dropped his head. "I'll take care of it."

Sal and Derek were together most days after that. They rarely saw Diane and Mandy and never for fellowship or even for friendly conversation. In the months ahead, Sal didn't entangle himself with any, other girls.

Seven

TONIGHT, WAS A COLD AND unpleasant Monday evening in late October. The season was changing in Pennsylvania and the trees had dropped most of their leaves. A steady rain was not sufficient to dispel the heavy fog. Sal and Derek drove to Allenby's Farm and Sport Supplies on the outskirts of town. Allenby's was a lengthy, un-fancy, warehouse type of building that appealed to men. The business was a favorite place for those shopping for farm, fishing or hunting equipment and apparel. The country location of Clairton University attracts some of the more rugged males, many of whom, in off-class hours, gravitate toward coarse jackets, fleece lined vests, flannel shirts, sweats and rugged jeans. That brings them to Allenby's. Most of the merchandise here is stacked on shelves rather than displayed on neat racks.

Derek had come tonight with Sal, who was shopping for a pair of insulated, sport boots that he had seen advertised in the daily paper.

When he was with Sal, Derek always rode as a passenger in the Lexus. That didn't bother Derek…and especially not tonight.

"This might have been a good night to stay home," said

Derek as they left the place and, battered by the rain, ran for Sal's vehicle.

"Do you want to bed down in my room tonight?" offered Sal. "Jake and I can push our beds together and make room for you."

"No, thanks," said Derek with a laugh. "I'll get home alright."

Surprisingly, as he exited the parking lot and waited for the light at the intersection, Sal didn't turn back toward town but instead turned right and headed in the opposite direction.

He answered Derek's unspoken question. "It's only 8:15 Derek. Jake will be watching game shows, and I can't stand that. I find it impossible to study, and I can't get to sleep this early. Do you mind if I take the long way back to the dorm?"

Derek had some classwork to do before he went to bed for the night. But he enjoyed Sal's company and wasn't overly concerned about driving home later. So, he answered, "That'll be alright."

"I'll keep it short," Salvatore promised.

Derek leaned back and tuned in to the music playing on the radio. Sal's choice in music was surprising to Derek. For no known reason, he would have supposed Sal would like light classical. This night, the radio was tuned to a Nashville station.

They talked about the coming election. Sal was very interested in the politics of this country and had a myriad of questions on the subject. It was a good challenge for Derek, who still considered politics as a possible career in the future.

Sal pulled off onto a country road. About six miles further on, it would connect with a main road leading directly to the campus. But the country road was not a wise choice on this night that was so dark, wet and heavy with fog. There were no white or yellow lines marking the side or middle of the road. There were very few, bright, state signs warning of curves. Sal slowed his vehicle and concentrated.

"This might not have been the smartest thing I've done today," said Sal.

They were both quiet as he focused intently on the roadway. Around the latest bend, the road was bordered by a corn field which somehow hadn't yet been harvested for silage. The lifeless, tan stalks glistened silver in the rain and provided a boundary-of-sort for the dark road. Sal was being very careful.

Suddenly, as they came around a sharp bend, they both noticed the back, tail lights of a car up ahead. Derek said cautiously, "I don't think that vehicle is moving."

Sal applied the brakes and then went forward in a crawl.

"Look! The headlights are aimed right into that field!"

"Yes," Sal replied. They were nearly upon the scene now, and Sal approached cautiously. Sure enough, the car ahead of them was off the road. The front headlights were lopsided as they pointed toward the field. Sal carefully maneuvered the Lexus off to the side of the road.

"It looks like the entire, front wheel on the passenger side has dropped into that gulley," said Derek. The troubled car was listing dangerously to that side.

Just then, a man stepped out from the glare of the headlights.

"Sal! That's Grunge!"

"Yeah," said Sal quietly.

Grunge had been in front of the car trying to lift that

wheel out of the ditch, while the driver of the vehicle, hoping to reverse, was spinning the back wheels. The right, front side of the vehicle was in a deep hole. Grunge was strong. But with no good place to get his footing, he was no match for this problem. Furthermore, he was covered with mud from the spinning, back-wheel residue. Even the back tires were now settling into the mud. The front, passenger side of the vehicle was firmly situated deep into the gully.

Sal and Derek reached for their door latches. The rain was driving sideways as they made their way to where Grunge stood. He was soaked, of course, and muddy. He recognized the duo but didn't speak.

Salvatore and Derek stayed back a space. Salvatore said, "Do you have a problem, Grunge? Maybe we can help?"

Leo had crawled out of the driver's seat. He stepped over to where the two men stood and, pointing to the problem asked, "Do you think you could help Grunge lift it out?"

Grunge was saying nothing.

"Sure," said Sal.

Leo hurried back to the driver's seat and checked for "reverse". Grunge silently moved over to make room for the other two beside the sunken wheel. With everyone in position, "At the count of three," Sal said to the other two.

"One. Two. Three!"

They all gave a heave. The back wheels spun, throwing mud far and wide!

The men were mud-covered and soaked. But the vehicle was out of the ditch!

"Is it drivable?" asked Sal

"Seems possible," said Leo. "It should get us back to campus."

"We'll follow just to be sure."

"Thanks," was Leo's reply.

"Sure," Sal responded.

Grunge was crawling into the passenger side. He still had said nothing.

"Thanks again," Leo said as Salvatore and Derek turned to go back to their own vehicle. Sal reached into the backseat and retrieved a blanket, which he spread for Derek and himself to sit on. He turned the heater to high.

On the drive back to town, Sal kept his Lexus a reasonable distance behind Leo's vehicle.

"They're going to make it back to campus. But I expect he'll need to get some repair work done before he drives very far. His vehicle will surely have a twisted frame from that accident," said Sal.

"Isn't that amazing?" Derek exclaimed. He was excited! "You took the long way back to campus. Who'd have ever thought of something like this happening?

"You treated Grunge real well, Sal," Derek continued enthusiastically. "Maybe he'll think better of the way he's been treating you?"

"Derek," Salvatore spoke quietly. "I can't tell you how often Providence has interceded on my behalf. I rather expect it," he said.

When they reached Derek's car, Derek accepted the blanket Sal offered for his seat. He was soaked, muddy and even chilled, as he crawled into his own car for the drive home, and he didn't have a heater. But his mind was on Salvatore's statement about Providence.

Apparently, there are some problems God can handle without my help, Derek thought wryly. *I've been a Christian for a while now. Salvatore is a Catholic....but he's a faithful Catholic.*

Lou...and Abel, too...had been urging Derek to attend church with the family. *I need to get into the church,* he decided.

After that night, Grunge still didn't speak to Salvatore in the hallway. But he gave no further problem to Jacob or Sal.

Sal and Derek always traveled together in Sal's Lexus. One evening, Derek had a question about Sal's choice of music. This evening, the radio was tuned to Old Favorites. Rosemary Clooney was singing, *Come on'a my house, my house-a come on.*

"Recently, you were listening to Country Western music. Do you like all music?" Derek asked.

"You can learn a lot about people, or an area, by listening to their music. I like most music, Derek. I rejoice to hear a soul break the bonds of propriety and release the emotion in music. I recently discovered Country Western. I guess you know that it's very popular in this area. I've spent some time examining the spirit of that music...and others." Then, he added softly, "But my heart is with the classical." He didn't elaborate, and they talked of other things.

In the days ahead, Derek noted that Sal never chose to play classical music when they traveled in his car.

Derek was early this Saturday morning...nearly half-an-hour early. Sal had a friend who owned a boat. He had invited Sal, Derek and another student to spend the day "checking out the Clairton River". Sal, who loved the greenery and river scene, was most enthusiastic to do so. Derek, too, thought it would be a fun adventure. He had arranged with Skinny to be free this, special day. And he agreed to meet Sal at 7 a.m. for breakfast in town before joining the others. He was so accustomed to rising early, and maybe a bit excited, too, that he arrived in town nearly half-an-hour before the appointed, meeting time with Sal.

This was a part of Clairton's campus that was practically unknown to Derek. He simply had no occasion to be on this side. For their adventure today, Sal had suggested they meet in the parking lot of the gymnasium building across the highway from the large, Catholic Church. He didn't explain why he chose that location, but it didn't matter to Derek anyway.

As he was early, Derek was driving slowly to pass the time. Maple trees fronted the well-kept houses on this street. He could see the Catholic Church up ahead. It was the largest church in Clairton and surely could be matched architecturally only in the big cities. It was most impressive. There was no traffic yet on this street, so Derek was taking his time and enjoying the scenery. Just as he was about to make the right turn onto the street leading to the gymnasium, he noticed something strange.

That looks like Sal's car, he thought. *But, no, it couldn't be....Sal wouldn't come to church at 6:30 a.m. Besides, there are no other cars parked there.*

As there was still no traffic, Derek slowed his vehicle to a crawl.

It is Sal's car! I can see that bright decal of Sao Paulo, Brazil on his back window. His car is parked in the side lot of the Catholic Church.

In fact, the Lexus was the only vehicle there, and it was in the back of the church...almost out-of-sight.

Derek was curious. He parked his Pontiac out front and walked around to the side, where Sal's car was parked. Now, he faintly heard music and stopped. It was beautiful, piano music. One expects to hear beautiful music coming from a Catholic church.

But at this time of the morning?...it isn't seven o'clock yet. Is Sal here? Are there others here, too? But I see only Sal's car... It's the only car here...

He looked across to the entrance of this building and noted that there seemed to be a number of expansive, stone steps leading up to the great, front doors, which were painted bright red. Would those doors be open this early in the morning? He'd never been inside a Catholic Church before. *Surely, everyone is welcome in a church,* he decided.

He tried the latch on the side door nearest to where he stood. It wasn't locked. Derek didn't make a habit of entering buildings uninvited, but he stepped inside and was in a hallway with doors on one side and a stairway on the other. It was dark except for one, small light that glowed at the far end of the hall. The music was coming from above. He decided that, since there was music, there had to be people here. Sal must be here. At the top of the stairs, he entered another hallway. This one was lined with thick, lush carpet. It was equally dark here. Now, he did feel like an intruder!

Though the doors were shut, Derek could see that the large, stone staircase at the front of the building opened into this hallway. Off to the side, he was confronted with a set of large, impressive, mahogany doors, which were also closed. The music was emanating from there.

Derek carefully opened one door just a crack. The music struck with force! Awesome!

This, large sanctuary had not yet received the early, morning sunlight. The beautiful, stain-glass windows were still shadowed and the interior of the room, with long rows of seating, was mostly dark. Everywhere, that is, but on the stage. There was a piano there with a lighted, floor lamp beside it and a bright light above it.

The music and the lights created a heavenly scene. Derek was awed! He had no knowledge of classical or of "high", church music. But the sound was entrancing, and he knew this music was being played by no ordinary pianist.

He was staggered to realize that Sal was playing the piano!

Just then, he felt a hand on his shoulder, and, alarmed, swung around to see the source.

"Father Alonzo is not yet in audience. Do you have a need?"

The words were spoken somewhat sternly. The man had seemingly, stolen up behind Derek, who was now momentarily speechless. How would he explain this unwarranted entrance into the church?

But the moment had created enough distraction to cause the pianist to stop playing.

"It's alright, Henri," Sal said quickly and hastily rose. "This is a friend of mine."

Henri dropped his hand from Derek's shoulder, and the two waited there, in the doorway, while Salvatore quickly gathered the sheet music, lifted the lid of the piano stool and dropped it inside. He turned the light switches, and then, hurried to the door to introduce Derek and Henri. Derek was informed that Henri was the primary caretaker of this church.

After the brief introduction, Sal quickly turned his friend to the stairway.

"We have an appointment, Henri. Give my regards to Father Alonzo. I'll see you soon."

"Good day, Salvatore," said the caretaker.

"We need to go, Amigo," Sal said to Derek and headed quickly to the stairway.

Before exiting, Sal raised an arm in a silent farewell to Henri, who had remained standing up above.

Neither of the young men spoke as they walked over to Derek's car. Finally, Derek found his voice.

"Sal! I didn't know you were a pianist! And not an amateur, either! You could become a professional musician!" Then, he corrected himself and said humbly, "You probably are, right now, as capable as any professional musician." Derek was confused. "Why do you not play openly? Why not join the music department and share your talent?"

Derek was trying to understand, but Sal remained quiet.

"How? ...where did you learn to play like this? You're a master pianist." He was a novice judge, but Derek knew that was true.

But why was Sal so quiet?

Finally, Sal did something he hadn't intended to do while in this country. He decided to share this very personal matter with his good friend.

"I was gifted with the piano skill at birth," he said. "Mi madre's hermano, Tio Ferdinand... (In his confusion, Sal was speaking in Spanish.)

"Excuse me," he said. Now, he consciously collected his poise and deliberately, carefully switched back to the English language. The accent was always obvious but Salvatore was very affluent in English.

"My Uncle Ferdinand," he spoke carefully in English, "is a flutist for the Chicago Symphony Orchestra. He has written a number of concertos that are played by that orchestra and others across this country. From my mother's side, music is my gift.

"As a toddler, I was fascinated by Uncle Ferdinand's talent. When he visited us and played his music, I would listen enthralled. As a young child, he let me play his instrument, and, even untrained on the flute, my gift of music was evident beyond my age. But when I heard the piano, that stirred me deepest. As a child, I had countless questions about music.

"My parents knew of my gift. But they offered no encouragement. At a very young age, I understood music was not to be my future. Neither they, nor I, discussed it. My...father.. (It was obvious Sal was still disconcerted, but he carefully, deliberately chose to speak in English.) "My father has chosen to ignore my gift. There has never been a piano in our home, though we could afford the finest.

"Madre is saddened for me, of course. She and I know that this is not unkindness by el padre but just an acknowledgement that influence demands sacrifice."

Sal was still mentally fluctuating between Spanish and English. Derek had never before seen his friend so unsettled. Obviously, this matter touched him deeply.

"My father is a powerful man in our country," Sal explained. "His enterprises are crucial, not only for our family but for a multitude of families and even for our nation. His influence sways government decisions. From earliest childhood, I've been groomed as his successor. It is vital that I be prepared to step into that role immediately, if necessary. Even at this age, my word carries weight in my homeland. I am the son of Fernando Salvatore Ridenti, III.

Derek was stunned by Sal's explanation. *But can this be right?*

"You have a brother...a younger brother," Derek said. "Could he be groomed for the family business?"

"Garcia?" Sal chuckled. "My little brother is a wonderful fellow, but he has a most ordinary mind. He's a zealous, soccer fan and starts his day in his Pele jersey...or sometimes Ronaldo. He can give you the statistics of Kaka's legendary feats in the 2002 World Cup. Garcia enjoys his modern gadgets. He has good friends and good times....and he takes care of Brutus...my dog," he said with a laugh. "Brutus is about the extent of his responsibilities. My little brother is of normal intelligence and normal interests....and I love him dearly," said Sal.

"But Providence...was right to choose me as Padre's successor."

Derek voiced his confusion. "You are gifted," he said to Sal. "but you're also accomplished. Could you master the piano to this extent without training?"

Sal chuckled. "Oh, I had training," he said. "The priests saw to that.

When I was a young child in the Catholic school at

Cacapava, my passion for music was discovered. Father Manuel came upon me playing the piano in the empty Cathedral. Though I never mentioned my father, he quickly discerned my predicament and arranged for me to have unhindered access to the piano. Very soon, I was practicing daily.

"From early childhood, with discretion, I would enter the silence of that cathedral and release my passion! And soon, Father Manuel, unobtrusively, arranged for a piano maestro to "just happen" to be in the sanctuary at that, same time to instruct me.

"Often, Father Manuel would come in, sit quietly and listen. 'The secret passions burn brightest,' he would say.

"As I matured in my education and moved on to a different city and a different parish, always, the priests passed the word of my gift on before me. It would "just happen" that an accomplished, piano maestro would be involved in that parish and available to counsel me. I received excellent training."

"Should they have done that?" Derek asked. "It doesn't seem quite right that the priests would go against your father that way."

"In fact, they had no word concerning this from my father...neither "for" or "against". He never mentioned my gift at home or away. For padre, my gift of music doesn't exist.

"When I would come to the cathedral to practice, the priests called it 'recreation time.' No need for my father to know otherwise. 'All children need recreation time,' they would say with a smile.

"Everywhere my schooling took me, I was given access to a prize piano, the teaching of gifted instructors and the kindness and encouragement of the priests."

Then, he added somewhat sadly, "I had good training, the best, music teachers....but it is not to be my career."

"You'll not make it your career?" Derek was saddened for his friend.

"Ah, Derek..... It seems you had a hard, family life in the beginning. You fought through that time to overcome. It has made you a man of strong character. And I'm so glad things are turning around for you and for your family. I rejoice with you. But for me, the well-being of many others is involved. Some situations cannot be rectified."

Sal turned and walked toward his Lexus. The subject was closed.

Derek drove his vehicle over to the gymnasium, parking lot and rode with Sal, as always. The day spent boating on the Clairton River was, indeed, an enjoyable experience for all, and maybe, especially for Derek, who had such limited, recreational opportunities in the past.

That night, Derek gave consideration to the new information he had learned about his friend. He was saddened by Sal's, future limitations. Only the past evening, he had pondered Job's lament:

Job 5:7 Yet man is born unto trouble, as the sparks fly upward.

Now, he could see that financial security, the finest schooling and even proper, home relationships cannot necessarily prevent limiting circumstances and hardships.

Lord, my determination to trust You to lead in my future is a wise one, he thought.

Eight

THEY WERE THREE MONTHS INTO the new, school year. It had been a busy three months, which was helpful for Mr. Harriger in getting his bearings without Cindy. At this time, he was standing in the hallway outside his room as the students hurried past. They greeted him enthusiastically. The teen girls were usually more reserved than the boys, but they all spoke to him.

Further down the hallway, Mr. Hardin's door opened and Rachael filed out with some classmates. Two other girls nearby called out to her, and she joined them. David was pleased to see that Rachael had obviously resolved that earlier problem. He recalled how JerriLynn had counseled her through that time.

Just then, JerriLynn came around the corner, and the three girls surrounded her. The chattering group walked along together. *JerriLynn never seems to walk alone,* he thought. *There are always several, young girls vying for her attention....or, just as often, there are four or five kids, both male and female. She is so very approachable. And she looks so young,* he thought. *She could pass for a student herself.*

As he was alone for a few moments, he watched the scene with amusement. *She's one-of-a-kind,* he thought....*a pretty* special kind. *JerriLynn is totally without pretense.* For some reason, he found himself comparing her with Cindy.

He remembered Cindy had drawn attention, too, when she walked down the hallway. *But the kids didn't treat her with quite this much familiarity. She was always dressed to a "T". She wore those high heels that gave her some stature. Cindy wasn't vain; she didn't seek attention. She just had beauty and class and moved with the grace of a model. She easily captured any scene in which she found herself.*

Ah, Cindy…..

True, he was thinking of Cindy. Even so, he found himself smiling as he observed the scene with JerriLynn.

She is cheerful, kind, self-forgetful, and most helpful, thought Mr. H. *JerriLynne is attractive, too. It has taken me a little time to realize just how attractive. It helps that she has abandoned the pony-tail or whatever it was she did with her hair when she first came. Her dark curls are cut short now. The new hair style makes her look a little older. And since she exchanged her glasses for contacts, one can see that she has really pretty, blue eyes.*

Today, JerriLynne was dressed in dark slacks. With the colder weather, she had retired the sandals and now wore a pair of flat, penny loafers.

She's so tiny, he mused. *It would be easy to mistake her for a student.*

Everybody likes JerriLynn, he thought, *including me. She comes across as a flighty, little butterfly. But she's quite accomplished in ministering to others. When JerriLynn appears, she brings acceptance, peace, fun and always service. She just unobtrusively begins to serve those, who are present.*

She turned her head just then and saw him watching her. JerriLynn blushed! *She always blushes when she's around me,* he thought with amusement. *But it's a bit flattering, too.*

He smiled at her and gave a short wave. She smiled back and then turned toward her "cave". That's what she called her Home Ec room under the stage, either "cave" or dungeon". In a building with over 500 students, there was little time or opportunity for anything more familiar than a smile and a wave. But the moment had been pleasant ...quite pleasant. The moment registered with JerriLynn, too. She scolded herself for blushing. *Why can't I be more poised,* she thought with despair? *I behave like a schoolgirl with a crush.*

Her despair deepened as she remembered she was twenty-six years old and still single. *I can hardly believe it,* she thought. *I'd love to be married. I want children...a houseful of children! It isn't like I never have a chance to date. Art Peterson has asked me out....rather often. Even Attorney Coulter has shown himself to be interested.*

But, always, her heart said, No.

JerriLynn Smathers loves David Harriger.

There, I admitted it. No surprise. Not for me and maybe not for the others, either. They surely see my blushes every time he shows me the slightest attention. But that relationship appears to be as dead-end as this job, she thought as she entered her Home Ec room. *My major is in English....English! Not Home Ec!*

Miss Sally, the head of the English Department, had announced that she'd be retiring after this year. JerriLynn had hopes that she might be rewarded with that job. She certainly intended to apply for it.

Fortunately, just then, several kids came bounding down

the few stairs to her room. They were quickly followed by others and the noise level rose to "high". JerriLynn forgot about herself and plunged into her teaching duties.

The next morning, she hurried into the lounge to prepare the coffee in advance of the entrance of the others. Mrs. Blake was first to arrive, and, this morning, she had brought a tray of brownies for the group.

"How's this for perfect weather? The nights are in their 40s and the days are in the 60s this week....pretty unusual for this time of year." Mr. Scott was talking as he took his seat and began munching on a fudge brownie with chocolate icing and nuts.

"They're good," said JerriLynn, who had seated herself across from Mr. H and was enjoying a brownie, too. Mrs. Blake's brownies were disappearing fast as the others arrived.

"How did you ever find the time to bake these?" JerriLynn asked. "When I watched Emily's, three kids last summer, I didn't even have time to fix their meals. We ate out a lot."

"They keep me busy," agreed Mrs. Blake. "But I enjoy cooking and baking. It's part of my 'fun' time."

"We've been missing Cindy's treats," said Mr. Wilbert.

Cindy Roberts sometimes brought Devil Dogs or Peanut Butter Fudge for the coffee break.

"I expect Cindy has lots of time to bake right now," said Mrs. Blake sadly.

All heads turned toward her. They all missed Cindy Roberts and were anxious to hear any news about her.

Mrs. Blake confided, "I had a letter from her this past weekend. I think I told you that she's working as secondary,

Business Instructor at #32 Senior High in Ultima. It's a large school. I think she said the student enrollment for Senior High is about 4000 students.

"I sure wouldn't like that," said Mr. Wilbert. "You lose a lot in the bigger schools. The slow students, especially, slip through the cracks."

"I don't think Cindy likes it too well, either," said Mrs. Blake. "But that's only a part of her present problem. She said that Clifford has returned to his dig in Egypt. She wanted to go with him. But she had committed to this school job, which he helped her acquire. Clifford wanted her to stay and fulfill her commitment. He felt it would impact his standing with the educational hierarchy in Ultima if she were to leave before the school year was over."

Several teachers shook their heads. Everyone seemed distressed to hear this news.

"Of course, she misses Clifford. She says she has no idea how long he'll be away. She's lonesome. She hasn't had an opportunity to connect with her fellow teachers yet. It seems there's not the camaraderie we know here," Mrs. Blake concluded.

The lounge had grown quiet. No one could imagine a group of people among whom Cindy Roberts would be lonesome.

"Is she getting to know Clifford's parents?" someone asked.

"The Edelsons? Clifford's parents are very wealthy and socially prominent in Ultima. I understand they have social gatherings most weekends. Clifford insisted they attend those parties when he was there this past summer. Now that he's away, Cindy is invited, of course. But she says she's uncomfortable in that lifestyle. She rarely tries to attend now. She uses her job as an excuse. But, in fact, she's quite lonesome."

Heads were down. They were all sorry to hear this news.

Mr. H pushed back his chair and left the room without a word.

The others didn't bother to try to make conversation. Fortunately, the bell rang just then, chairs were shuffled back, and they all went to their classrooms.

Throughout Derek's, high school years, basketball, at Alton High, was the predominant entertainment of the students and the town during the winter months. The citizens of Alton attended the games as enthusiastically as did the students.

Derek was spending more time with Salvatore, and he was making an effort to introduce his friend to life in this country, namely in his home town of Alton. Skinny had employed a young, tenth-grade student to help him on the evenings Derek had...or in this case, wanted....to be away. Derek would not take advantage of Skinny's kindness. But he did want to give Sal a taste of life in the little town of Alton, Pennsylvania.

This evening, he and Sal were attending a basketball game at Alton High. As they drove up to the school and began looking for a parking place, Sal commented, "Derek, I know you are quite intelligent, perceptive, morally astute..."

Derek glanced over at him, wondering where this conversation was taking him.

"It's just hard to believe you received your foundational education in that little building," said Sal, as he nodded toward the tan, brick, high school. "How did you ever get enough learning here to be able to grasp the greater education offered at Clairton University?"

Derek didn't respond immediately. Sal became occupied in the crush of traffic as they drove past the school and continued to look for a parking place.

"There's room just beyond that driveway," Derek pointed.

Sal carefully maneuvered his Lexus into the area indicated. He turned and looked at Derek. "Of course, your major is English …..and Social Studies," Sal said thoughtfully. "And I know you read much outside the classroom. I suppose you could supplement your education that way. But what do the science majors do in a tiny school like this? How can they graduate with enough knowledge to go on to college?"

"As a matter of fact," said Derek, "my best friend is a scientist. Bill Tonkins is one of the chief officers in NELCO EASTERN….a chemical company that only recently won a lucrative, government contract.

"Alton High has an up-to-date, Science wing that is suitable for the high school level.

"We didn't have a large, teaching staff, but Alton has a superior administration and excellent teachers. We learned the basics well. Schools are failing in our nation today. Many kids are graduating, who never learned the basics. Of course, they can't move on.

"Then, too, this little town is united in their efforts to pass on values that will enable their offspring to compete honorably and well in society.

"Values and basics are the bedrock of education. If students are taught and comprehend those early in their schooling, the rest that is necessary for a successful career can be added."

Sal said nothing. He was considering what Derek had just said. They walked the block-and-half to the school. The area was jammed with citizens making their way inside.

Derek spoke to a number of townspeople at the entrance to the gym. He had opportunity to introduce Salvatore to the janitor, Calvin Carson.

"I'm very pleased to meet you," and the janitor offered his hand. Derek briefly explained his acquaintance with Salvatore, and shared that his friend was from Brazil.

The place was too noisy for conversation. "I hope you will enjoy your stay in our country," was about all that could be heard. The two, young men made their way further in and found seating high in the bleachers.

Another group crowded into the entranceway. Following close behind was Attorney Samuel Coulter.

"Who was the black guy?" he asked Cal.

Calvin didn't answer immediately. He had hurried to prop open the door for another group entering. As they passed, he released the door again to keep the cold air outside. Then, he turned to the attorney, who had waited for him to answer his question. Cal was momentarily confused. He had to jog his memory to recall the attorney's question.

"Oh. You wanted to know who came in with Derek?" said Cal. "That's a friend of his from the college."

But the attorney obviously wasn't relating to his explanation, so he added a bit of explanation. "The young man is a friend of Derek Metcalf. You do know Derek, don't you … … Lou's son?"

"Oh. Sure….Derek Metcalf. I knew him when he was in high school. He looks considerably older now. The guy with him seems to be foreign," he added.

A loud cheer went up, and Attorney Coulter pressed forward to see what was happening. Cal seized the opportunity to move away.

Mr. Harriger had noticed Derek and Salvatore enter. He, too, noted that the young man seemed to be foreign. True, Alton had few, foreign visitors. But that's as much thought as he gave to the matter. Mr. H was coaching the Junior High, basketball team this year. Early this fall, he had been hired for that job, after Mr. Adams resigned to take a more lucrative position at Clairton High School.

Mr. H hadn't played that sport in college, but he had been on the basketball team in high school. Mr. Lombard, Alton's head, basketball coach, had a good relationship with the man, and he knew his "boys" respected this teacher, so David was invited to take the position.

The school year was busy and challenging. But David Harriger needed more than that to occupy him. There was little entertainment outside the school happenings in Alton, PA. When asked to apply for the Junior High, basketball job, he did so readily. He would rather be involved than be a spectator. As he was sufficiently respected by the administration and school board, he was quickly hired. He found that he enjoyed the challenge.

All the lights were lit in the gymnasium and the bleacher seats were filled. The place was alive with chatter, hum and motion. Spectators climbed past others to scale the bleachers, students raised their voices in excitement, and townspeople bumped shoulders and greeted one another. Friday night basketball was a noisy event in Alton.

As his boys sat quietly awaiting the next quarter, Mr. H. looked around at the bustle. He always enjoyed this scene. Earlier, he had noticed JerriLynn enter. She was the only, woman teacher who regularly attended the basketball games. Miss Roberts had never attended, when she taught here. Mrs. Blake was too busy with her family. He had never seen Ms. Conrad in attendance. In fact, he rarely saw any other, female teachers in attendance. But JerriLynn never missed a game. He knew that, for he rather looked for her each time. She came alone, but she was never alone long.

Tonight, she was dressed in dark slacks and a Navy blue, long sleeved, cotton top. She wore a gold band around her hairline. Black/blue/and gold were the school colors. Her feet were enclosed in sneakers, which made her seem shorter. Dressed this casually, she could easily have been mistaken for a student. Just as soon as she entered the building, she was greeted by students. She didn't have many of the students in her Home Ec classes or the newspaper detail, but they all related to her in a most casual way, and she knew most of them by name. She could be seen chatting with two or three for a brief moment. Then, she moved on. As usual, the kids on the lower seats quickly moved closer to make room for her.

Mr. H smiled to himself as he observed that. For some reason, he took pleasure in knowing JerriLynn was present and truly interested.

The bell rang; the action started, and he was lost in the game.

A little later that evening, with a lull in the action, he looked across the gym again and noticed Attorney Coulter was still lingering in the entranceway and visiting with anyone who came or went. There were no vacant seats now; the first quarter was nearly over. The attorney continued to look around rather than watch the game. He seemed more interested in the crowd than in the action on the field.

Samuel Coulter's dark-brown hair was cut short. Though it was no longer the style, he had recently grown sideburns and a mustache. His hazel eyes twinkled and matched his ready smile, except when in the courtroom. There, when the matter was serious and the jury intent on his delivery, his eyes would turn dark and intense, seemingly holding the jury spellbound.

Samuel wasn't classically handsome but had the appeal of a successful, confident rake. Women were much attracted to him. Men easily discerned the "gentleman" artifice. They didn't put a lot of stock in his character, but they wryly figured it probably made him a good attorney.

He was single, and the object of a number of female eyes.

Attorney Coulter was too intimidating for the young people to greet him with familiarity. Mr. H. noticed a town businessman make his way over to where the attorney stood and the two were engrossed in conversation for a time.

A female, town citizen noticed the young attorney and whispered to alert her friend.

He always draws attention, thought Mr. H. *Samuel Coulter is held in high esteem. Personally I don't care much for the man.*

Mr. Harriger turned his attention back to the game and became intently involved. It was not until late in the third quarter that he again glanced toward the stadium entrance.

He was surprised to notice that Attorney Coulter, who had disappeared for a span, was again standing in the entranceway. But now, he was talking to JerriLynn! Why had she left her seat to talk to him?

He had no way of knowing that JerriLynn had removed herself from the noisy auditorium to answer her cell phone. She noticed that the call was from her sister in Oregon and moved quickly outside to talk to her. When she re-entered, Mr. Coulter was in the entranceway and standing in such a way that she could not easily pass.

"Well, young lady, I feared you had given up on the team and gone home," he said.

Their team was behind by three points.

"Oh, no," said JerriLynn with a smile. "I just had a call and needed the quiet of the outdoors to answer it."

It was hard to make her voice heard over the crowd. She would have gladly hurried back to her seat, but he persisted in talking to her. He was still blocking her path.

"Well, I'm glad for the call you received," he said. "Otherwise, I might not have had this opportunity to visit with you."

Thankfully, just then the stands erupted in a cheer. The attorney was distracted, and JerriLynn grabbed the moment to slide past him. "Oh, I'm keeping you from the game," she said, as she did so. They both knew it was the other way around. But he smiled at her subtlety and with a wave of his arm, ushered her on.

Mr. H had looked across the room just in time to see that exchange. Of course, he had no way of knowing why

JerriLynn had left her seat and was talking to Attorney Coulter. He chided himself for even thinking about it and returned his attention to the basketball court.

His team lost their game this night. That, no doubt, was the reason the coach found himself so out-of-sorts as he returned to his apartment. But his mind kept drifting back to that incident with JerriLynn and the attorney. *What business is it of mine if JerriLynn befriends Attorney Coulter,* he asked himself grumpily while climbing into bed?

Following the game, Derek and Salvatore visited the local restaurant. Sal observed how the entire town seemed to be here. Despite the team loss, the crowd was loud and boisterous. The place was almost as noisy as the gym had been during the game.

Derek introduced his friend every chance he had. For Salvatore, it was a new experience. He had been to games in great stadiums. He had sat in city bars and restaurants following an exciting game with a noisy crowd, but this was different. These folks all know each other. There was a sense of camaraderie that he had rarely experienced...if ever. In truth, he felt a tinge of envy for Derek, who lived in this small-town.

He dropped Derek off at his home. Sal was thoughtful as he drove back to Clairton U. He was glad he had chosen a small town in Pennsylvania to experience life outside of Brazil.

The town of Alton offers little recreation apart from school events. There had been endeavors in the past to allow fancier restaurants and bars. But the citizens always unanimously voted the town "dry". There was no movie theater or roller rink. The closest, bowling alley was just outside Clairton. Really, beyond the church or school events, the only recreational spot in town was the pool hall behind Hank's catch-all "grocery, hardware, little-bit-of-everything" business at the edge of town. It stayed open weekends until the wee hours. The ladies in town would have gladly included that place among their banned entertainments. But this was a favorite haunt of the working men in town, and the women knew better than to challenge that.

The citizens of Alton mostly observe Sunday as a day of rest. The restaurant and garages stay open. But Skinny's Market, the pharmacy, Tom Karn's hardware and other, small businesses are closed.

Weekends in Alton could be long and boring. For sure, Mr. Harriger found it so. He did not frequent the pool hall. Of course, there was no basketball practice. He attended the Presbyterian Church on Sunday morning. After that, there was professional football on the TV. After that... .....well, after that, the evenings were long. There were always papers to grade and lessons to plan,but he needed respite from that.

This cold, Saturday evening in December, he did what he did most weekend evenings. He donned a jacket, no hat, and walked down to the restaurant for his evening meal. He struck up a conversation with several other men who were there alone. Usually, these townsmen wanted to discuss his basketball team, the last game or the next game. If they only knew, Mr. H wanted his weekend to be wholly un-school related. But he smothered his groan and talked the game with them.

They were leaving as Colonel Abel Saunders entered the

doorway. David was glad to see Abel. They'd become well acquainted through a number of similar meetings here at the restaurant.

Abel spoke to this one and that as he moved past the counter customers. He teased the waitress, who nearly tripped as she hurried by with her tray. And he headed directly to the stool beside Dave.

"Good evening, David," he said congenially.

"Well, it's improving. I'm glad to have some company finally. Is Lou working again?" he asked.

"She's teaching her art again. She has a large class this time. I think she said there were seven women....or girls... anxious to learn how to knit."

"It will be a good pastime for them," said David. "JerriLynn Smathers,....at the school...(he explained)..."

"Yes, I know Miss Smathers," Abel said quickly.

Mr. H continued, "JerriLynn has long lamented that no one is teaching the young women to sew or knit. Her values are those of the women of the past."

"Well, good for her," said Abel.

David would have been considered old-fashioned, but he, also, believed sewing and knitting were commendable arts for women to learn.

The two men talked for forty-five minutes before Abel had to leave. David finished his coffee. Then he rose, slipped on his jacket and exited the building. Except for that short respite with Abel Saunders, this had been a long and lonesome day. There were always people with whom to talk. He was part of the school personnel, so there was usually someone with whom to engage. But the conversation never reached that lonesome spot within.

He walked down the steps intending to turn toward his apartment. That was when he noticed her coming up the street. JerriLynn had been visiting her older sister and family. She was headed for home. Like Mr. H, and even with her family in town, she found weekends lonely. The evening was cold, but there was no wind blowing. She was wearing jeans, a pair of high, brown leather boots, and a beige parka with a fur-lined hood over her head. Her gloves were brown like her boots. She walked with her head down, so she didn't notice him watching her. Actually, he was now waiting for her.

A look of shock crossed her face, as he stepped out of the shadows. Then, she realized it was David Harriger who stood there.

"Oh! Hi, Mr. H," she said as she came to a stop beside him.

"JerriLynn, how long have you known me?" he questioned her.

"Why...several years now," she said hesitantly.

"Could you not call me Dave?" he asked. "You make me feel very old with your 'Mister' address.

"It's Dave, then," she said with a laugh.

"What brings you out on this, dark night?" he asked as he fell into step beside her.

"I was visiting my older sister, Emily, and her family. They're the kids I watched last summer," she said. "I just love them."

"It would be nice to come from a big family," he said. "I had only one brother. And Stu....Stuart," he elaborated... "lives in Chicago with his family. He has three boys. I sure wish we lived closer."

Dave looked down at her. *She's so small*, he thought,... *scarcely more than a kid herself.*

181

"How old are you, JerriLynn?" he asked. *Why did I ask her that?* he wondered.

She didn't seem insulted or embarrassed but answered him easily.

"I'm twenty-six-years-old." She didn't mind his question. But she was still a bit awed that he would choose to walk with her. He had stepped to her side and was matching her stride as they walked toward her home.

"That old?" he said. "I always think of you as a kid. I guess I'll need to revise my thinking."

She smiled up at him, and their eyes met.

JerriLynn is very pretty, he realized. *She is finally wearing contacts, and she is indeed pretty. Why have I not noticed that before?*

They walked a short time in silence. They were both thinking their own thoughts.

Finally, she said with reluctance, "This is where I live."

"Oh. I guess I knew that," he said, as he glanced toward the house. "I was so comfortable with my companion that I just forgot."

JerriLynn was without words. *He is comfortable with his companion,* she thought. *He actually said that. And, he's making no effort to leave.* She looked up at him and realized he was studying her.

It seemed so natural when his arms went around her. The kiss was so right.

He looked, with puzzled intensity, into her eyes. Then, his arms fell away, and he said softly, "Goodnight, JerriLynn."

"Goodnight…. David…." she replied. JerriLynn turned toward the short walkway that led to her door.

David Harriger slowly walked away. He was admittedly confused.

Why did I do that? Am I that lonely?

But…..it was nice, he thought. *That kiss was sure nice… ….*

The following week, JerriLynn was much aware of his presence in the lounge, but Mr. H made no particular effort to talk to her. There was that one time, though, when she was fussing with something at the coffee counter. He had stepped up behind her, slipped an arm around her shoulder and leaned over close to reach beyond her for a cup. Her heart danced at his nearness. But he made no comment. She wondered if the others noticed. The talk had continued undisturbed.

The ball game was at home on Friday night. During half time, one of the students handed her a sealed note.

"Mr. Harriger asked me to give this to you, Miss Smathers," she said.

JerriLynn's fingers shook as she opened the seal. She read, "Can I stop for you after the game?"

There was no signature. But she looked across to where he was sitting. He had watched her open the note. Now, they both smiled.

David stopped at her house. JerriLynn still lived with her parents. It had never seemed important to have her own, living quarters. Now, she thought it was ridiculous to be twenty-six-years-old and still living at home. *I need to do something about that this next summer,* she thought. Tonight, her mother was already in bed. Her dad was watching a game show.

"I'm going out for a short time, Daddy," she said as she leaned down to kiss his cheek. Her dad gave little thought to her comings and goings, and tonight he asked no questions. She would explain to her mother tomorrow. JerriLynn hurried out to where David was waiting by the open, car door to assist her.

He took her to Clairton this night. On the drive over, they talked about the game and some school-related subjects. The restaurant he chose was three miles beyond the far side of the town. The only, other building nearby was a large, busy, gas station. As this restaurant was near a confluence of interstate traffic, it was usually busy. JerriLynn looked around when they entered. There was a large, circular counter with seats facing a TV on the wall ahead. A few, solitary men, who were seated there, were engrossed in a sport's program. On either side of that counter there were four booths. Tonight, three of those booths were occupied. She knew none of the patrons. David helped to remove her jacket, which she then folded and placed beside her on the seat.

They sat quietly and waited for the waitress.

"If you're like me," said David, "you're famished. I never have much to eat before a ball game. I fill up afterwards."

She just knew he'd be more comfortable if she ate something. So, she ordered a cheeseburger and a chocolate milk shake. He asked for two cheeseburgers with his milkshake. After that, conversation was easy. JerriLynn wanted to know anything about this man that he would share with her. And surprisingly, he seemed equally interested in her life.

In fact, David Harriger was delighted with the company. When the ballgames were over, he commonly sat alone in a restaurant. His obsession with Cindy Roberts had left him with no desire for other companionship.

But tonight he discovered he much enjoyed JerriLynn's company.

It was nearly one o'clock when he stopped at her home and walked her to the door.

"That was a very enjoyable evening, JerriLynn. Thank you for keeping me company."

"I enjoyed it, too," she said sincerely.

He made no effort to kiss her. *But, why would he,* she chided herself. *He forgot himself last week when he kissed me. We are just friends.*

He's more than that to me, though, she thought as she lay in bed remembering his every word, even his every smile surely.

The following Friday, the game was at Middletown. JerriLynn did not attend the far-away games. That morning, when the bell rang, the teachers exited the lounge and headed to class as always. She was quickly wiping the coffee counter before she, too, needed to hurry to class. She sensed someone behind her, and when she turned, Mr. Harriger was standing there.

He smiled at her. "Are you busy tomorrow night, JerriLynn?" he asked.

"...n-no," she stammered.

"Could I take you to dinner?" David was smiling down at her.

"I'd like that," she said breathlessly.

"I'll stop for you at six," he said.

The next afternoon, JerriLynn searched for the right outfit to wear. She decided against slacks. That would remind him too much of her school uniforms. She chose, instead, a mid-length, print skirt with an elastic waist. It was cotton lined and flared when she walked. A soft blue, sweater with a wide, dipping neckline matched the print in the skirt. Around her neck, she wore a small, black velvet band centered with a tiny embroidered, blue flower encased in a silver showcase. The outfit looked fine with dressy, flat shoes. JerriLynn was still not comfortable in heels.

That Saturday night, David took her to Burnswick to the Regal Lounge for an evening of dinner and dancing. As he led her onto the floor after dinner, they both remembered a dance they had shared several years before. They had been chaperoning at a student affair. As the music played and the students danced on the floor, David had stolen a dance with her in a private alcove. The momentary pleasure was disrupted when their janitor, Calvin Carson, came into that area. They had no further contact after that. But JerriLynne had known, even back then, that she was in love with David Harriger.

Tonight, David's right hand encompassed her tiny waist. Her soft hand fit snugly into his. He was glad JerriLynn had finally acquiesced to her sisters' admonitions and purchased contacts. He was a bit bewitched as he looked into those, blue eyes. *She's a good dancer,* he thought, and *it feels very good to have her in my arms.*

When he walked her to her door later, he held her again. Everything about JerriLynn was beginning to feel right. This night, he kissed her.

Nine

THE FIRST SNOW WAS LATE this winter. There are times in this area when snowflakes fall late in September. They don't often stay on the ground that early, but they're a warning of changing seasons. This year, on December second, the first, cumulative snow gathered on the ground. When Derek left his last class to head home, Salvatore did not meet him as usual. Instead, he was waiting in the parking lot. Sal had a snowball in his hand that was hidden in his jacket. He aimed it squarely at Derek's head!

"Hey!" shouted Derek as he ducked just in time. He quickly joined the game and exchanged a shot. Soon, there were five guys in the lot throwing snowballs. Several girls joined the melee, and the battle raged until so many students were returning to their cars that they had to quit. But it had been a glorious, fun though brief time!

"We don't get snow in Brazil," said Salvatore. "I love it!"

At Christmas break shortly after, Salvatore flew home to visit his family.

Derek realized what a blessing it was to have Sal's friendship. With Sal away, he was quite lonesome. He spent this vacation time from school at home with his family. Lou made much ado about the Christmas holiday. Even so, those weeks over the holidays were long and lonesome for Derek.

I miss Penny. Wouldn't you think I'd be over that by now, he chided himself?

It helped some to have Bill and Debbie in town for a few days. Derek had dinner with them on two, different occasions. But, alas, that proved to be a reminder of the times he had spent with Penny, in their presence. He endeavored not to let his heartache show and scolded himself for not moving beyond this, lost love.

Derek loved the time he spent with Sal at school and here in his home. But he was realizing how long it had been since he, as their older brother, had given adequate time to his sisters. He had so few evenings at home anymore. He was still working at Skinny's Market four evenings a week and Saturday until two now. He usually spent Monday evening with Salvatore. Then, too there were the occasions he had to spend in other, school-related activities. He felt he needed to be more involved in his sister's lives. Sal had arranged for an extra week of time off from school. Derek determined he would use the time to re-connect with his family.

This Sunday evening early in January, Abel and Lou had gone out to dinner together, leaving the girls at home with Derek. After their parents left, he put everything aside, including some school work that needed his time, and went to the family room. He seated himself in one of the comfortable, over-stuffed chairs and, ignoring the TV, flipped through yesterday's newspaper and waited quietly.

Very shortly, Joy came bouncing into the room. When she saw Derek, she skipped over to the chair and perched on the arm, swinging an arm around his neck and leaning close. Derek smiled. He had forgotten how Joy skipped everywhere inside-and-outside the house.

"Hi, Joy. What's up with you?" Derek asked. He loved this little sister's easy affection. "Are you glad to be back in school," he asked?

The girls had returned to classes several days earlier.

"Yes!" she said cheerfully. "We had a career day yesterday," she informed him.

"What's a career day?"

"Every so often, Mrs. Burchfield invites someone in the community to come in and tell us what they do in their job," said Joy.

"Well, who did you hear from this week?" Derek asked.

"Mrs. Campbell, who has the catering service," she answered. "She told us how much food she has to prepare for a graduation party...or a birthday party....or a wedding reception."

"Oh, I'll bet Mrs. Campbell's talk was interesting," Derek said.

"It was. But the best part was the little cakes she brought for us to eat. They were decorated with orange icing that had yellow flowers on top... 'In anticipation of spring', she said. They were so-o-o-o good!"

Joy squirmed about on the arm of the chair, as she told that story. She had leaned into him, wrapped her arm tighter around Derek's neck and never moved it while she talked. He sat still, let her squirm and listened intently to everything she had to say.

Joy is such a delight, he thought. Derek much loved his sisters. They both loved Uncle Abe, as they called their step-father. But Derek had been there for them from birth. They had never known their dads, so Derek knew he was a father-figure to them.

Joy was too intent on her stories to notice Rachael enter the room. Derek saw her and spoke to her quickly lest she should turn and leave again.

"Hey, Rachael, come on in and sit with us a bit," he said.

Joy turned then, and seeing Rachael, she climbed off the chair and stood quietly for a moment. Rachael had that effect on the family now. She was in her moody, teen years and none of them ever quite knew when she might just suddenly turn and leave the room. They all wanted to draw her closer.... back to that closeness of their past. Joy much missed the fun she'd had with Rachael. Tonight, Rachael walked slowly into the room.

"How are things going for you, Rachael?" Derek asked.

Joy quietly moved across the room, dropped to a cross-legged position and began to occupy herself with a paper project of some sort.

"I'm good," Rachael replied. Actually, she loved Derek, and she too rather missed that closeness. She took a seat on the sofa opposite him and picked up a magazine.

"How's school going?" Derek asked. His mother had confided that she was troubled by Rachael's attitude toward school. For such a smart girl, her grades did not reflect that.

"She's so smart, Derek. Why won't she study?" Lou had asked.

Tonight, Rachael answered Derek's question with a mumbled, "It's ok."

"Are you getting your math alright?" he asked. Math had always been her hardest subject.

"It's ok," she muttered.

"Is it just 'ok' or is it really 'ok'?" he asked. He didn't want to tell her what Lou had shared. "Are you making the honor roll, Rachael?" he asked.

Joy had looked up and was listening to their conversation. Now, she offered her thoughts. "Rachael got a 'D' in Math on her last, report card," said Joy.

"You old tattle-tale!" said Rachael sharply.

"Well….you did…." Joy answered defensively. But she turned back to her project and pretended to be busy. She didn't want to further alienate Rachael.

"Rachael, you're smart enough to be on the honor roll."

"I don't like Math," she muttered.

"What does that matter?" asked Derek. "You have to get good grades in all your subjects."

"Why?" Rachael asked. "I'm never going to like math!"

"You're in the upper grades now. What do you plan to be when you're out of school?"

"I'll be a journalist!" she said with assurance. "I'll travel around the world and take pictures and write stories," she declared.

"You won't get hired if you don't have a college education," he said.

"And you won't be accepted at the good colleges if you don't have good grades."

Rachael was quiet now.

"If you need help with your math, you can ask me," Derek continued.

"You're never here," she responded defensively.

"Well, I'll be here," Derek committed. "There's still time in this school year. You can get that grade up before the year is over. Is Mr. Harriger your teacher?" he asked.

"Yes," Rachael said..

"He's a good teacher. And he'd be glad to explain anything you don't understand."

Derek suddenly remembered a kid he had tutored, who was failing math because he didn't like Mr. Harriger. "Do you like Mr. H?" he asked, using the nickname the kids had given that teacher years earlier.

Rachael responded, "Yeah, he's cute....."

Cute! Is this how girls measure their teachers, wondered Derek?

"I'll be here on Sunday evenings to help you. We'll go over your math for the previous week and make sure you understand what you were expected to learn that week. Do you have your math book home tonight?" he asked.

"No," said Rachael.

Derek was frustrated. She got a "D" in math, but she didn't bring the book home to study!

But he chose not to say that. "You get busy this week and try to catch up. Ask Mr. Harriger to help you. He can even solicit one of the other students to tutor you. Bring your math book home next weekend, and we'll study it together."

"Ok," said Rachael.

Abel and Lou walked in shortly, and Derek's time with Rachael was at an end. But, at least, he knew now how to help her.

Later, he reminded himself of the commitment he'd just made to her. He determined he would keep it.

When Salvatore returned, he mentioned, with concern, that his mother was experiencing a return of the symptoms of illness she had the previous year. That was the reason for his additional, vacation time.

"She insisted I must complete the school year," said Sal.

And so, they moved into the New Year, a new school term, different classes and new challenges. Derek welcomed them. Once again, he had Sal's companionship.

Lou was expecting a baby now. She was to give birth late in June. Abel was almost beside himself with joy. He thought his wife had never been more beautiful.

Sal's Saturday evening visits at the Saunders' home were now a regular part of their week. Jacob was invited, also. But he always declined.

As the season progressed, Salvatore was overjoyed with the winter landscape in Pennsylvania. He would arrive at Derek's home around six o'clock on Saturday evening, and the two guys would play in the snow with Rachael and Joy. There were snowball battles, of course. The ridge behind the house offered excellent sled riding. These two, young, college men acted like kids again.

Derek observed Rachael during those evenings. It was impossible not to see that she was enamored with Sal. That was obvious to Abel and Lou, also. And it's certain Sal had to notice, as Rachael managed to find ways to get his attention. She dropped her mittens near him; he stooped to rescue them for her. When they climbed to the ridge to sled ride, she cajoled, "Sal...my sled is so hard to pull." And so, with Rachael walking at his side, Sal pulled his sled and her sled, too. Whatever the maneuvers she chose, Sal would always oblige. Once, she asked him to please zip her shoe-boot, and she proceeded to seat herself expectantly on the edge of the veranda. As Sal knelt to work with the boot, he caught sight of his scowling friend off to the side. He could barely conceal his amusement.

Even so, Sal carefully kept his distance from Rachael in word and touch.

Lou would prepare a late dinner. Then, they sat around the fireplace and visited. Though he was invited to spend the night, Sal always went back to the dorm to be with Jacob.

Thus the month of January passed pleasantly.

In Pennsylvania, February is arguably the gloomiest month of the year. It's often the coldest, and the days are commonly so overcast that one can forget the warmth of the sun's rays. Fresh layers of glistening, white snow, mingle with the now murky banks of January's snow fall, and the roads are a mess of slushy salt.

The holidays have faded from memory, with springtime and Easter seemingly far away. At Clairton U. the teachers were laying on the assignments thick and heavy, as they aimed to complete the material their students would surely need in the future.

Derek was feeling the winter blues. In truth, he always missed Penny and had no hopes that loss could ever be replaced. This morning, when Sal's Lexus pulled up beside the curb, he didn't hesitate to climb in. Sal's company might lift his spirit.

But he soon found that was not going to happen this time.

"I've got a problem, my friend," said Sal, (He commonly used the English term now.) He turned his vehicle toward town. "This problem is my own fault", he muttered. "I should have known better."

Derek said nothing. Sal was busy with the traffic. He'd wait. The Lexus offered better comforts than the six-year-old Pontiac that Derek was still driving. The heater in his vehicle had stopped functioning some time ago. It felt good to be in a warm car.

There was a quiet, little restaurant tucked in amongst the better businesses on Main Street. It did much less business than the restaurants nearer the college or those on the outskirts of town. In the past, these two had found an escape here on those rare occasions when they felt the need of serious conversation. That Sal had chosen this restaurant was evidence that he was in earnest about his problem.

It was only 9:45 a.m. The business district was barely awake yet. The lighting in this little restaurant was muted, and the walls were quaintly decorated. On one wall, there was a sprig of tree branches with tiny lights on the tip of each. Large, wooden, red, yellow, and white blossoms with three-dimensional depth were scattered together in another place. On the opposite wall, a dark, wooden planter offered bright flowers for the colorful, sipping hummingbird ...also made of wood. The knickknacks seemed to be the design of a particular artist. Derek always liked the feel of this place.

This morning, only two of the six booths were occupied. An elderly man was reading the morning paper at the counter. The tables and chairs were empty. After they were seated and awaiting service, Derek found himself reading the plaques:

"The richest person is not the one with the most, but the one who needs the least." (anonymous)

"You've got to do your own growing no matter how tall your grandfather was. (an Irish proverb)

He had read them all before. Nevertheless, they always drew his eyes.

When the waitress came, Derek ordered coffee and Sal asked for a Pepsi.

"What's up, Sal?" Derek asked. He was concerned there might be bad news concerning Sal's mother. To his surprise, Sal said, "It's about Diane, Derek."

"Diane? But, you haven't been seeing her anymore.....or have you?"

"No. Not since that night in October when you and I agreed to terminate the association with Diane and Mandy. I haven't been with her since then. That's been more than three ....no...four months ago."

Derek did the Math privately and concurred. "What's the problem?" he asked.

Their drinks came just then. They thanked the waitress and waited for her exit.

Derek was observing Sal, who looked very upset.

"What's the problem, Sal?" he asked again.

"Diane's pregnant," said Sal quietly.

Derek was stunned! He looked at his friend, whose head was down. When Salvatore offered nothing more, he finally asked in concern, "Are you the father?"

"NO! No, I'm not!" said Sal vehemently. "I'm not the father. But she's claiming that I am!"

"Could you be?" asked Derek. "Is it possible you could be?"

"I'm not, Derek! I stopped seeing her back in October. She says she's three months pregnant. It's been more than three months since I stopped seeing her. And I know at least three other guys who've been with her since.

"She went to that place just off campus, the ABC Center, to ask for information about an abortion. Not surprisingly, the ABC Center... 'A Better Choice Pregnancy Center'", Sal explained, "convinced her to keep the baby. When they asked her to name the father, she named me!"

Sal was in turmoil. Derek was silent. Neither of them spoke for a few minutes.

Then, Sal offered, "I got a paper in the mail today from the ABC Center informing me of her claim. They are requesting an interview next week." He said glumly.

Derek knew about pregnancies. He had aided the doctor who delivered Rachael. And in his senior year in high school, his former girlfriend, Penny, had become pregnant to another classmate. He had observed all the turmoil that pregnancy had created for Penny. Now, along with the town of Alton, he was witness to her unhappy marriage that followed.

But he had given no thought to the complications inherent in disproving paternity. That was what Sal was facing, it seemed.

"Do you have to go to that meeting?" asked Derek. "What will they do if you don't?"

"They'd probably track me down eventually with their legal mumbo-jumbo. They might go to the school authority and, then, I'd have to go for the interview anyway.

"I'm not the father!" he said vehemently. "I'd rather get

this over quickly ....and hopefully before my parents hear of it. If the law doesn't deport me, they would!"

Then, he added sorrowfully,"....Mi padres doesn't need this now...not with the cancer concern."

Then, still worrying the thing in his head, he asked, "How can Diane do this? She knows I'm not the father!"

"How can I help?" Derek asked quietly.

"I guess there's nothing. I just needed to share it with someone."

They were both quiet for a bit. Then, Derek said, "I'll be praying for you, Sal. I know prayer is important."

"Yeah, it is," Salvatore answered glumly.

Sal offered no more conversation. They finished their drinks, paid at the counter, and then Sal drove Derek back to the parking lot.

"I have a friend who knows about things," said Derek. "I'll ask his advice...without naming you, of course."

"...ok...," said Sal, but with no evidence of optimism.

That Saturday, before going to his job at Skinny's Market, Derek visited Alton High School. It had been some months since that last visit. His visits were rare now. His life was busy. Besides that, he seemed to have a better handle on his problems, at this age, than he had back in his high-school years.

Cal must be nearing retirement soon...surely just a couple of years, thought Derek. *The school will be losing a fine janitor, but much more than that,* he knew. Calvin Carson had mentored a number of troubled students, including Derek, during his years as janitor here. Derek understood, beyond question, that he would not be a student at Clairton University today had it not been for the wise counsel and encouragement he received from this janitor in those earlier years. He hoped Cal might have some good advice today.

He opened the door that had seemed so heavy and cumbersome when he was a student here. It closed with enough noise to alert Cal that someone was in the building.

Derek descended the steps in a run, not because he had to, but he was just naturally impatient to get to the point of things.

The boiler room hadn't changed an iota. *But, then, boiler rooms don't usually get redecorated,* he thought with a bit of humor. The equipment didn't appear to have been updated since his graduation. Even so, with Cal and his crew in charge, it surely got expert maintenance. There were plenty of lights down here and, he noticed anew, there were no cobwebs. In his years of almost daily visits, he couldn't remember ever seeing a cobweb....or a bug even. This basement was clean.

The radio was offering a commercial for anti-acid medicine. Assuredly, when the commercials ceased, the airways would be filled with weather reports. Cal obviously listened to the news when he was at home, for he was well informed. But, during school hours, the janitor listened only to the weather channel.

Calvin had risen from his straight-back chair to await the approach of whoever was coming.

"Well, Derek! How good to see you," he said, with genuine delight.

The two shook hands. But Cal held to Derek's hand for

a space and just feasted his eyes on one of his favorite, young friends. The love was mutual.

"How good to see you," he repeated. Then, motioning to Derek's stool...the makeshift seat Derek had fashioned in his high-school days...Cal turned to the coffee pot to fill two cups.

"How are things, my friend," Cal asked.

"I'm good, Cal," said Derek. "How are you doing? You look good. But, ...do I notice more of a limp now?" Derek asked with concern. He had observed the uneven gait as Cal fussed with the coffee.

"Aw, Derek, it's just the ravages of age....old age. Nothing serious," said the janitor.

"Are Al and Jason still with you?" asked Derek.

Al and Jason had been Cal's aids when Derek was in school here.

'They're both still here, and both excel at their work. When I'm gone, either one could easily manage this job," said Cal proudly.

"Well, they sure had good training," said Derek.

"Thank you. Now, tell me, what's new with you. Is everything going alright?"

"With me? Yes. But I have a concern for a friend with a problem. Maybe you could give me some advice. It's a 'girl' thing. Sometimes I think every problem is a 'girl' thing."

That brought a laugh from Cal.

"Did I ever tell you 'thanks' Cal, for the good advice you gave me about my 'girl' thing in high school? The further I go, the more I realize how important it is to get that part of life under control. I've seen so many students treat sex casually. Then, they find themselves in a maelstrom of problems that were really inevitable, if they'd just thought about it."

Derek had been in love with Penny Crawford in his eleventh year of school. They dated that spring and most of the following summer. But the relationship was getting ever more serious, ever more physical.

When Derek sought Cal's advice, he was warned to "flee" the relationship until they were older and capable of proceeding legitimately. Hard though it was, Derek had broken-up with Penny just before their senior year.

He had tried to explain his sexual concerns to Penny. But he didn't do it well, and she had been very hurt.

"I'm glad you took my advice, Derek, and broke off the relationship with Penny before things got out-of-hand."

"Yeah. I am, too," said Derek. But Cal heard the sadness in his young friend's voice.

"It's too bad about Penny," Cal said softly.

Another classmate, Michael Houston, befriended Penny after her break-up with Derek. To Derek's dismay, Michael and Penny became a couple that winter. She was nearly five months pregnant by the end of the school year. Michael and Penny married later that summer.

The ordeal had broken Derek's heart....and Penny's, too, if the truth be told. The marriage of Michael and Penny was not a happy one.

Derek still loved her.

Now, shaking off the remembrance of that unhappy time, Derek brought his present concern to Cal.

"I have a friend.....He's a Brazilian citizen here on a government exchange program for college students. He got involved with a girl this past October. Now, she's pregnant and accusing him of being the father. He insists he wasn't with her during the necessary months. They had broken off the relationship prior to that time.

"At least three other guys have admitted to him that they were with her.

"My friend is from a wealthy family. That, and the fact that he's not a U.S. citizen, makes him very vulnerable to her accusations.

"I believe him when he says he couldn't be the father," added Derek.

"Ah…too bad," said Cal. "His exciting adventure to the U.S. is now clouded with this concern."

"Yeah," said Derek. "And he's a nice guy. He should have had more sense. But now what can he do? The girl has gone to the local, pregnancy center. They've notified him they want a meeting."

"He needs to agree to the meeting. They will counsel him on his options to disprove her claim."

"Is there nothing he can do now?" Derek asked.

"He can pray that the young lady will tell the truth," Cal replied. Seeing Derek's dismay, he added, "Hopefully your friend has learned from the ordeal."

"I think he has," said Derek. "That's your advice then. He needs to follow it through."

"Yes," said Cal.

They spent a little more time together discussing current affairs in Alton.

The two shook hands in parting, and Derek headed to his job at Skinny's Market.

Sal left his Lexus in the parking lot and walked. The building he sought was a short distance up the street from the campus. His Lexus, parked in front of that house, would surely have stirred the gossip.

This area of town had once been populated by the wealthiest citizens in Clairton. The houses on the street were beyond large. They had once been the residences of the richest folks in town, back in a time when servants were common. Many of those, large buildings were now converted into college residences for fraternities and sororities. There were three, such houses on this street. They, like those on other streets, needed paint now. The porches, that circled three corners of the house, were cluttered with book cases filled with paperbacks, chairs, lamps, dishes in boxes and a variety of "stuff" collected by college-age youth.

But Sal's mission was in the first house on this street. It was much smaller, newly painted and the yard was neatly manicured and tastefully planted with shrubbery. The sign in front read, *"ABC Center."* This pregnancy center offered free testing for pregnancy, a free sonogram and counseling. Because that counsel emphasized the blessing of the young woman raising her child or giving the baby for adoption by others, many of the college students commonly referred to the center as *A Better Choice Center.*

The workers at the center hated abortion. But they didn't let that affect their counsel to the young women. They treated their-concerned-and-mostly- young clients with respect and sensitivity, willingly allowing each to make her own choice.... though that was difficult. Abortions were not offered here, nor even counsel regarding one.

Sal wished for rain. He would have welcomed a dark and

gloomy sky. But the sun had chosen to shine today, and all was bright and cheerful. As he hurried down the sidewalk, up the three steps and across the porch, he felt like he was the star in a movie being watched by the entire town. When he reached the door, he hesitated. There was a doorbell! Do you ring a doorbell before entering a pregnancy center?

He decided to ignore the bell and opened the door. An inside clanging announced his presence. Stepping within, he quickly assessed his surroundings. The room was small. The walls were beige colored. Flowered curtains covered the double-pane window. Under his feet was a soft, thick, green carpet. A cabinet, off to the side. held some parenting books, vases and womanly decorations. On another stand, there was a computer, telephone and communication necessities. There were three, comfortable chairs along the one wall and one chair on this side of the desk. The woman seated behind the desk looked up, as he entered. She stood to her feet and held out her hand.

"Mr. Ridenti, I assume," she said pleasantly.

"Yes, ma'am," he replied and hastened to shake her hand.

"I'm Mary Jo Young," she said simply.

Mary Jo was a friendly-looking lady in her late forties, he guessed, though her hair style helped to make her look younger. She wore her brown hair clipped short around her ears. Parted on one side, the bangs crossed her forehead and covered the brow opposite. The simple style seemed right for this seemingly serous woman. But her smile was sincere, and Sal actually relaxed a bit as he took the seat which she indicated across from her.

"Thank you for coming," she said.

"I figured I didn't have a choice," Sal replied truthfully.

She smiled slightly.

"May I say you speak very good English, Mr. Ridenti," said Mary Jo.

She knows something of my background, he thought. "It's Salvatore. Most people call me Sal," he replied. "And thank you," he responded to her comment about his English.

"I'm sorry for this problem," she said, "…problem is not quite the right term."

"I'm sorry, too. But Diane is lying!" he added quickly. "I haven't had any contact with her since the middle of October. If she's pregnant, I'm not responsible."

She looked at him silently for a minute. He didn't lower his gaze. Sal wanted her to know he was speaking the truth.

Finally, she spoke.

"Actually, Salvatore," she said softly, "I know you are speaking the truth."

"What did you say?" Sal was quite confused and thought he might have heard wrong.

"I said, I know you are speaking the truth." She spoke kindly. "Diane has admitted you're not the father."

Sal could not remember ever being more relieved than this. He felt as if chains had fallen away from him.

Now, unable to keep the bitterness out of his voice, he asked, "Why did she accuse me?"

"Diane is only twenty-one years old. She's a conscientious girl. Diane didn't want to have an abortion. I think, even if she hadn't come here, she would have chosen to keep the baby.

"She wishes, most of all, not to be pregnant. But she is. Why did she accuse you? She's old enough to know better, but I think she was looking for the easiest way to solve the problems she faces. I believe she thought you were rich enough to pay her a large sum of money. You're an exchange student from another country. She thought you'd be willing to pay to keep the matter quiet and away from the authorities and your family.

"It was an unwise, unkind and ridiculously transparent ploy. But, as I said, Diane is twenty-one-years-old and in confusion."

Salvadore lowered his eyes. He was furious! It was good that Diane wasn't in the room at this moment. The words that were fighting for release in his head would have shocked both women. He felt none of the sympathy for the twenty-one-year-old mother-to-be that Mary Jo Young seemed to be urging.

The counselor understood and waited quietly for Salvatore Ridenti to regain some control.

"You're angry," she said finally. "And that's understandable. But may I ask you, Salvatore....did you have intimate relations with Diane?"

He didn't answer immediately.

That was an answer.

Finally, he said defensively, "Diane was willing! I'd even say, she encouraged it! And she isn't seventeen. She's twenty one! There was nothing to prevent her from saying, 'No!' No one was forcing her!"

Mary Jo sat quietly, waiting for Salvatore's calm again. Then she said, "You could have resisted, Salvatore. You could have taken the responsible, manly role and resisted her overtures."

He was looking hard into her eyes now.

"You're a man, Salvatore. Whatever any woman does in your presence, you are capable.....and accountable...for your own response."

Again, she waited for her words to penetrate his thoughts. He still hadn't looked away. She felt the hope that he was receiving her truth.

"Intimacy is for marriage, Salvatore. Many women are in disregard of that truth today. The woman may be blatantly, sexually wild! But that is no excuse for any man to surrender his God-given responsibility. You alone are answerable for the choice you make.

"You can find excuses for yourself. Or, you can acknowledge your foolish submission to her enticement, ask the Lord's forgiveness, and hold yourself to a higher standard in the future."

The room was still. The young man was staring at her intently. *The truth is penetrating,* she thought hopefully.

She said no more, but just waited.

"You're right," he finally said. The hardness had faded from his eyes.

"You're right," he repeated thoughtfully.

They sat quietly for a moment. Then, he rose and offered his hand.

"Thank you, Mary Jo Young. I understand. I really do," he said.

Salvatore walked to the door and exited.

As the door closed, Gina Fallings, the counselor's assistant, stepped into the room. She had been listening to the exchange from the slightly open door into the inner chamber.

"Do you think he really does understand?" she asked.

"Yes. I believe Salvatore received the truth," said Mary Jo.

"That's why you had him come in," said Gina. "I wondered

why you didn't just notify him that he was in the clear when Diane dropped her charges against him. Now, I know why."

"Yes," said Mary Jo. "We need to educate these men to their responsibility as well as educate and minister to all the 'Dianes' out there."

Derek left his last class and was anxiously looking around for Salvatore. *Is that meeting over yet,* he wondered? He had offered to go with his friend, but Sal wanted to handle this alone.

"I'm a man, Derek. I will do this myself," he had responded.

"Derek! Over here!" called Sal.

The Lexus was behind three, other vehicles, the last being a large U-Haul. It was hindering Derek's view. Now, he hurried over and crawled into the passenger side.

"Well? How did it go?" he asked anxiously.

Sal didn't answer at once, but instead maneuvered his vehicle into the lane of traffic, turned out of town and toward the country. Finally, he said to Derek, "Diane has admitted the truth. She told them I'm not the father."

"WOW! How great is that?!" Derek responded excitedly.

"Yes. It's a relief," said Sal quietly. His demeanor was confusing to Derek. They rode without speaking for a minute.

"I'd think you'd be more exuberant," Derek said finally. Then, anxious to hear the details, he asked, "What was the lady like in that place?"

"Mary Jo Young?....that was her name. And she is a lady....a very wise lady," Sal added. "She helped me to see how foolish I've been... how foolish my responses have been."

Derek studied his friend. Sal was different.

"This sort of thing will never happen to me again," Sal said thoughtfully and with certainty. "When I am around women....any woman...even a woman like Diane....I will respond like a man."

He had driven several miles out of Clairton on the busy highway. There was a small turnoff onto a country road just up ahead. There, in the field where the two roads meet, a Bowling Alley was situated. Sal pulled the Lexus into the gravel lot and parked amongst the other vehicles.

He turned to Derek and asked, "How good are you at bowling?"

"As a matter of fact, I've never played the sport," Derek replied.

"Well, it's time you learned," said Sal. "We're never too old to learn new things," he added thoughtfully.

And the two spent the next several hours relaxed and aiming for the pins.

The calls from home were a burden to Salvatore. He could hear, in his mother's voice, the weakness she was experiencing. She was not responding well to the treatments now. His father could not hide his concern when they spoke, and it was an underlying weight in the emails Sal received from him. Even so, both of his parents were aware of how much Sal had enjoyed this time in the states. His mother insisted he must finish this school year at Clairton.

Sal glanced at his watch. His first class had ended at 10:15 a.m. It was now 10:23 a.m. as he entered the student lounge. This was a notoriously noisy place much of the time. It was a place for the students to unwind from the rigors of their classes. But it was still relatively early, and Sal was one of the fewer students who had an empty space in the second period. During this time, he usually stayed in his room or went to the library to study or prepare for his next classes of the day. But, today, he chose to go to the student lounge. He had a purpose.

As he entered, Sal was immediately greeted by a number of friendly voices. The place was not crowded this morning, or any morning at this time. There were plenty of empty tables and chairs. Off to the left, his name was called.

"Hey! Sal! Come join us," said one.

"Hi, Sal," said others in greeting. He was well-known. He greeted them all with a smile and a wave. But he didn't stop. He was looking for someone.

She sat alone at a table on the far side. She had chosen a seat by the window looking out on the small, enclosed pavilion. This building and another were joined by a partially enclosed walkway on either side. In the center, the small, open space had become a pavilion, where a wild cherry tree grew. Of course, that tree had only stark, empty branches as it was only March. But soon it would be covered with rosy pink blossoms and later with green leaves. On either side of the walkways, long planters were placed. Spring planting would be happening soon, and the planters would be filled with bright flowers and bordered with marigolds. In late spring, this window seat was a welcome place.

But this was still early March, and Diane's view today could only be desolate. Those were Sal's thoughts as he made his way across the room. He was so noticeably Brazilian, an exceptionally bright and friendly student. Salvatore Ridenti was now recognized by most on campus. Diane had been a popular cheerleader. A few of the students here....maybe quite a few...had heard the story of Diane and Sal. This morning, the chatter grew quieter, and a number of the other diners watched as he walked deliberately toward her table.

Her head was down; her fingers worried the rim of the cup that was now nearly empty. Lost in her own thoughts, she hadn't heard his name called. Nor had she noticed his approach.

When he pulled out the chair across from her, she looked up. Her face flushed and she quickly dropped her eyes to the table.

"Hi, Diane," he said. "Is it alright if I sit here with you?"

"I don't know why you would do that," she replied in a small voice. As he continued to hesitate, she said softly, "Of course, it's alright."

Sal sat down and waited for her to gain some composure. "How are you, Diane?" he asked finally.

"I'm alright," she murmured. Then, she looked up, and her eyes clouded with tears. "Sal, I'm so sorry! I'm so ashamed," she said, and a sob escaped her lips. She fumbled for a tissue and wiped the tears that had begun to run down her cheeks.

"It's alright, Diane," he said kindly. "We all do some unwise things when we're in a crisis."

She looked directly at him now. "You can forgive me?" she asked woefully.

"Of course," he said. He reached across the table and put his hand over hers.

It took a few minutes for her to become calm. The room returned to normal activity. In fact, with passing minutes, more students had entered. Most glanced at the couple over on the pavilion side. There were whispers exchanged. No one chose to sit nearby.

Sal was known by most of them. But Diane was known, too. She had been a beautiful and popular cheerleader on the football team, albeit for only a brief time.

Her pregnancy was evident now.

"What are your plans, Diane?" Sal asked. "It seems you intend to finish this year...?" He left it as a question.

"Yes," she said. "My parents want me to complete this semester in Clairton. Then, I'll return home to live with them until the baby's born."

"I'm so glad they're supportive," said Sal.

"Oh, yes. My mother's excited about the baby....The doctor says my baby will be born on July 25th," she added with a slight smile.

Sal was glad to see the smile. It evidenced her motherly instincts.

"You'll have a busy summer. What about the remainder of your education?" he asked.

"Oh, I'm going to complete my education," Diane said with determination. "My sister, who has two children of her own, will watch the baby while I return to classes....locally, of course. Do you remember, I'm from Frederick, MD? There's a college not far from my parent's home....Hood College. It's small, but it's a good college...."

There was much uncertainty now, and her voice wavered.

"You'll make it, Diane. You're a strong woman...and smart. What about the father?" Sal hesitated to ask.

Diane looked away again. Then, she said, "Neither of us want further relationship, but he has agreed to pay child support."

Finally, she added, "Maybe, in time, we can work something out to help the baby know his father..." She was speaking with uncertainty now.

"I hope everything goes well for you," Sal said.

He rose to go, but then he hesitated.

"Diane," he said. "I'm so glad that you haven't harmed the baby...you know....abortion...."

"Oh, no! I couldn't!"

She looked into his eyes. "Sal.....I'm so sorry....," she said softly, as she tried once more to erase the harm she had tried to bring on him.

"I know you are. And I forgive you. You know, I'm not so proud of my treatment of you, either.

"I'll see you again," he promised.

Diane watched as Sal exited the room, speaking to one, waving to another.

True to his word, in future days, Sal came to the student lounge again during this period. Once or twice a week, he made it there. Always, she was seated on the same side near the windows. They talked and laughed and became better friends as they watched spring advance in that little pavilion on Clairton College in Clairton, Pennsylvania.

As the semester year advanced, Diane's pregnancy was quite noticeable. She was regaining her confidence following the friendship she now had with Sal. Gradually, as the other students saw the two of them comfortably chatting together, they began to wonder over to that table. Sometimes, they had a word for Sal. But it was also common to hear someone ask Diane how she was doing in her pregnancy.

Once, Derek's professor hadn't shown for class, and he had an unexpected, free period. He knew Sal had befriended Diane. That morning, he made it a point to go to the student lounge to visit with them. As he pulled out a chair and sat,

Derek could only smile. Diane had a glow. Of course, she was just naturally lovely. But pregnancy had highlighted that beauty.

One April day, knowing they would part after this semester, (and maybe forever) Diane had a question for Sal. "What is your middle name Salvatore?" she asked.

"It's Pablo.....Salvatore Pablo Ridenti," he said. "You would say 'Paul'."

Then, he was curious. "Why do you ask?"

"The baby's father is not someone with whom my son would be proud to share a name," said Diane, whose eyes were down.

"It's a boy, then?" asked Sal.

"Yes." Now, she raised her head and looking into his eyes, she said "He would be proud of my friend, Salvatore. Would you mind if I call him 'Paul'?"

Her words brought a lump to Sal's throat. "I'd be most honored," he said sincerely.

Ten

FOLLOWING THEIR DATE IN BURNSWICK, David Harriger began to see JerriLynn every weekend. The winter was passing quickly, and for these two, joyously. They danced; they went to the movies, and sometimes he just drove randomly, and they talked. He realized he was becoming attached. Always, he only kissed her goodnight. They kept their dates outside the school, and outside the town of Alton. Even so, the air was charged when they were together, and the lounge crowd was beginning to suspect something.

One evening, they had again dined and danced. But, this time, instead of taking JerriLynn home, David pulled his vehicle to a stop in front of his apartment and turned off the motor. The house was completely dark. Mrs. Faller would have been in bed some time ago.

JerriLynn felt her heart drop. She grew very still.

Turning to look at her, David quietly asked, "Will you come up with me, JerriLynn?"

She understood what he was asking. It seemed like forever before she could find her voice.

She kept her head down. Her words were spoken quietly. "No, David," she murmured.

He said nothing. She knew he was still looking at her. Finally, she lifted her eyes to him and said very firmly, "No."

He looked away then, turned the key in the ignition and took her home. As always, he walked with her to the door. He even kissed her and said, "Goodnight, JerriLynn."

Her heart was crushed, as she turned away. That night, she lay in her bed and wondered, "Is it over now?" She cried some and slept little.

David didn't sleep well, either.

Now, why did I do that, he asked himself?

Why did I put JerriLynn on the spot like that?

I've never done anything like that before.

....But then, I've never been this attached to any girl before.... that is, to anyone other than Cindy Roberts. But Cindy and I never even shared a kiss.

... ... I am attached to JerriLynn Smathers, he admitted. *I'm very attached.*

And I wanted her to say, No. What would I have done if she had said, Yes?

David knew he would have been disappointed.

Is JerriLynn angry with me? he wondered.

The next week, there were no glances between them in the lounge. There was no contact all week.

On Thursday, after school hours, David made his way to the Home Ec room. She was there, as was her custom. Living with her parents gave her too little privacy at home. Emily's children and other family members visited in the evenings. He knew JerriLynn found it necessary to do some book work after hours here. He stood in the doorway and observed her. Never had he been more sure of what he was about to do.

JerriLynn sensed a presence and looked up. He didn't speak, and she was speechless, as he came down the few stairs and walked toward her. David pulled out the chair beside her and sat down. Their eyes locked. He took her hand. With the other hand, he held out the ring.

"Will you marry me, JerriLynn?" he asked.

She was truly shocked! Tears sprang to her eyes.

"Yes," she said softly but firmly.

It was good that he quickly drew her into his arms, for JerriLynn found her strength had just melted away.

David would have liked to whisk her off to a pastor this very moment. But the Smathers' family was large and conservative. There would be a church wedding, he knew. They would fuss and plan, as women do.

Then, ...radiant in her white gown, beautiful and unashamed, JerriLynn would come to him.

David would be patient.

The school heard the news the next day. It was a rule that school personnel were forbidden to date or have personal contact during school hours. But these two were so respected and everyone was so excited that the rule was a bit relaxed.

A steady stream of students, mostly young girls, stopped by JerriLynn's Home Ec room to see her ring. Melissa and Rachael were ever so excited.

Mrs. Blake, like all the other teachers, was delighted with the prospective union of David Harriger and JerriLynn Smathers. Even so, that evening, with reluctance, she wrote to her friend, Cindy Roberts, to share the news.

Cindy received the letter three days later. She had just returned home from another lonely day in the large, #23 Ultima Senior High School. She was finding it difficult to make friends there. The hallways were so busy and noisy that there was no opportunity to talk to her neighboring teachers between classes.

There was a teacher's lounge. It was a big room, surrounded by windows on two sides. The floor was covered with a tweed carpet. The tables and chairs had the lacquered look of a hospital, cafeteria setting. A coffee machine offered any flavor you could want. Or, there was cocoa, tea or milk. Another machine offered a variety of sandwiches for those who did not choose the cafeteria. The machine that sold chips, cookies, packaged pies, was nearest the door and usually busy.

Teachers mostly came in as couples or with three or four talking boisterously and choosing to sit together. They smiled and spoke to her and then walked on.

After school, she headed home to her lonely apartment in the strange building in this strange city. *Oh, will I ever feel comfortable here?* she wondered. She had not imagined her married life would be like this. Cindy Roberts longed to start a family. Now, having passed the age of thirty, she was beginning to feel urgent about this. But when she suggested her desire for a family to Clifford, he brushed it off. "My work is too consuming right now," he said impatiently. "We'll talk about it another time."

Today, her spirit surged to find the letter from her friend, Sandra Blake. Dropping it into her handbag unopened, she hurried to her third floor apartment. When she turned the key in the lock and opened the door, she had the same, sinking feeling she now knew so well.

It's a nice apartment,…I guess, she thought.

The walls were a soft gray color. The carpet was a thick blend of two shades of gray and offset with burgundy. Clifford had chosen the oversize, leather bound, black sofa and lounge chair. Beside the reading lamp, there was a tan-and-brown, tweed rocker with a matching footstool. Admittedly, it looked out of place. It was the only thing in the room that Cindy had chosen and, indeed, had insisted upon. Her mother had an old, scratched and faded, tan and brown rocker. As long as she could remember, that rocker had rested just inside the sitting room beyond the kitchen. Cindy knew she had been rocked in that chair. Secretly, she imagined she would one day be rocking her baby to sleep in this rocker.

Velvet drapes, a rich burgundy in color, were drawn over the patio windows. She hurried there first to let the sunlight in. At her side, the entire wall was floor-to-ceiling bookcases with impressive tomes in matched bindings. There were spaces, between the books, that were set aside for selective, expensive Egyptian artifacts.

On the opposite side of the room, long rows of shelves displayed Egyptian pottery. The vases and bowls, most of which seemed to be made of red clay, were all sizes and shapes.

Another wall held numerous paintings…all Egyptian origin. She always thought the characters in those paintings had a wooden look. The lines of their head, bodies and clothing were sharp angled, as if created with a ruler. In one painting, the artist had drawn a little girl standing beside a swan that was much larger than she! Today, Cindy shook her head and again admitted that she couldn't understand Egyptian art.

With a sigh, she pulled the drapes aside, turned away

and reached for her purse with the letter from Alton, PA. She was so anxious for this mail that she tore it open while still standing. She read.....

> Dear Cindy,
>
> ....
> ....
> .... (When had she stopped breathing?)... ... ...
> "They seem to be very much in love," Mrs. Blake continued.

Cindy read the letter three times. "They seem to be very much in love."

Just then, the phone rang. She reached for it thoughtlessly. "Cindy?"

She heard his voice as in a hazy distance. It was Clifford, and he was so far away.....

"Cindy?" he repeated. "Are you there?" Clifford sounded excited. "Let me tell you what I found today!"

.....*No...*, thought Cindy sadly.....*Let me tell you what I lost today.....*

But she walked over to her rocker and sat down to listen.

David didn't want to wait for the end of the school year, so the date for the marriage of David and JerriLynn was set for April 24th. With the Easter break and a long weekend, the happy couple would have ten days for their honeymoon.

The wedding would have an impact on the Saunders'

family. Lou was asked to make the bridesmaids' dresses. Since her marriage, Lou had cut back on her sewing commitments and had turned down similar requests.

But she would honor this one. Mr. H had shared with Abel how helpful JerriLynn had been to Rachael during that difficult period earlier in the year. JerriLynn was far-and-away Rachael's favorite teacher and had even become a friend.

Apparently, JerriLynn felt the same way. Though she came from a large family with other, young girls to include in her wedding party, she made room for Rachael and Melissa, too. Both girls often stopped at her Home Economics room. These two girls were asked to stand in the church alcove and pass out the wedding bulletins, as the guests arrived.

That meant they would be wearing special dresses. They would have their hair done in a special way and be included in all the excitement of this wedding.

Joy quietly observed it all. Lou gave her special attention and drew her into the occasion as best she could. Derek and Abel exchanged many a bemused glance as they heard the "woman-talk" about the big wedding.

April of that year would always be special for David Harriger. It was the day that JerriLynn Smathers became his bride.

JerriLynn's parents were Methodists. That large, white, wooden church sat on the block just behind the restaurant. On their wedding day, not only the parking lot, but also the streets on all sides were lined with cars. The townsfolk fairly burst with excitement.

A deluge of rain had fallen overnight, and the weather

continued to be less than co-operative. Folks came dressed in their fanciest clothes. The women held wispy scarves above a carefully fashioned hair-do, as their men tried to shield them with umbrellas that threatened to collapse.

This was a joyous occasion. Both sides of the church were packed. Mr. H's parents were present, as was his brother, sister-in-law and their sons.

The staff at Alton High was in attendance, as was the janitor, Calvin Carson, a close friend of Mr. H.

Bridal showers, wedding rehearsals and receptions had kept Rachael and Melissa in a flight of excitement that entire month. They were accorded special hair-dos and even makeup for the occasion. And, for the wedding, the young girls looked beautiful in their three-quarter length dresses of a soft, blush hue.

The bridesmaids wore floor-length dresses in a brighter coral color. Lou, who had fashioned the gowns, carefully examined each as they walked past and breathed a sigh of relief that all was well.

David could not remember ever being so happy, as he was the moment he saw his bride, escorted by her father, start down the aisle toward him. She wore a soft, white chiffon gown with a delicate, floral design. A simple band of white circled her tiny waist and settled in a bow, with the long ribbons trailing down her gown in back, atop the brief, bridal train.

Occasionally, her toes peeked out from the pretty, white, two-inch heels. A wispy veil covered her face. But when she was a few feet away, he could see her beautiful, blue eyes. JerriLynn looked radiant.

Rachael would always remember this wedding. It placed a hope in her heart that she might one day find similar happiness.

Penny Crawford Houston heard the talk about the marriage of JerriLynn and Mr. H. But she had lost her illusions about marriage ending "happily ever after"...at least for her. Life had not been easy since she married Michael in the summer after graduation. She was five months pregnant at the end of their senior year at Alton High School. Michael had been relatively decent about marrying her back then. In the conservative town of Alton, it was considered the right thing to do, and in those days, he still cared to look respectable.

They'd moved into a rented apartment on Hickory St. There were four rooms and a bath, all upstairs over an abandoned, downstairs apartment. Their first year wasn't too bad. Max was born late that summer after the wedding. Married life was new and Michael still showed a modicum of interest.

She had intended to find out about birth control pills. This wasn't something she could talk over with her mother. Mom had never shared private things like that with her. She would get her courage and ask her doctor. But the new baby kept her busy, and she just hadn't done that yet. Besides, she wondered how they would pay for the pills.

She got pregnant just two months after Max was born. Things changed quickly when she told Michael that she was pregnant again

He yelled at her. "We can't afford another kid!"

During that pregnancy, he was rarely sober at night.

She had known he was a drinker, when she dated him in high school. She wondered, now, how she could have so completely fooled herself. When they dated, he always had a six pack in his car. He even got drunk on their wedding day! But, by then, she had to marry him. She held to the hope that things would get better. *Michael will settle down and become a family man*, she would tell herself.

That never happened. The drinking was bad enough. But there was something even harder. There was the fact that she still loved Derek Metcalf....and always would. And Michael knew that. No, she never told him. She never spoke Derek's name. But Michael knew. And when he was drunk, he would throw words at her.

"You still love that ---------- Metcalf!"

When Michael was drinking, there was no point in arguing with him. And besides, she probably couldn't argue contrary to that truth persuasively. Penny just closed her mouth and waited for him to fall asleep. On the rare occasions when Michael was sober, the thought of Derek seemed to be buried and festering in him.

He now spent his weekends drinking and gambling. Weyland and the "boys" at the local, pool hall realized what was happening with Penny and her toddlers. They did not make Michael welcome there. So, he did his gambling in Burnswick.

Penny never left her boys alone with their dad. He commonly showed bad humor with them. She had learned to walk-on-eggshells when Michael was home. He had a good job at Burnswick Asphalt and went to work faithfully. But when he got home in the evenings, he wanted things to be quiet and orderly, both of which were not always possible with two babies under the age of two.

Last night, when Penny was cleaning up from the evening meal, she had the boys with her in the kitchen. Max, her oldest, wanted to be in the room where she kept his toy box, but she had learned that it was best to keep the boys with her. Michael had no patience with them. Eugene was not feeling well. He had been restless and complaining all day, when he wasn't crying, and that was a big part of the time.

Michael had shouted at her. "I work all day long. Can't you keep them quiet, so I can hear the television?"

When she got the kids to bed, she went out to the living room to visit with Michael. They had little to talk about anymore, as he was uninterested in the boys, who were now the biggest part of her life. But she continued to try to build a relationship with him. Her boys needed that.

She sat quietly beside him as he watched a silly sitcom. Finally, she went to bed, and he might not have even noticed.

Today was Friday, and the weather was finally warm. This afternoon, Penny had brought her boys down to the small backyard behind their apartment. She sat on the ground and watched them playing in the sandbox, which was just a very large, wooden box that Mr. Briscuit had given her recently. The kind grocer had even gone to the local hardware and filled bags with sand. Max was excited, as Skinny lifted the bags from the bed of his old pickup and poured the sand into the box for them.

Mr. Briscuit is so good to us, she thought, as she recalled his kindness.

Her boys had been playing there, with their plastic trucks,

for nearly an hour. Now, her youngest was disturbing the road Max was building, and Max was frustrated.

"Mommy!" he cried. "See!"

See what he's doing! That's what he meant, but that was too much grammar for this emergency. She smiled and picked her baby up, placing him on her lap. He was tired and rubbed his face with his sandy hands. Now, he had something to cry about, and cry he did!

Penny quickly wiped his hands with the wet cloth she had brought for just such an emergency. Then, she stood and said to her older son,

"We need to be going inside, Max. Your daddy will be home soon."

I hope, she thought. ….. *I hope he won't stop at the bar first.*

Penny sighed, as she heard the front door close. Tonight was Friday. It was Michael's habit, now, to spend his weekends at Burnswick, where he drank and gambled. Penny never seemed to lose the hope that this would be the weekend he'd choose differently.

This night, Michael came home after work, took a shower and changed. As they were eating supper, she said to him, "Tom and Ginny, (her brother and his wife) have invited us over for a barbecue tomorrow evening."

Michael said nothing.

"He suggested we come around five o'clock," she added softly.

Still no comment.

Eugene was fussing. She knew he needed his diaper changed and reluctantly left the room without the answer she hoped to hear.

As she was changing the diaper, she heard the front door close. Michael was leaving without a word to her. She knew he wouldn't be back until the early morning hours, and he would be drunk.

He did return at that time and in that condition, . When he crawled into bed beside her, Penny lay with her eyes closed and pretended sleep. She much disliked when he wanted to be amorous in that condition. Tonight, she was spared. He fell asleep quickly and with the loud, snoring sounds that so often accompanied his binges. The room reeked of alcohol. But she didn't dare move.

She had attended the Baptist Church, on occasion, when she was in high school. She recalled some of the things she learned there. Tonight, Penny did what she'd begun to do in recent months. She prayed, and, sometimes, she quietly cried.

In the morning, when the boys awakened her, she quietly crawled out of the bed, so as not to waken Michael. She was in their room helping them dress, when she heard the front door close. Michael had quietly risen. She knew he would be gone now for the day, and most of the night, too. She and the boys would go to the family get-together without Michael. It was the pattern of their lives.

Money was tight in their household. Often Michael let Penny know she should have found a job rather than get pregnant a second time. He always got paid after work on Friday. He spent most of the weekend away from home. His drinking and gambling always came before he shared with her on Sunday.

This Sunday morning, Michael got out of bed about eleven o'clock. She gave him his coffee and offered to fix him breakfast. He gruffly refused.

"Michael," Penny said cautiously. "I need groceries. We're out of milk and bread, and Eugene needs baby food."

"Well, I don't have any money to give you," he said with less volume than usual.

"Didn't you get paid?" Penny asked with concern.

"I don't have any to give you," he said with a louder voice. Then, he pushed his chair back from the table and rose.

"Michael…?" she spoke with uncertainty.

"I told you I don't have any money!" he shouted at her.

"Were you gambling again?" she asked with dismay.

"So I lost once! You don't complain when I win, which is most of the time! You don't mind helping me spend my winnings! But you sure nag if I lose on occasion!"

And with that, he left the house.

Max was watching his mother with concern.

"Mommy… …I'm hungry," he said.

"Oh, honey," Penny drew him into her arms. "We'll be alright. You get your shoes and we'll visit grandma," she said.

That brought a happy response from Max

Once again, I'll need to ask Mom for money to buy our necessities, she thought, as she gathered the baby and prepared to leave the house.

Mrs. Crawford had a good job at the office in the Clairton Hospital. Thankfully, she was able to help when Penny and the boys showed up and in need, and that was rather often.

Mom was asked to work that morning, so Penny left herself into the house and prepared to feed her boys.

This was her life now.

Eleven

SAL HAD BECOME A REGULAR visitor at the Saunder's home on Saturday evenings. He was relaxed among these friends and spoke easily of his native land now.

Rachael's problems, at the start of this school year, were forgotten. Nearing the age of fourteen, she was once again the typical, independent teen. Previously, she had to be coerced by Lou to spend some time with the family. But with Sal present on Saturday evenings, Rachael was readily a part of the group.

Spring auto racing had begun in the area and, this evening in April, Sal and Derek planned to attend an event at Burnswick. Sal was most interested. Derek, still a boxing enthusiast, was only mildly interested in the auto races. But he enjoyed Sal's company and was attending for his friend. Sal would be driving the Lexus, as always, and had arranged to pick Derek up at his home.

Salvatore came to the kitchen door, as usual. But it was Rachael who opened to his knock. The kitchen lights were off and the light in the inner rooms was unusually dim. Anytime Salvatore was going to be present, Lou always made sure that Rachael was dressed appropriately. Tonight,

Sal knew at a glance that Rachael was not dressed in usual style. Her red shirt, with several buttons open at the top, was tight and revealing. She had tied the ends, so that there were several inches of bare skin between her shirt and the tight jeans she wore. Diamond-studded clogs enhanced the bright red, nail polish on her toes. Rachael is a beauty, and Sal caught his breath.

"Hi," she said with a smile, as she indicated Salvatore should come in.

Much aware of an uncommon stillness, he entered the room cautiously. "I told Derek I'd meet him here," he said with uncertainty.

"Derek will be here in a minute," said Rachael. And with an inviting smile, she indicated he should follow her into the living room. They walked through the unlit, dining room, and into the living room. The lights there were dim, too.

"Are your parents not home?" Sal asked. He intuitively hesitated to follow her into the room.

"Mom left something at the shop, and Joy went with them. They plan to stop at the restaurant for ice cream. They'll be here soon," she assured him. "And Derek will be coming," she said.

Her eyes were bright and teasing as she motioned toward the couch. When Salvatore walked over and warily sat down on the sofa, Rachael seated herself beside him. Then, with a twinkle in her eyes, she suddenly slid over close to him, very close. He could smell her perfume. He had sisters, and he recognized that fragrance....Black Diamond.

Salvatore had to smile. He was, after all, quite experienced with the opposite sex. He had not led a sheltered life in Brazil. And his college escapade earlier this, school year was still fresh in his mind. Rachael was young, but he knew she was well aware of the effect she had on men, and that she was using him for sport.

But she's just a kid.....did Derek say she was thirteen? Sal was considering how to handle this, when suddenly, Rachael perched herself on his lap and reached up to twirl the hair hanging over his forehead.

"Rachael!" Sal exclaimed with a laugh, as he tried to lift her off. "Derek will have my head!.... And, if he misses, Abel won't!"

Rachael stayed where she was and purred in a teasing tone, "Are you afraid of me, Sal?"

His friends back home would never believe that Salvatore Ridenti would respond with reserve at a moment like this. The temptation was great. *Rachael is a beauty,* he thought. *And, young though she is, I'm most definitely attracted to her. But .... this is Derek's sister. I know the family.*

"Yeah," he answered her tease truthfully. "Of course, I am."

As she leaned in to play with his hair, he endeavored not to look below her eyes. *She may be only thirteen,* he thought, *but Rachael is surprisingly developed.* He put both of his hands on her shoulders. He was determined to move her off his lap.

At that moment, the back door opened, and Derek was speaking as he entered. "Sal," he said, "I'm sorry I'm....."

But stopping just inside the doorway, he could see the scene on the couch. A red color rose up Derek's neck and spread to his face. The pleasant greeting was forgotten, as Rachael righted herself.

"Oh!" she exclaimed and stormed out of the room.

Sal had risen, too, and was endeavoring to straighten his clothes. He pushed his hair back, off his forehead, and struggled to meet Derek's eyes.

"Hey," he said. "Nothing happened… ….. You know I wouldn't," he implored, hoping to see a more reasonable expression from Derek.

"Where are my parents?" Derek asked abruptly.

"Rachael said your mother had to return to her shop. Joy went with them," Sal explained quietly.

Derek's emotions were in turmoil.

Mom knew Sal was meeting me here, he thought. *But, of course, she hadn't known I would be late. Even so, I will definitely speak to her about leaving Rachael alone at times like this.*

Sal was embarrassed. "Derek, nothing happened," he repeated. "Rachael was just teasing me. She knew I wouldn't do anything… …You'd have my scalp, and she knows that."

He knew Sal well now. In spite of that folly with Diane, Derek trusted him. And Derek knew Rachael was probably the instigator of any playfulness that had occurred between them. He sought for calm and decided to put a reasonable interpretation on the moment. Though frustrated, he finally mumbled, "She has a crush on you, Sal. I trust you to handle Rachael wisely."

Inwardly, Sal realized he was a bit enamored with Rachael, too. But, what he replied was, "Of course."

Rachael has interfered enough for one evening, thought Derek.

Sal and I need to leave at once.

"We're going to be late," he said. And the two, young men left the house together.

On the drive to Burnswick, Sal expressed what Derek was thinking.

"I have sisters, too," Sal said. "They drive me crazy. They should be locked in the house until they're given in marriage!"

"Are they as pretty as Rachael?" Derek asked morosely.

"Rachael is very pretty," Sal agreed.

"And, she doesn't have a bit of sense about men!" The thought stirred Derek's anger again. Then he chose to dismiss it. There was no further discussion about Rachael.

Later that night, as he prepared for bed, Derek let himself think about his sister's actions. *Why can't Rachael be like Joy,* he fretted? *How should I handle this?*

He didn't want to tell his mother how Rachael had behaved with Sal. He had no ideas. Fortunately, he was too tired to stay awake and worry.

As for Sal…sleep evaded him. He couldn't erase the memory of the beautiful, teasing young ….girl?….woman?…. who had sat on his lap.

All of the family were present on Sunday. There was no opportunity to speak to Rachael alone.

Derek was earlier than usual when he entered the kitchen on Monday morning. He set his books aside and leaned down to kiss Joy on the forehead. Then, he poured himself a cup of coffee and joined Abel at the table. This was not his usual routine.

Lou was surprised. "Do you have time for breakfast this morning, Derek?" she asked.

"No thanks, Mom." Derek answered the question in

her eyes. "Actually, I thought I'd drop Rachael off at school today," he said.

Both Abel and Lou knew Derek would have a purpose for this. But he was a man now. Since he chose to say no more, they didn't question him.

It was about ten minutes before Rachael appeared in the kitchen carrying her school books. Though Lou pushed and insisted, Rachael never wanted breakfast. Sometimes, Lou won and sometimes she didn't. It usually depended on how much time Rachael had before she had to catch her bus. This morning, Lou let the matter pass.

Derek was usually gone when Rachael came down in the morning. When she saw her brother, she guessed the reason.

"I'll drop you off at school today," he said to her.

Her dark look was evidence that she wasn't happy about this. But she knew she had no recourse but to agree.

Derek rose from the table with a "See you," aimed at the others and then preceded a sullen Rachael out the door.

Abel and Lou exchanged a look. "What do you suppose that's about?" he asked.

"I have no idea," said Lou. But she was always so thankful for the responsible role Derek played in the lives of his younger sisters. He was as protective toward them as a good father would have been.

If Derek wants me to know what this is about, he'll tell me, she mused. *Otherwise, he will handle this....and handle it well.*

Rachael sat quietly as Derek maneuvered the car out the

driveway and onto the main road. She waited for what she knew would be coming.

"That was a really stupid thing you did the other night," said Derek. "You put Sal in a bad situation."

"I was just teasing," Rachael muttered.

"You're too old for that kind of teasing," Derek said. "Sal could have had a real problem because of this.

"And," he continued, "if it had been someone other than Sal, you could have been in danger!"

Rachael didn't respond. She realized she had acted a bit foolishly.

"If you don't learn how to act, you'll get a bad reputation, and the nice guys won't want to date you," Derek continued.

"Mom will never let me date anyway," she muttered. Rachael had already broached the subject with Lou, who told her it was too soon for that.

"Sal is my friend," said Derek. "If I can't trust you to behave properly when I bring my friends home, I won't be able to do that anymore."

Oh, Rachael wanted to see Sal again.

"...ok....," she said.

Derek offered no further conversation on the short drive to school. Actually, Rachael was sorry to have disappointed him. Everyone admired Derek, including herself. But she was sometimes a bit jealous, too. Derek seemed to do everything right. And she seemed to always do things wrong! But she really loved her older brother. And she knew he loved her.

That day in school, Rachael behaved properly.

Derek let the car idle a moment to watch Rachael walk into the school building. He considered what Sal had said last night. He knew his little sister was very pretty. When had Rachael stopped sprinting here and there with Joy on her heels? At only thirteen-years-of-age,...well, almost fourteen... today her movements were practically those of a woman...a very attractive, young woman.

Ah,....she's beautiful, thought Derek. *And she's almost fourteen. Rachael looks older, and she has our mother's beauty.* Remembering his mother's history, that concerned him.

Joy is quiet, timid and shy. But Rachael is confident, adventurous and somewhat aware of her attraction to men.

I can hardly keep Rachael from maturing. She sure has changed in recent months. Her figure is more developed.....and she's so pretty.....and so headstrong!

With a deep sigh, Derek turned his vehicle toward Clairton.

The school year was passing so quickly. This semester, Derek and Sal usually met after 2:30 in the afternoon. But, today, when Derek left his first class of the morning, he was surprised to see Sal waiting for him outside. He could see from his friend's demeanor that something was wrong. Sal fell into step beside him without speaking for a minute.

Finally, he said, "Derek, I'm being called home."

Derek looked at him in confusion. This was not exactly unexpected. Sal had informed him recently that his mother was experiencing a serious setback. Even so, there were less than six weeks in this school term. He had supposed Sal might complete this year, at least. Now, it was necessary to face the hard truth. His good friend would be leaving.

"How long will you be gone," Derek asked sadly.

"It's permanent. The doctor has said that, optimistically, my mother has three months," Sal said sadly. "I want to be there for her. And my father wants me to remain home to help with the business and the family."

They were both momentarily without words.

"I'm really sorry," Derek said finally. They walked slowly and in silence.

"I'm concerned about Jake. Would you look in on him, Derek?" Grunge no longer bothered Jacob, but neither had Jacob made other friends.

"Sure. I'll check on him daily," Derek promised

"I've urged him to attend a school in Pittsburgh next semester and live at home. His mother is lonesome, so she may now be willing to let him do that."

"Yeah. That would be best," Derek agreed. He understood Sal was preparing for his return to Brazil to be permanent.

"Smitty, at the car dealership, has agreed to sell my Lexus on commission," Sal continued.

Asking the car dealer to sell his vehicle while he was out of the country would guarantee a short sale. Sal would have preferred to gift Derek with the car. He could well afford to do so. But he didn't offer, as he knew Derek wouldn't want that. A gift of this size would mar their relationship, which had been one of equals without regard to the bank account of either.

Again, there seemed nothing to say. Both were feeling the sadness of the coming separation.

"My plane departs Pittsburgh Airport on Sunday afternoon at 2 p.m.," Sal said.

"That soon? What about your schooling?" Derek asked. "...We're so near the end of the term?"

"The Administration has been very considerate. They're arranging for me to complete this school year via the Internet. My professors are being helpful, too. They're organizing lesson guidelines that will prepare me for the final exams."

"Can you come to dinner on Saturday?" Derek asked anxiously. "Abel and Mom will want to see you before you leave...the girls, too. I can come for you," said Derek. "You could spend the night at our place, and I'll take you to the airport on Sunday."

"I'd like that. But no, I can't spend the night. I have too much to do to get ready for departure on Sunday. There's the packing. And there are so many friends I want to see...I can't spend the night. But I'll look forward to Saturday evening with your family," he said. "And, if you want to drive me to the airport on Sunday, it would be a big help."

"Of course," Derek replied.

They had reached the building in which Derek took his next class.

"I have some interviews in the office later today. I won't be meeting you after class this afternoon."

"We'll see you tomorrow evening then," said Derek sadly.

Derek's family was very sorry to learn of Sal's departure. He had become a regular, weekend guest in their home this past year, and they'd come to know him well. When he arrived late, Saturday afternoon, Lou hugged him and expressed her sympathy for his home situation.

"We'll miss you. But I know your mother will be so glad to have you home," she said.

"I'm sorry I won't be here to greet this little guy," Sal said, indicating the baby Lou expected to deliver in June. She had wanted to have the baby without knowing the gender. But Abel simply could not wait. When the sonogram showed a boy, he was beyond proud.

Discussion around the dinner table was spirited as always but tinged with sadness. Lou was quite conscious of her older daughter's demeanor. Rachael was uncommonly quiet. There was none of the sparkle and flirting, albeit somewhat discreet, in which she had engaged during Sal's past visits. Her spirit was subdued this evening. Sal glanced across the table at her frequently. But rather than meet his eyes, Rachael kept her eyes lowered much of the time.

Sal noticed that. *Ah, little one,* he thought. *You're just too young.....*

That evening, he had to leave earlier than usual, saying he still had much to do to prepare for his trip. The night was warm, and the family stepped out onto the lighted veranda to say a final goodbye. Lou handed Salvatore a picture of their family. "To help you remember us," she said.

"Oh, there's no danger I will forget," said Sal. "But I'll treasure the picture."

With tears in her eyes, Lou hugged him. Abel abandoned the handshake and hugged Sal, also.

"Goodbye, Sal," said Joy shyly. "I'll miss you."

"I'll not forget you, Joy," he said as he drew her close and kissed her forehead.

Then, he turned to look at Rachael. They all turned toward her. She had drawn back a little from the tight, family gathering around Sal. There she stood, off to the side and with her chin up, seemingly defying him to hug her. She gave every indication this was not a momentous occasion for her.

That brought a tender smile to his face. "Will you miss me, too, Rachael?" he asked teasingly, while being careful not to violate the distance she had placed between them.

With her chin still high and her eyes unwavering, she offered a defiant shrug of her shoulders. "Maybe," she said carelessly.

That made him smile. He looked at her for a long moment.

"I'll be back....when you're older," he said softly. His eyes were crinkling, but he rather meant that promise, too...

Derek walked with Sal to his car.

"I'll see you tomorrow then," said Sal. "7a.m. wouldn't be too early to suit me. I'd like to get to the airport plenty early. We can visit some until my plane takes off.

"I'll be there by 7, then," said Derek.

It took Salvatore longer to pass through the lines at the airport than Derek imagined it should. Of course, Sal had extra baggage. Still...why are they spending so much time with him, Derek wondered? He found he was suspicious that it was Sal's coloring and obvious accent that was drawing the extra attention toward him.

But Salvatore showed only respect and patience throughout the procedure. And when he had his clearance, Derek and he found an area that provided a place to sit and talk.

"What will you do about your education now?" Derek asked.

"Oh, that isn't optional," said Sal. "I'll continue it. I'll probably enroll at the Catholic University again. I may need to take some on-line courses for a time…"

Sal looked so sad, and Derek understood he could not speak with certainty when his mother was so ill.

"The Ponteficia Universidada Catholic of Sao Paula is an exceptionally fine university. They offer an excellent program on the Science of Agronomy.

"You're fortunate, Derek." There was a note of sadness in Sal's voice. "You can choose whatever career you desire. Maybe you've noticed that I love trees? That's what drew me to Clairton. If I had the liberty, I would have chosen Forestry rather than Agronomy."

(He makes no mention of his music, Derek noted sadly.)

"Brazil has 60% of the Amazon rainforests," Sal continued. "I'd love to be involved in that…..But the choice isn't mine."

When his call came to board the plane, Sal and Derek exchanged sad glances.

"You are my friend, Derek. You know more about me than any other person ever has."

They hugged.

"We'll stay in touch," Sal promised.

Derek felt ever-so-much like crying. The lump in his throat actually hurt. But he stood stoically and watched Sal step through the doorway and onto the ramp.

He stayed at the airport window until the plane was out of sight. Then, Derek turned, walked to his car and began the lonely future without his friend.

"Hold on, Buddy," said Derek, who was struck on the shins by the charge of the little boy. Derek was leaving Skinny's Market. The child was in advance of his mother. The ramp was on the opposite side. She couldn't take the stroller up the steps and had bent over to remove his baby brother. The young mother was Penny Houston, who had once been Derek's girlfriend.

Penny put the youngest on her hip and was reaching toward the other child, who was toddling ahead of her toward the steps.

"Max, get back here!" Penny scolded.

The little boy staggered as he ran into Derek, who quickly reached out to catch him. "What's your hurry, big guy?" he asked.

The child righted himself and backed up carefully to snatch onto his mother's pant leg.

Penny drew the retreating toddler to her side.

"Derek, I'm so sorry!" she said.

"It's alright, Penny," Derek responded with a laugh. "I recall how I hurried at his age, too."

The two adults were suddenly silent. They lived in the same, small town, attended many years of school together, and even dated at one time. But at this moment, as they stood face to face, Derek could think of nothing more to say. Penny, too, was without words.

Derek saw this past girlfriend rather regularly. He still worked at Skinny's Market, and Penny shopped here several times a week. But if Derek was present when she came to the store, even if he was the one to wait upon her, the two of them avoided eye contact and exchanged only the most necessary words. This confrontation between Derek and Max broke through that carefully erected barrier.

"Mommy.....?" This oldest child, not quite two years old, seemed to sense their discomfort and was puzzled by his mother's silence.

Derek purposely fixed his eyes on Penny. She had gained, Derek supposed, an additional twenty pounds since he had dated her. That was at the end of their eleventh grade of high school and the summer before their senior year. No doubt these two children accounted for the additional weight. But she was still pretty. In fact, standing there with one child in her arms and another clinging to her side, Derek thought Penny, with her babies, was quite beautiful.

Derek and she had been in love back in high school. At least, he knew he had been in love. And, yes, he would say with confidence, Penny felt the same. Derek had ended the relationship. He felt it was too much of a temptation to hold her in his arms and never cross the line with her. Penny had been as passionate as he. And they still had a long way to go before they could make a commitment. So, he stopped dating her. He didn't date any of the other girls. Penny had his heart. He had told her that, too, as he tried to explain.

But Penny began to date Michael Houston shortly after their break-up. Michael was in their class at school. He was a nice enough guy but always out for a good time. Derek feared how that would evolve. And it did. By the following spring, Penny was pregnant. The couple married the summer after graduation. These little boys were the offspring.

This day, Derek finally broke the silence. "How have you been, Penny," he asked?

"I'm good," said Penny politely.

"Two children must keep you busy..." he said and turned his gaze to the other boy.

"This is Eugene," she said, indicating the lad she held. "And the one who ran into you is Max."

"They're handsome boys," said Derek sincerely. He looked into Penny's eyes and was struck by the sadness he saw there.

"Thank you," she murmured.

Then, the child on her hip began to wriggle, and Derek reached behind himself and opened the screen door for the little family to enter the store.

"Thank you," Penny said again. The little trio entered, and the door went shut. Derek hastened down to his car. He was admittedly shaken by the meeting. He'd been in Penny's presence often. But this time their eyes had connected. And he once again greeted the pain he had lived with throughout his senior year of high school and ever since it seemed. He was finishing his second year of college, and he hadn't dated another girl. Of course, there was Mandy. But they didn't actually date. They just accompanied Sal and Diane, who were actually dating...sort of....Derek knew Sal had not been as serious about the relationship as Diane was.

There had almost been a relationship with Alison Brinker. But he just couldn't bring himself to go forward with that.

After this meeting with Penny, he wondered if there could ever be another girl for him.

The marriage of Michael and Penny was rumored to

be troubled. The couple lived in an upstairs apartment on Hickory Street. Michael had taken a job at Bud Cross' asphalt plant in the nearby town of Burnswick. It was considered a rather well-paying job. But the talk in town was that Michael was drinking too much and playing cards every weekend.

As he walked away from Penny and her boys, Derek climbed in his car and eased it onto the roadway. He determined he would aim his vehicle, and his thoughts, in another direction. At least, he would try.

Skinny noticed the tears in Penny's eyes when she came into the market. He had seen the unplanned meeting between the two just outside his door. He well remembered the close relationship this couple had in the summer before their senior year.

"Hi, Penny," he offered. "How are my two, favorite boys?"

"They're doing fine, Mr. Briscuit," she replied.

"Can you guess what I have for you, Max," Skinny asked?

Max shook his head, but his eyes were glued to the grocer. He was fully expecting a treat. Skinny always kept something special for the visit of this, little family.

"Would an elephant do?" asked Skinny.

"Yeah!" said Max, who was totally excited.

Skinny reached beneath his counter and found the baggie with the large, elephant cookie he had hidden there. Mildred had put blue icing on it.

"Yeah!" Max yelled again as he reached for the treat. The other child was looking at him now, and Skinny said to Penny, "I expect he's too young for an elephant cookie?" It was a question.

"Yes, he is," Penny agreed. She had reached into her pocket and found a pacifier for Eugene.

Skinny was glad to notice this scene with her boys had distracted Penny. She had regained control. *She's a really good mother,* he thought. *But why did she get involved with Michael Houston? Everyone knows things aren't going well for the couple. Derek is a far better man than he,* Skinny knew.

Penny made known her order, and Skinny set about filling it. She shook off her sadness, as she fussed over her children. But Skinny's heart was wounded as he watched her leave. He had a real fondness for this young woman he had known most of her life. And Derek had found a degree of affection with this grocer equal to that of a son.

With a sigh, Skinny returned to his duties.

That night, Derek did what he commonly did when he sought comfort. He loved Sal and missed his friend. Tonight, it was Bill Tonkins with whom he shared his heart. Bill had known him in his high school years when he first fell in love with Penny.

Bill's wife, Debbie, and Penny were best friends during high school. Derek had been told that Penny still exchanged letters with Debbie regularly.

Bill received Derek's letter at 10 a.m. on Wednesday morning. He was busy, as always.

Even so, he reached for the letter Sherry had carefully laid on top of a pile of mail. Swinging his chair away from the desk, he faced the large section of window, which overlooked Seventh Avenue, and opened it. Derek had written:

Dear Bill,

I saw Penny today. Does that sound strange? We live in this same, little town. And we meet two or three times a week. But for the past .....nearly two years?....I've managed to look at her and not see her! I actually believe she'd say the same. I became very adept at filling her order at Skinny's and never meeting her eyes. It was easier that way.

This afternoon, I met her on the steps outside, as I was leaving work. Her oldest boy ran into my legs. Penny was so embarrassed. I caught the little guy and looked up to say, "It's alright. No harm done" and found myself looking into Penny's eyes. It was too late to look away. Time seemed to stand still.

She looks so sad. That's always the impression I get when she is near...her sadness. What can her life with Michael be? I wanted to reach out and take her in my arms! What kind of a dunce am I? She belongs to another. She's been married almost two years. Wouldn't you think I'd be over this by now?

I'm not.

You sound so happy with Debbie. I'm glad about that. Give her my love.

Until later,
Derek

When he read the letter, Bill was grieved for Derek. Debbie and he were so very happy. That made him even more conscious of his friend's heartache. He loved Derek like a brother.

Penny had been Debbie's best friend all through their school years. She and Penny continued to communicate regularly. Debbie knew the marriage of Michael and Penny was not happy. Though Penny never said so, Deb believed Penny's heart was equally tied to Derek.

Bill was sad at this situation. And there was nothing that could be done.

"I can see you miss your friend," said Calvin Carson. Derek had stopped to see his old friend, Alton High's janitor. Calvin was now handing him a cup of coffee.

"Travel is relatively easy today. In a few years, you'll be out of school and free to do some traveling. No doubt, you can visit him in Brazil. And he will be able to visit you again."

"Actually, Salvatore is more apt to come back to see Rachael," Derek said with a laugh.

"Rachael?" asked Calvin in obvious confusion.

"That's a family joke," Derek explained. "Rachael had a crush on Salvatore. He never said so, but we thought he was sort-of interested in her, too.

"Oh, nothing happened," he quickly added with assurance. "Sal wouldn't. But Rachael isn't shy, and she usually gets what she wants. We can probably be glad Sal is gone."

Derek knew his statement had truth in it.

"Well," the janitor assured, "I've observed Rachael in the hallway, and I've never seen her do anything out-of-line."

"I wish you'd let me know if you ever do," said Derek sincerely.

He left the school shortly and walked to Skinny's Market for his usual job there. *My life sure is routine,* he thought.

Summer had brought, with it, a slower pace for Derek. He enjoyed having more time for his family. He appreciated the evenings at home with his younger sisters.

Sal had called him several times and wrote on occasion, as he knew that was Derek's preference. His letters were brief. His father was consumed with his mother's illness. Sal was immersed in family and business matters.

This is so like Bill Tonkins, thought Derek. *Bill's dad died; Sal's father is still living, but like Bill, Sal has to assume responsibility in the business with little training. That has to be hard.*

Derek was pleased to have completed his second year of college. His classes had gone well, and he had excellent grades. He regretted that his political activity was at a standstill. Politics suited him well. But that was a closed door for now.

So many students were gone for the summer, and those who were in attendance were in summer-mode. There was no structured, political activity on campus.

Derek had enrolled in two, summer courses. With Sal gone, he had no interest in visiting the student lounge. That place was rather quiet in the summer anyway. He was glad he still had his job at Skinny's.

Admittedly, he was restless.

The ridge wasn't as conveniently reached from the family's new home, but he would make his way up there and sit quietly for long periods of contemplation. He was seeking direction for his life. Thus far, nothing had quite clicked.

Lou watched him silently these summer days. Once, she came upon him sitting on the veranda and staring at nothing. She slid into the chair near him. "Is everything alright, Derek?" she asked.

He didn't answer at once. Then he said simply, "Yeah, I'm fine, Mom."

But she knew Derek was lonely. Her son had a devoted heart. It had been two years since Penny married Michael Houston. But Derek's love and his loyalty were unchangeable. He loved Penny still.

Lou didn't offer platitudes.

"I understand," she said.

And she did. She had lived with an aching heart for Charles. Charles was Derek's dad. She was still grieving many years after he vanished from her life. He just disappeared. Finally, she learned he'd been killed in a military maneuver eighteen years earlier. Only then, when she knew he was dead, did her heart begin to heal.

"It seems like I lose all the good friends I make," he said sadly. "Bill… ..Sal… ….." Of course, he had contact with Bill and Salvatore. But though he didn't say her name, Lou understood that, for her son, Penny was the biggest loss of all.

"I'm sorry, Derek," she replied. She hesitated about speaking further, and then decided to do so. "I think Michael is not very good to Penny," she said sadly.

"Yeah. I can see that," said Derek. "We never talk, but she always looks so sad."

"I understand he's drinking too much." *Oh, maybe I*

shouldn't be spreading gossip like this, she thought. *And it can't help Derek to know this.*

They sat silently for a space. Then, Derek gave her a rueful smile and said, "It's ok, Mom....really it is."

She smiled gently, rose and, with a kiss to his forehead, she turned and went back indoors.

Late in June there was a major change in the Saunders household. When they planned the house, Abel and Lou had included a nursery. And to the joy of all, this summer Lou gave birth to a boy, Marshall Abel Saunders, Jr. Abel refused to have him called Junior. Both "Marshall" and "Abel" were too grown-up a name for such a little boy. He came screaming into the world, and in the early months his voice was heard loud and clear. His Dad laughingly called him, "Sarge". The name stuck.

"Sarge wants his bottle."

"Sarge needs a nap."

Sarge never lacked for attention. His two, older sisters doted on him. Derek showed the same love and care for this little boy that his sisters had enjoyed. He hurried home in the evenings to see his little brother before Lou put him to bed for the night. And she arranged the baby's schedule to accommodate Derek's visitation.

His daddy nearly burst with pride at the boy's every, minor achievement. Colonel Abel Saunders was discovering the happiness of his very own family.

Strength, dedication, courage, skill, determination, perseverance, endurance...even satisfaction, these were words that were central to Abel's being. They had shaped him. They made him an excellent, military commander; they had seen him through the battles.

But contentment, joy, happiness, those words had been less associated with his life. That is, until he met Lou and took her as his wife. He loved her; he loved her children, and now he loved his son. Abel knew a depth of joy he'd never had before.

Lou continued with her sewing shop. Abel could see how much she enjoyed it and let her decide. Lucy helped with the baby at home. And Abel was there much of the time. Lou had never learned to drive, so Derek or Abel transported her to-and-from the shop, where an older woman was hired to assist. That gave Lou considerable freedom. She spent much time with the new baby. And sometimes, she took Sarge with her to the shop, and the ladies in town fussed over him.

Twelve

THE TOWN OF ALTON WAS shocked by the tragedy that occurred in the early hours of a foggy, Saturday morning on the first day of July. Michael Houston was drunk when he departed from a Burnswick bar. He was driving too fast and lost control of his car. It caromed off the road and sideswiped a tree on the driver's side, before coming to a stop on the embankment. He died instantly.

Derek didn't attend Michael's funeral. He didn't even visit at the funeral home. That was odd, for Michael had been a classmate at Alton High. But he couldn't bear the thought of Penny's pain, so he stayed away.

Rumor said Michael had left his car insurance expire, so the vehicle would not be replaced. No one imagined Michael would have been responsible enough to have life insurance. The churches in town, including Pastor Lowe's church, where Penny attended before her marriage, took up a collection. Someone put a jar on the counter at Tom Karn's Hardware Store and another at Skinny's Market. The guys at the pool hall passed a hat. The town was generous. The family's, immediate needs would be met, but there would be nothing toward the future.

Penny and her boys moved back home with her mother.

Mrs. Crawford was working daytime hours now in the office at Clairton Hospital. As she was available to watch the children in the evening, Penny took a job at the restaurant, always working evening hours. The restaurant was open until 10 p.m. From 10 to 11 p.m., the staff cleaned and prepared the place for the next day.

The first week of August, Derek hurried with his clean-up at Skinny's. He didn't skimp but endeavored to get that work done by 9:30 p.m. He even informed Skinny he would be leaving earlier. Skinny had no concerns about this employee's work. Derek walked up the street to the restaurant and arrived half-an-hour before closing time. He took a seat at the bar, and ordered pie and coffee. He talked with anyone who sat near.

As the days went by, that became his routine. The townsfolk noticed his regularity with approval. In fact, Derek's "seat" was usually vacant and waiting for him. Penny found herself watching the clock, looking for him to come. The two of them shared no conversation other than in her sphere of service. Derek could see that the work was good for her. The townspeople were friendly ....even kind to her. It was not unusual to see her take, from her pocket, photos of her boys to share with someone who asked. As they looked at the pictures, Penny's face would glow.

The guys had begun to tease her some. Penny was becoming more confident. Her personality, which had been stifled in her unhappy marriage, was beginning to break through again.

Summer was nearly gone. Derek would be back in college in a few days. This was his third year. He was glad to be back. He had known much loneliness this summer and welcomed the mental challenge and activity of college. On his way to Skinny's this Saturday morning, he saw Penny coming out of the post office. While descending the few steps, her head was down as she sorted through the mail. *Mrs. Crawford would be home today*, thought Derek. *She is obviously watching the boys*, for Penny was alone.

She was dressed casually in a pair of tan, capris slacks, a sleeveless yellow top and sandals. Penny always tanned easily in the summer months. She had her boys outside most afternoons, so her brown hair had red highlights from the summer sun. She seemed to have regained her pre-childbirth weight. *No*, thought Derek as he reconsidered. *She is thinner now. But she looks as young as she did in high school. And just as pretty.*

Derek waited up ahead on the sidewalk.

Penny looked up just then and noticed him. She realized he was waiting intentionally. Her cheeks flushed, as she stopped near him. She knew this man so well; their hearts once beat as one. Now, she found it uncomfortable to look at Derek. She was fearful her emotions would show and lowered her gaze to the sidewalk. They were silent for a moment.

"I'm very sorry, Penny," Derek said.

It had been nearly two months, but this was the first time he had spoken to her of her loss. In fact, it was the first, personal conversation he had had with her in years.

"I know," she murmured in reply.

There was an underlying sadness about her. What should he say to her? He wanted to reach out, pull her into his arms and comfort her. But that wasn't reasonable. They stood silent again, and she was looking down.

"What are your plans?" Derek finally asked.

"I have my boys to care for," she responded quietly.

Neither spoke for a moment. Then Derek softly said, "They'll need a father…."

Penny caught her breath and raised her head quickly to look into Derek's eyes. What she saw there, gave her hope.

Derek continued quietly, "I still have two years of college…."

It wasn't right that either of them should say more…not so soon after Michael's death.

But, that night, Penny wrote this to Deb: "If Derek still wants me after he graduates, he will find that I was faithful this time."

When his classes started again at college, Derek could not be at the restaurant every night. He was still working at Skinny's. He was finally finding an avenue of involvement in politics. That occupied him on most Friday nights. Skinny was understanding and urged him to become involved.

"I'll find all the help I need, Derek," he would say. "There are always high school kids asking for work. You let me know what times you want off; we'll work it out."

Derek was so thankful for this man's kindness. *People in town have sure been good to me.* And, then remembering some bad encounter in the past, he would revise that and think, *Most of them have been kind to me.*

It concerned him that Penny would not understand his evenings of absence. If he tried to tell her, she would know that he was coming just to see her. *Does she already know that,* he wondered? *Does everyone know….?*

Finally, he spoke to her when she had a rare, un-busy moment.

"I'm back in school, Penny," he said as she refilled his coffee cup.

"Yes, I know. Everyone says you're doing real well in school."

It was the most personal conversation they had yet had. He sensed that she was glad for this moment, too.

"I won't be using this seat so often in the future," he said.

The townsfolk were still avoiding the seat in which Derek had chosen to sit. Many of them knew that Penny and Derek had once been a couple. They also knew that Penny's marriage to Michael was not happy. If Derek and she got back together, it could only be good for Penny and her boys. That was the gossip now.

"I'll miss you, Derek," Penny said softly.

He was so glad to hear that. "I'll be here every time I can be," he said.

"Yes," she said. *Yes, Derek, come...and come often.* That was her thought. And he understood.

That's how it went that fall. Any time he had the opportunity, Derek slid into the seat at the restaurant. Penny no longer concealed how glad she was to see him.

Between her customers, they began to share their lives.

When December came, Derek knew he was losing his reserve. It had only been six months since Michael's death. They needed to wait at least a year before seeing each other. But the Christmas season tends to weaken one's defenses. *Maybe I could see her just one time,* he thought. *Just once...it's Christmas.*

Penny always drove to the restaurant, though she lived only a few blocks away. She liked to walk and would have welcomed that, but she'd have had to walk home alone at 11:30 p.m. at night.

It was just a week until Christmas. The night was cold but clear. With a fresh covering of snow, the town looked like a Christmas postcard. And Derek could wait no lomger. He took his seat and waited for Penny to have an opportunity to visit with him.

When she did, he quietly asked, "Penny, do you think we could go for a walk after you get off work tonight?"

"Yes! Yes, we could," she replied equally quietly.

"I'll meet you at your place after you take your car there," he whispered.

Other than the porch light, there were no lights on at her mother's house. Penny parked her car, and as Derek stepped out of the shadows, she joined him. They started to walk. It was all so familiar. Derek didn't have his license when they dated in high school, and they had always walked. Tonight, neither of them talked. They instinctively turned at the school road. They walked slowly past the high school. It brought back memories for them both.

My life could have been so much better if I had just waited, thought Penny. *I had Derek. How could I have been so foolish?* There were tears in her eyes for the wasted years, and for the pain she had endured and the pain she knew she had caused Derek.

Derek was saying nothing. He didn't know what he could say. He was afraid if he opened his mouth, he'd declare his love for her. But there were so many reasons why he shouldn't... couldn't...do that. So, they just walked. Their feet took them to the ball field. It was a cold night. There were several inches of snow on the ground. But Penny seemed to be dressed warm, and she was wearing boots....

They walked, by habit, over to the cold, wooden bleachers. He brushed off a place and used his hanky to wipe it dry. Then, they sat. Derek put his arm around her, and she leaned into him. With his hand, he tilted her face toward him. Only then did he see she was crying.

"Penny?...."

The tears began to roll down her cheeks. He wrapped his arms around her and pulled her close. Penny was sobbing, deep, heart-wrenching sobs. He held her tight, and she cried. She couldn't seem to stop crying.

Finally, she muttered, "Oh, Derek, I'm so sorry. I'm so sorry for the pain I caused us. I loved you so much. I'm so sorry," and she cried some more.

"It's ok, Penny. It's alright," he said trying to soothe her. "We're together now."

The sobs finally ended, but he continued to hold her. They kissed, and the years fell away.

That night, they talked for a long time. They never once felt cold. They agreed they would marry, just as soon as Derek finished college. He knew he needed the education, if he was to support Penny and their boys as he should. (Derek already welcomed her boys as his responsibility.)

Penny understood. "I can see you all that time," she said. There was still a hint of fear, so he quickly said, "Of course. We'll never be apart again. Never!"

That evening, the stars fell back into their proper course. The earth sang sweet songs. The night sky twinkled with joy. And Derek felt whole again. The missing part of his heart was back in place.

Derek and Penny endeavored to be discreet. But they didn't exactly hold to the proper time frame expected for a mourning widow. She walked to work on the nights he could be with her. When the weather was too bad, Derek waited for her with his car. Most often they walked through town in the quiet of the night.

She shared, with him, about her boys.

"Max asks about his dad," Penny said. "I never say anything bad…"

"Oh, no. You should never do that," said Derek.

"But I find it so strange. Michael was not a caring father." She looked at Derek and added, "He wasn't a good father, Derek."

"I know that," he responded.

"It's just so strange that Max remembers him…and even asks. 'Where's daddy?' he asked the other day."

"What do you tell him?" Derek wondered.

"I said, 'God wanted him to come up there.' And Max asked, "…there?…"

"Up to heaven, honey," I said. "They're such good boys," she added almost defensively.

Derek wished the next year-and-a-half away so he could make a home for them.

And eventually the time passed.

The sun was shining brightly on this last weekend of May. Lou stood at her living room window and looked out at her world. The dogwood trees were just casting their flowers. The peonies were up and blooming....the rhododendron bushes were heavy with blossoms.

Across the road, there was a pasture field, unused at present. And beyond that was a high hill that was thick with green pines, their limbs so tightly entwined that no light could be seen between them. She had never lost her awe of this scene.

It was Derek's graduation day, and the Lord had given them a perfect day. She took the moment to express her thanks, before the many needs of her family were tossed her way.

Rachael would soon be sixteen-years-old. And Joy was thirteen. Lou was so proud of her girls and of their little brother, Sarge.

But this was Derek's day. He would graduate from Clairton University this afternoon. She would have liked to stand here and let her memory drift back over the years of watching this son grow and mature. But... ... *I guess that's for old age,* she thought, as she turned and embraced the needs of her family.

Penny attended the service with Abel and Lou. There were only the three tickets. But Rachael and Joy would share in the celebration dinner afterward.

Lou had made arrangements with the restaurant to reserve the side room for their celebration.

Lucy would bring Sarge. He was two years old now and "full of ginger," his mother would say. When they took him out among people, his daddy's proud eyes seemed always to be on his son.

Penny's two boys would be there, and her mother, Mrs. Crawford.

Lou invited Calvin Carson, and his sister, Della. They were both precious friends to her family. Bill and Debbie Tonkins had come home this weekend to attend. Bill's mother was invited. And, though it brought a groan, Derek suggested they probably should invite Debbie's mother, Agnes Rudolf, ... just as a courtesy to Debbie.

Mrs. Price said she would attend. And Pastor Lowe and his wife gave a positive response. Skinny planned to close the market for several hours so he and his wife, Mildred, could be present.

"The town will just have to understand. I don't plan to miss this event," he said.

There were a few of his high-school teachers invited, as well as Professor Graff, his college mentor. In his last two years of college, the professor had found opportunities for Derek to be more involved politically, including using him as speaker at different rallies. He expected a notable future for his prize student and let Derek know that.

The Dereksons, his grandparents, were too elderly to attend, but they sent their love and for a gift, a photo album containing pictures from his dad's early years. Abel and Derek went through the album together, and Abel told him stories of that time. Derek treasured their gift.

Sal couldn't attend, of course. Derek and he had kept in touch. For this occasion, Sal wrote a very long letter to his friend expressing his joy in their friendship, reminding him of some special experiences they had shared, and assuring Derek of his prayers for a successful future.

"I'm expecting you and your bride to visit me in Brazil soon," he urged in his letter.

Derek carefully placed Sal's, precious letter in his Bible for safe keeping. He still had his mother's long-ago note, in which she had shared a very brief account of his dad's, background information. He liked to consider how the years since then had been blessed.

Altogether, there were thirty-two guests expected to attend his graduation party....all dear friends and all had responded positively to the invitation. Lou was so grateful for God's goodness to herself and her family.

She found it hard not to cry as she looked up on the stage and saw Derek there. She reached over and placed her hand into Abel's. He looked at her and smiled. He loved seeing Lou so happy.

Penny had tears in her eyes. She glanced down at the diamond ring on her finger. Then, she looked up at the stage and saw that Derek had been watching her. He had a front row, prominent seat as he was among the honored group. He had seen Penny look down at her hand. They exchanged a smile. Derek rejoiced that she was wearing his ring. They would marry in just two weeks. *And I'll take care of her,* he thought. *Penny needs a strong man,....and I need Penny. I need her gentleness, her comfort, her love.*

In a letter to Bill, he had written,

"I've had more than a year to get to know Penny's sons. They're wonderful, little boys. I know what it is to be raised without a father. I'll be a good dad to them. And Penny and I hope to enlarge our family. We both want more children."

With Professor Graff's endorsement, Derek had been offered and had accepted a job as an aide to Representative

Caldwell. He was given a month to get his affairs in order before relocating to the Washington, DC area. He and Penny had found an apartment outside of Washington in a smaller town below Silver Springs. It was a starting place.

Derek's heart was full to overflowing today.

The chancellor walked onto the stage and the ceremony began.

The market had been busy that morning, and Skinny had no help. Andy, his newest worker, was away with his parents this weekend. At least, that's what he said he would be doing. Andy wasn't nearly as dependable as Derek had been.

"You could use some help," said Sonny Berger. Sonny was the barber in town.

"That's just what I was thinking," said Skinny. His speech was pleasant …though he was feeling the strain. There were two, other customers waiting, and Agnes Rudolf.

Agnes was last to come into the store, but she will expect to be served first. She always imagines she is someone important.

Those were Skinny's, uncharitable thoughts as he rang up the barber's few items.

"Big doings over at the college this weekend," the barber said as Skinny took his bill. "I hear Lou's boy will be among the graduates."

"Yes," said Skinny. This was a subject that was sure to bring a smile to the old, grocer's face. "Derek did real well, too. He's graduating Magna Cum-Laude. He has accepted a job as an aide to Representative Caldwell.

"I can't think of anyone I respect more than that young man," he added.

"Derek is a tribute to our school system," said Agnes Rudolf. Upon hearing the discussion about Derek's graduation, she had sidled up to the counter. "I had the boy in eighth grade, you know. He was a good student. Of course, his home life back then was a handicap for him. But I always made certain he got treated fairly. And I gave him extra attention, as I still do for any of the underprivileged children."

Neither Mr. Berger nor Skinny responded to her statement. The town was aware of Agnes Rudolf's less-than-charitable treatment of the less privileged kids. The two men passed a knowing glance between themselves as Skinny counted out the change.

"I've been invited to attend the celebration at the restaurant later today," Agnes said proudly.

Skinny was invited, too, but he didn't say so, as he didn't wish to continue the conversation with Agnes Rudolf.

All morning long, others, too, commented on Derek Metcalf's graduation from Clairton University. Most of the townspeople were sincerely delighted with Derek's achievements. The older folks well remembered the young, fatherless boy who hung around town and the pool room talking with the older men. Back then, it didn't appear that he had much of a chance in the future.

Today, many of them were proud of what he had done with his life.

There was no one who rejoiced more than Skinny Briscuit.

When it was finally noon, Skinny put his CLOSED sign in the window glass of the door. That was a rare happening.

Skinny could remember only a couple of times he'd ever closed his store on a normal, business day. He was too conscientious for that. But today, he had no qualms about it.

This is a special day, Derek's graduation-from-college day.

As he turned from the door, Skinny's eyes fell on the photo that had a prominent place just below the large, round, white-rimmed clock on the wall behind the counter. It was a picture of Derek and himself at work here. In the photo, he was behind the cash register, and Derek was packing a bag of groceries. Both Derek and he were smiling. On the opposite side of the counter, Tom Karnes was the customer who was chatting with them as they worked. The three were unaware the photo was being taken.

Someone, Skinny couldn't remember just who it was, had snapped the picture. It was precious because it was such a typical moment....Derek and he working together. The sensitive photographer gave the grocer the snapshot. Mildred had it enlarged and put in a nice frame. Derek laughed when he saw it. Since then, the picture has hung behind the counter on this wall. In time, the photo had become so familiar that it is, now, mostly ignored.

But today, Skinny gazed at the photo with a lump in his throat.

The kindly, old grocer let his thoughts wander back to the little family who had lived in that trailer on the other side of Alton. Lou had been so young then; Derek was just a baby when they moved here from NJ. He remembered how concerned he was that Lou and her son were off by themselves, out in the country.

Even as a little boy, Derek was responsible. When he was

quite young, Skinny remembered, *Derek tried to look after his mother.*

Lou was strong and healthy, but it was more than a mile out to their trailer. Skinny had done his best to help Lou by delivering her groceries. When Mildred learned that Lou was anxious to do mending and hemming, she had taken her wardrobe needs to her. Other women did that, too.

But assuredly, as Lou was so lovely, she had inspired criticism and insinuations.

Skinny recalled how saddened he was by some of the decisions Lou made in those early years, when she lived in that trailer. Assuredly, she did harm to her reputation and subsequent harm to her family.

Like the town, Skinny could only stand-by and watch as the two, sweet, little girls were added. Admittedly, Lou had not been wise in her relationships. Neither of the fathers stayed to help her. Lou had to raise all three of her children alone.

The town's grocer was privy to all the gossip that surrounded the family. As Derek matured, Skinny observed that even Lou's boy seemed to be judged harshly, and by suspicion, rather than truth. He knew that Derek didn't deserve the social stigma he endured. It concerned Skinny, but there was so little that he could do.

When Derek finally got to high school, Skinny had been heartened to learn that Calvin Carson had taken the boy "under his wing". Those, with wisdom among the townsfolk, knew there could be no better counselor for the young man than Cal.

Skinny recalled that day, early in his eleventh grade, Derek came into the market and asked him for a job. He was glad to find work for the boy. *I have been amply rewarded*, he thought today. *Derek has been a hard and conscientious worker ..*

In spite of all the nay-sayers, Pastor Lowe helped Lou to find peace with the Lord and get her own life in order.

Today, she is married to a fine man, Colonel Abel Saunders. They'll make a good home for those, two, young girls and their, baby brother.

Lou and her family are triumphing today. The thought brought much satisfaction. *Derek is graduating from college and has a promising future ahead.*

There was a mist in the old grocer's eyes.

Yes, indeed, Lou's boy has done real good.

Printed in the United States
By Bookmasters